Julianne and the Judge

Julianne and the Judge

MELODY CARLSON

This is a work of fiction. All characters and events portrayed in this novel are either fictitious or used fictitiously.

JULIANNE AND THE JUDGE

WhiteFire Publishing
13607 Bedford Rd NE
Cumberland, MD 21502

ISBN: 978-1-941720-89-9 (print)
978-1-941720-90-5 (digital)

1

Early June 1890
Colorado Springs

Julianne Blackstone was nobody's fool. Except perhaps when it came to her parents. But after two years of finishing school, she planned to outsmart them. So when she got back into Colorado Springs, instead of returning to their fancy new home like they fully expected, Julianne hired a wagon at the train station.

"I want you to take me to the Double W Ranch," she told the young man.

"The Double W?" He tilted his cowboy hat back to give her a closer look.

"It's only a few miles outside of—"

"Oh, I know the Double W Ranch all right, and I'm more'n happy to take you there." He grinned. "Or anywhere."

Naturally that offer made her uncomfortable, but she was desperate. Despite coming home a day sooner than expected, her fear was that her father would show up and escort her home. Well, to his home anyway. It sure wasn't hers.

She gave the young man a stiff nod. "Thank you, but I only need to get to the Double W, and I will reimburse you for your time."

"No need to pay me, I'm headed that direction anyway." He grinned again.

She rewarded him with a polite smile, and he jerked his thumb to where porters were loading a crate onto a boxcar. "I just brung in a heap of cowhides for the east bound then I'm headed home. Got an empty wagon and no one to keep me company."

"That's mine." She pointed to her trunk just unloaded from the baggage car. "If it's not too much trouble, I hope we can leave directly." She attempted nonchalance as she coolly glanced around the train station. Hopefully no one had tipped off her parents about her early arrival.

The young wagon driver, with the help of a porter, got her heavy trunk onto the wagon bed, then, removing his hat to display a messy head of poorly cut tawny hair, he introduced himself as Ned Greer. "And don't you worry none, Miss, cuz the Double W is right on my way home."

He helped her onto the buckboard then clucked his tongue, snapped the reins, and they were on their way—straight through town. She hoped he wouldn't notice her hunkered down slightly, using her hat's wide brim to shield her face as his wagon rumbled down Main Street. She wanted to sneak a glance at her mother's dress shop up ahead but feared she might be spotted. And so she turned away, fixing her full attention on the driver.

"It was so fortuitous that you happened along right when you did," she said in an overly bright tone.

"Huh?" His brow creased as if confused.

"I was very lucky you were at the train station," she interpreted. "Just when I needed a ride too."

"Oh, yeah. That was lucky. For me too." He beamed at her.

She smiled back at him, not because she wanted to lead him on, but because they were now passing the dress shop and she could imagine her mother gazing out the plate glass window in front. "I haven't been home in so long. I'm very eager to see the beautiful countryside again."

"You mean the Double W is your home?" He cocked his head to one side. "You related to the Davises or something?"

"Delia Davis is my older sister." She almost added half sister but didn't think it necessary. By now she recognized Ned. They'd probably met at a church picnic or barbecue or something. He was several years older and from a neighboring ranch. But he obviously was unable to place her. Probably because she'd still been in pigtails and pinafores at the time.

As they left town behind them, he chattered away about local goings on, but she only half listened as she soaked in the rolling hills of the Colorado countryside, the red rock formations contrasting against the intensely blue sky. June was such a pretty time. And the rain must've been abundant this year because the hillsides looked lush and green. Hopefully there'd be no water rights battles going on this year.

"So you're Mrs. Davis's little sister?" Ned drawled out for what must've been the third time as he finally turned into the long drive that led directly to her sister's gracious ranch house. It all looked as lovely and inviting as ever. Roses were even blooming on the trellis next to the wide front porch. "But I know you're not Miranda. That's just as plain as the nose on your face."

"That's right. I'm Delia's youngest sister." Julianne reached for her satchel, which she'd stowed at her feet. Eager to escape this overly friendly fellow and his endless chitchat, she spoke quickly. "Miranda married Jackson O'Neil. And now they have two children and live over at the mine—"

"Oh, yeah, yeah, I know Jackson. He's a good man. But I don't recall Mrs. Davis having another full growed sister."

Julianne forced a smile. "Well, she does. And I'm her." She pointed to where the drive curved in front of the house. "Just stop there. Thank you."

He told the team to whoa then looked up at the tall white house then over to the barn and outbuildings. "I always thought this was the prettiest ranch I ever seen. Sure was a shame when Winston Williams got killed like he did. Shot by his own foreman too. People still talk about it sometimes."

She nodded as she tossed out her satchel, ready to depart her talkative driver. "Yes, I wasn't here then, but I heard the story. Very sad."

He hurried around to help her down.

"Just put my trunk there," Julianne instructed. "One of the hands will take it up to the house." She thanked him again, reaching for her satchel, but he grabbed it first.

"So Mrs. Davis has got two full growed sisters? One that's married and one that's not?" Leaning against the sideboard, he peered curiously down at her.

"I realize it's a little confusing." Julianne never enjoyed trying to explain their slightly fractured family. "You see, Delia—Mrs. Davis—came out here from the East Coast to see her father, Winston Williams. As you know, this was his ranch. His second wife was Miranda's mother, which makes Miranda his stepdaughter, and Delia's stepsister, but no actual relation to me." She reached for her satchel, but he held it ransom.

He scratched his head. "So how're ya related to the Double W?"

"Delia is my half-sister. We have the same mother." She couldn't hide her exasperation.

"So your last name ain't Williams?"

"No. My brother Julius and I have a different father than Delia. We are both Blackstone—"

"Is Jefferson Blackstone *your* pa?" Ned's brows shot up.

Julianne cringed then nodded. She knew her father had acquired quite a reputation as a politician in the fast-growing mining town. She also knew from Delia's letters that his progressive politics weren't popular with everyone. Particularly ranchers. But nothing surprising about that since Julianne didn't get along too well with her father either.

"Sorry to say my pa don't cotton up to Jefferson Blackstone much." Ned grimly shook his head as he leaned back against the buckboard. "Don't like outsiders coming in and trying to change things. Specially things they don't know nothin' about."

"I'm sure your father is not alone in his opinions about, uh, Mr. Blackstone." She tried to be patient as she waited for Ned to unload her trunk from the back of his wagon, but knew she was at his mercy.

"So you're little Julianne Blackstone." He nodded like some kind of light had gone on. "Delia's little sister. I remember you now. You were just a kid last time I saw you." He set down her satchel to reach for the trunk.

"Uh-huh." She snatched her satchel and stepped away, hoping Ned might take the hint, but he was still just standing there gawking at her with way too much interest. "I'm very eager to see my sister." She peered over toward the bunkhouse, wishing one of the hands would notice her and come over to help with the trunk, which Ned seemed to have completely forgotten, but no one else was around just now. So she reached for a handle herself.

"No, no," he told her. "I'll get that." He tugged the heavy trunk to the edge of the wagon bed then muscled it down to the ground. "There you go." He grinned at her, standing tall and squaring his shoulders, as if she'd be impressed by his manly strength. She was not.

"I thank you very much for the lift," she told him. "Very neighborly."

"Oh, yeah, I can be right neighborly, Miss Julianne. Our ranch is just a few miles thataway. I s'pect I'll be seeing lots more of you now that you're home from that fancy school you was talking about during on our nice little ride."

As eager to escape Ned's overly accommodating company as she'd been to escape finishing school, she thanked him for what she hoped was the last time. Then clutching her satchel, hurried up to the house.

It wasn't so much that Ned Greer was an uncivilized, unsophisticated, rough-hewn, clodhopping cowboy, although he was. Julianne wasn't a snob—at least she hoped she wasn't. After all, she'd always had great respect for the hands that worked her sister's ranch. But something about Ned Greer's interest in her made her very uneasy. Probably because it was a stark reminder of what her parents had in store for her. According to her mother's last letter, Julianne was prime marriage material now, and they already had a number of influential prospects all lined up for her.

2

"Julianne Margaret!" Delia shrieked happily when she opened the front door. "What on earth are you doing here?"

Julianne stuck her lip out in what was probably meant to be an offended pout. "Aren't you the least bit glad to see me?"

Delia laughed as she grabbed her baby sister into a big bear hug, holding her tightly. "Of course, I'm delighted!" She finally released Julianne, and still holding her by the shoulders, just stared at her. "You're a sight for sore eyes."

Julianne was smiling, but her eyes were misty. "You are too."

"And you're all grown up—and what a beauty you've turned into."

Julianne shrugged with nonchalance as she unpinned her wide-brimmed blue hat, the same color, Delia noticed, as her sister's eyes.

"But what are you doing here?" Delia asked. "And a day early too."

Julianne quickly explained her plan to outwit her parents. "It's as if history is repeating itself, Delia." She unbuttoned her gloves. "According to Mother's last letter, my father is determined to arrange a marriage for me. Just like he did for you before you ran away."

Delia grimaced to remember. "So I've heard."

"And you didn't even warn me?" Julianne slapped her gloves across her palms with a scowl.

"I was trying not to interfere." Delia didn't want to admit that she wasn't exactly on speaking terms with Julianne's father, or how that made things awkward with their mother.

"Well, I'm hoping that you'll let me stay here on the ranch with you." Julianne looked imploringly at her with wide blue eyes. "I can help with the children, or the kitchen, or with horses, or—"

"Of course, you're welcome to stay." Delia put her arm around Julianne's shoulders. "For as long as you like."

Julianne pointed to Delia's split skirt. "Are you going for a ride? Or coming back from one?"

"On my way out. I try to get my ride in while the children are napping. I ask Ginger to sit up there with them. It gives her an excuse to put her feet up."

"Want any company?" Julianne looked hopeful.

"I'd love it." She grinned. "I already pulled out your old riding clothes and gave them a good airing out. Just in case you decided to come visit after you got home."

"Home?" Julianne glumly shook her head. "Where is that anyway? Not with Mother and Father. Not if I can help it."

"Let's not think about that now. Your riding things are all laid out in the guest room, which you can use for as long as you like. Go get changed and I'll see to the horses. Most of the men are out moving cattle today, but Caleb was getting Dolly saddled up for me, but I'll let you ride her."

"Not if you planned to—"

"I know how much you love that horse. I really prefer Jax, but I've been trying to keep Dolly in shape. I've been taking turns with them, so she'd be ready for you."

Julianne hugged her again. "You're the best sister in the world!"

"I'm your *only* sister." Delia laughed as she reached for her dad's old cowboy hat. "Now, hurry and get changed. We're burning daylight!"

As Delia strode out to the stables, she wondered about her mother. Jane Blackstone wouldn't take it lightly that Julianne had come to the Double W first. And her stepfather…well, Delia didn't care to think about Jefferson right now. Why spoil a perfectly good afternoon?

Julianne almost felt guilty for enjoying herself so much on the ride with Delia. What would Mother say if she knew? Hopefully she had no idea…yet.

"That was perfectly wonderful," Julianne told Delia as they walked the horses into the corral. "I haven't had that much fun since I was last here."

"Was the whole time at finishing school that bad?" Delia swung out of the saddle.

"It's not that it was terrible exactly." Julianne patted Dolly's sleek neck. "It's just that it wasn't here. I love it so much, Delia, I wish I could live out here forever."

"No reason you can't." Delia looped her reins over the rail.

"Howdy, ladies." Old Caleb approached them with a wary expression. "So that's where Jax went off to. Can I help you with those—" His eyes popped open wide. "Well, I'll be hogtied and hornswoggled, if it ain't Miss Julianne all growed up." He tipped his hat. "Good to see you, missy."

Julianne smiled at him. "Good to see you too, Caleb. You're looking well."

"For an ol' cuss." He rubbed his grisly chin. "You know I'm past seventy now."

"Well, you seem to be holding up just fine."

"He sure is," Delia agreed. "He can run circles around some of the younger hands."

"Just the lazy ones." Caleb reached for Dolly's reins.

"Speaking of lazy, where's that no good brother of mine?" Julianne teased.

"Julius ain't got a lazy bone in his body," Caleb defended. "He's out roundin' up cattle with Wyatt right now. But he didn't expect to see you till Saturday. Delia's planning a welcome home shindig for you. Reckon that won't be much of a surprise now." He winked at Delia. "Sorry."

"It's all right, Caleb. Julianne would've heard about it anyway since she'll be staying here."

"Reckon you'll like that," he said to Delia. "You always being outnumbered by men folk."

Delia nodded. "Having Julianne here will be a real treat."

"I haven't even told my parents yet," Julianne confessed.

Caleb chuckled. "What they don't know won't hurt them none. Welcome home, little lady."

"Please don't tell Julius I'm here," she said. "I want to sneak up on him."

"No chance of that today," Delia told her. "He and Wyatt won't be home until late day tomorrow."

Julianne adjusted her hat's brim against the afternoon sun. "Then it'll just be us girls and the children."

Delia nodded. "Speaking of children, Billy and Baby Lil might be awake by now."

"I can't wait to see them. I wonder if Billy will remember me, and I've never even met little Lilly."

"Billy knows you by the photo you sent us from school, and he's been very excited to know that Aunt Julianne's coming home."

"Home." Julianne sighed happily. "It does feel like home."

"Julius is looking forward to seeing you too." Delia paused on the front porch, turning to look out over the ranch. "He might not show it much, especially since he works so hard at trying to be a rough tough cowboy, but he has missed his twin sister."

"Really? He never bothered to write me a single letter."

"You know he's never been too interested in things like reading or writing."

Julianne rolled her eyes. "I'm well aware of it. Plus Mother has written to me about it enough times. She and Father weren't very pleased with Julius's choice to stay on here as a ranch hand."

Delia pursed her lips. "Believe me, I know. But it is his life. I hope they can respect his right to choose for himself."

"And for me too?" Julianne peered curiously at her sister. "Would you support me in my decision to live my own life too?"

"You know I would." Delia wrapped an arm around her as she opened the front door. "Unfortunately, you're going to need my support."

"Mama, Mama!" A towheaded blond boy came barreling down the stairs at full speed.

"Billy," Delia called out, "we walk not run in the house. Now come say hello to your aunt Julianne."

Billy stopped mid-step, staring hard at Julianne. "You're my aunt?" he asked with a furrowed brow.

"Of course." Julianne knelt down with her arms widespread. "Don't you remember me? I used to take care of you when you were little." She grinned. "But look how big and grown up you are now, Billy Boy."

With a shy smile, he cautiously continued, but just a few feet from Julianne, he stopped. His expression grew wary, as if about to bolt. But before he could escape, she swooped him up into a big bear hug. "I missed you so much, Billy Boy!" She landed a big kiss on his warm rosy cheek then tickled his tummy just like old times, and laughing and squirming, he wriggled away from her.

"I gotta tell Baby and Ginger that Aunt Julianne is here," Billy hollered as he took off for the stairs.

"Come and meet Baby Lil." Delia reached for the stair rail. "I'm sure she's awake by now."

After a happy reunion with Ginger and a quick cuddle with her sweet baby niece, Julianne went to change out of her riding clothes. She took her time now to look around the guest room. The linens were fresh, and on the little side table was a small vase of pink roses. Had Delia been actually expecting her? While she'd been riding, someone had moved her trunk up here.

As she unpacked a few things, Julianne was grateful for Delia's invitation to remain at the ranch. Oh, she knew the offer didn't come with any promises of a long-term situation, but Julianne felt she'd be welcome. The only fly in the ointment would be her parents. But as she dressed, she practiced the excuse she would give her parents. Delia had a lot to take care of, and Ginger was slowing down with age, and Daisy had her hands full with cooking for the ranch. Delia would need help with the children and running the household. And Julianne would do everything possible to make life easier for everyone on the Double W. And she would also make herself indispensable to her sister.

As pleased as Delia was to have Julianne home, and as happy as she felt to have her little sister stay on at the Double W, she knew this would come with a price. Her mother would be upset that Julianne had come out to the ranch first. Especially since she'd been so eager to show off her new home. A home that Delia knew they could scarcely afford.

As Delia changed out of her riding clothes, she thought about the frilly pink room Mother had set up just for Julianne—including a closet filled with the latest fashions. Some dresses seemed a bit impractical with their ridiculously large, puffed sleeves, but Delia had kept her thoughts to herself. She knew that Mother was eager to have Julianne under her roof. And that Jefferson was even more eager to have Julianne under his thumb.

Delia could just imagine how her stepfather would act greatly offended when he discovered Julianne's plans to remain on at the ranch. Jefferson was an expert at putting on dramatic airs. Especially when it suited his purposes—or his politics. Truth be told, Delia wasn't too concerned over his reaction, but she didn't want to hurt Mother. Especially since she'd worked so hard to restore their wobbly relationship these past few years.

But she kept these thoughts to herself as she and Julianne played outside with the children. It took no time for Billy to completely warm up to his aunt, proudly showing her all around the farm and introducing her to every animal. Then, during supper with the children, she listened to Julianne's rather dismal tales of finishing school. Although Julianne had learned many skills that might aid her in becoming an admirable wife and mother, she clearly had not enjoyed the experience. It sounded nothing like Delia's college days, a time she still remembered with gratitude.

"The worst part was being stuck indoors all the time and no horses," Julianne said glumly. "I'm so glad it's over with."

"Did they teach you to cook?" Daisy asked as she started to clear the dishes.

"They tried," Julianne told their cook. "But I'll never be as good as you. Your biscuits are still amazing."

"I'm sure Daisy will be glad to continue your training." Delia winked at Daisy as she picked up her plate. Daisy giggled as she carried the dishes to the kitchen.

"So what was the best part of being at school?" Delia asked Julianne. She hoped they could end this conversation on a happier note.

Julianne's brow creased for a long moment, and then she held up a finger. "Type writing!"

"What's that?" Billy asked.

"You use your fingers on a machine." Julianne wiggled her fingers up to show Billy. "And the machine prints the letters out on paper nice and neat. Just like you'd read them in a book or newspaper."

"Type writing?" Delia repeated this with interest as she extracted sleepy Lilly from the highchair and onto her lap. "Were you good at it?"

Julianne nodded proudly. "Very good, according to the school secretary. I was allowed to work with her three afternoons a week. *That* was my favorite thing. If I had to earn my living, I would become a type writer in a nice office somewhere."

"Interesting." Delia felt amused to imagine her little sister working as a type writer, but wondered what their mother would say? Before she could mention this to Julianne, Ginger came in and announced it was time for the children to bathe and get ready for bed.

"Let me help," Julianne insisted. Jumping from her chair she swooped Baby Lil from Delia's lap. "You just sit here and relax, sis. Ginger and I will take care of everything."

Delia was reluctant to remain behind, but then just decided to enjoy it. Who knew how much time Julianne would actually get to be out here with them on the ranch? While the children were being readied for bed, Delia made a pot of tea then went upstairs. After she tucked the children in, listened to Billy's prayer, and kissed them both good night, she invited Julianne to join her for tea.

"Let's take our tea out to the porch," Delia suggested. Partly because she wanted to be out of earshot of anyone while she broached the subject of Mother and Jefferson, and partly because it looked like they were in for a beautiful sunset tonight.

After they were settled in the rockers and enjoying the colorful June sunset, she asked Julianne the hard question. "So…how do you plan to tell Mother and, uh, your father about your plans to remain on here at the Double W?"

Julianne let out a long, loud sigh. "I haven't completely figured that out yet."

"It's not exactly simple, is it?"

Julianne sipped her tea. "I do plan to explain that I think you can use my help here, Delia. In the house and with the children. After all, Ginger *is* getting older. Daisy helps when she can but running the kitchen and keeping our ranch hands fed is a full-time job. And Billy, I'm discovering, is quite a handful. And it probably won't be long before Baby Lilly is walking. Then you'll really be busy chasing the two of them around."

"I would definitely appreciate the help. Especially if it allowed me more time to be outside overseeing more things on the ranch. The larger livestock keeps Wyatt pretty busy, but I like to take care of the chickens and gardens and things. Billy's learning to help and acts like he knows it all sometimes. Like he did for you this afternoon. But you can't expect a four year old to do all that."

"He's very smart for his age." Julianne smiled. "And so much personality."

"That's for certain."

"Anyway, I'm hoping Mother and Father will understand and respect my decision." Julianne's tone sounded a bit uneasy.

Delia nodded, unsure of how to respond. Julianne couldn't really expect her parents to support her in this decision, could she?

"And if they don't like it, well, why should that concern me? It is my life after all." She looked hopefully at Delia. "Right?"

"I agree, but if Mother and Jefferson do put up a fuss—and they probably will—I want you to be prepared for it."

"I have no doubts my father will put up a very big fuss, Delia. And to be honest, I don't care what he thinks." Julianne stuck her chin out with a defiant expression. "I know he has definite plans to marry me off. Mother has said as much in her letters. Oh, she wraps it all up in nice words, saying how we'll all socialize with picnics and parties and gatherings and such. But I know my father is ready to marry me off to his wealthy influential friend. I'm sure he's pressured Mother into believing it'll be a perfect match—and that I'll be happy about it." She scowled.

"Mother's mentioned this to me as well." Delia wasn't sure how much to say, but felt Julianne deserved the truth.

"Of course, Father's reasoning for this arranged marriage is entirely self-serving. He obviously has no concern for my feelings. I can tell by Mother's letters, they believe sending me to that expensive finishing school, gave them the right to marry me off to the highest bidder." She turned to Delia with tear-filled eyes. "I didn't want to go there in the first place. And now this. Well, they won't get away with it. Women are not chattel. We may not have the vote, but we still have rights."

"I know. And I agree." Delia cringed to remember the time her stepfather had pulled this same thing with her. No wonder Julianne was upset.

Julianne reached for Delia's hand. "I'm so glad you support me on this."

"I do support you. But if it's possible, I don't want to make this too hard on Mother." She quickly explained how she'd been restoring that relationship. "And, really, I don't think she's as sold on this idea as Jefferson."

"Maybe not. But do you think she could stand up to him?"

Delia considered this. "She's gotten stronger these past few years. Running the dress shop has been good for her. And thanks to the local mining successes, her business is doing quite well. Mother can hold her head high now."

"She owes that much to you, Delia. You're the one who helped get her started in the first place."

"I was glad to help. It's been good seeing Mother stand on her own two feet for a change. But I have to warn you, she still talks as if it's *their* business. As if Jefferson is her partner somehow, or that he contributes in some way. But as far as I know, the only part of the partnership he shares is in the profits."

"That's exactly what I thought. And that fancy house they're in—Mother has shared in her letters that they really can't afford it. Father is still trying to keep up appearances. And you know how that goes."

Delia nodded glumly.

"I think it's so he looks like the big man around town. To help him in his political pursuits." Julianne set her teacup down with a loud clink. "Well, I refuse to be part of it."

"And Wyatt and I support you in that decision." Delia cleared her throat. "Wyatt has actually met the man Jefferson picked out for you." She didn't want to admit that she'd sent Wyatt on an investigative mission several weeks ago.

"Really?" Julianne's fair brows arched then she leaned over with interest. "Tell me more."

"His name is Royal Dayton, and he's older. A widower with no children. And it sounds like he's a pretty smooth talker with political interests."

"No surprises there."

"And..." Delia wondered how to say this next part. "Wyatt mentioned that Mr. Dayton is considered a *handsome* gentleman."

Julianne tilted her head then frowned. "You mean for an *old* man?"

"He's probably around forty, and it seems he's quite wealthy. He's established several businesses close to an active mine near Cripple Creek. He got in on the cusp of this recent rush and bought up most of the nearby land and is about to establish a township called Dayton Springs. Right now it consists mostly of a store, hotel, and a few other businesses, mostly owned by Mr. Dayton, and he's turning quite a profit from it."

Julianne almost seemed interested now. "So far Royal Dayton doesn't sound too terrible, Delia. Why would someone good-looking and wealthy need an arranged marriage?"

"That's a good question. As you know, there's always a shortage of good women in the West."

"Yes, but that's changing."

"Also, like your father, Royal Dayton has political aspirations. I think that's how they became friends."

"Sounds like a match made in heaven. I mean my father and Mr. Dayton."

Delia smiled. "So if Mr. Dayton hopes to succeed in politics, it could explain his need for an attractive, respectable bride by his side."

"And one just fresh out of a respectable finishing school?" Julianne pursed her lips.

"That probably wouldn't hurt."

"What you're saying doesn't necessarily contradict Mother's letters, Delia. It makes me wonder if I've overreacted. Oh, I certainly have no interest in an arranged marriage. Or any marriage in the near future. But maybe I've been too hasty to judge this Royal Dayton. Do you think I've been wrong?"

Delia slowly shook her head. "There's one thing I haven't mentioned. According to Wyatt, Mr. Dayton's character isn't exactly reputable."

"Ah-hah."

"To be fair, it could be just rumor and innuendo. But Wyatt is under the impression Royal Dayton, besides being an opportunistic businessman, is a bit of a philanderer too."

Julianne wrinkled her nose in disgust. "A ladies' man, of course. Now it all makes sense."

"But we don't know that for certain, Julianne. So let's not think about it for now. Time will tell." Delia forced a smile. "Let's just enjoy this beautiful summer's eve and being together."

"You're right." Julianne took in a deep breath then slowly exhaled. "Tomorrow will take care of itself."

"And if you write a note to Mother before you go to bed tonight, informing her of your early arrival and whereabouts, I'll see that one of our hands takes it to town first thing tomorrow."

"Thank you." Julianne beamed at her. "For everything."

Delia squeezed her hand. "You're more than welcome."

3

Julianne had just taken Billy outside to feed chickens and gather eggs—or maybe he was taking her—when she observed a sleek, black buggy coming down the long drive at a pretty good pace. "Wonder who that can be?"

"It's Grandma!" Billy exclaimed.

"Grandma? She drives her own buggy?" Julianne squinted against the morning sun to see, and sure enough her mother held the reins harnessed to the high-stepping chestnut horse.

"I'm gonna go meet her." Billy dropped the empty egg basket and bolted across the side pasture, and scrambling over a fence, waved vigorously as he raced across the front lawn.

"Might as well get this over with," she muttered to herself as she followed his trail. But instead of jumping the fence, she opted for the gate by the house and, forcing a smile, waved to her mother.

Jane Blackstone called out a loud "*Whoa!*" and, pulling back on the reins, brought the buggy to a stop in front of the house. "Julianne Margaret!" she cried out. "Is that really you?"

"Grandma, don't you know *Aunt Julianne*?" Billy asked importantly.

"Of course, I do. Hello, Julianne!"

Julianne greeted her mother, then, with Billy's help, walked the mare to the hitching post. "I'm so impressed that you drive your own buggy, Mother." She lent the older woman a hand as she climbed from the buggy.

"I'm so happy to see you." Her mother hugged her tightly then held back at arm's length with a scowl. "But I'm not happy for the way you did this, young lady. Skulking into town on an early train, sneaking off to your sister's ranch. I demand to know the meaning of it."

"Mother," Delia called as she emerged from the house with Baby Lil in her arms. "What a pleasant surprise." She hurried over, chattering about the baby in an obvious distraction tactic. "Did you know that besides saying Dada and Mama, she can say Beebo for Billy now? Isn't that cute?"

Jane smiled and cooed at her grandbaby. "Now you need to learn to say *Gramma*."

"And Aunt Julianne too," Billy added.

"That's a mouthful," Julianne told him. "Maybe just Auntie."

"Come on up to the porch," Delia told them. "Julianne, why don't you go ask Daisy to make us some tea?" She exchanged a look with Julianne then nudged Billy. "Why don't you help her, son? Daisy was making cookies. I bet they're done by now."

Billy didn't need any more encouragement. Running ahead of Julianne to the kitchen, he didn't even notice when she motioned to Ginger. "Could you keep Billy occupied?" she whispered, "so that Delia and I can speak privately to our mother."

Ginger nodded knowingly. "I have just the thing."

"And do you think Daisy could bring us some tea to the front porch?" she asked.

"You'll get tea and sympathy," Ginger assured her.

Julianne thanked her then returned to what she knew would be an uncomfortable conversation. But at least her father wasn't there.

Delia and Mother were already seated in rockers, both watching with amusement as Baby Lil, with the aid of the porch railing, attempted to walk by herself.

"It won't be long now," Jane said. "You were already walking by her age."

"I'm in no hurry for her to grow up," Delia assured her.

"I don't blame you for that." Julianne sat down with them. "When Lilly starts to walk you'll have *two* little ones to chase around the ranch, which is precisely why you need extra help around here." She glanced at her mother, wondering if she'd caught the hint or not.

"They can be a handful," Delia agreed. "And Julianne is such a natural with children. I remember how much she helped me when Billy was a baby. She was the best nurse a mother could want."

"That's good experience for when Julianne has her own home and her own children." Jane smiled at Julianne. "And hopefully that won't be long. Imagine having your own babies growing up with their cousins just a little bit older."

"Mother." Julianne frowned. "Isn't that a bit like getting the cart in front of the horse? Speaking of which, when did you learn to drive a buggy. I couldn't have been more surprised seeing you managing that by yourself this morning."

Jane waved a hand. "I've become a rather independent woman in many ways these past few years." She turned to Delia. "Thanks to a lot of prodding from you."

"I call it encouragement," Delia said lightly. "But I'm proud of your achievements, Mother. Running your dress shop and driving a buggy. It's impressive."

"Well, Jefferson has asked me to leave the managing of our dress shop to someone else." She glanced at Julianne. "Someone younger. That way I can spend more time being the lady of the house. Your father believes a woman's place is in the home, and I must say I agree."

"But I thought you enjoyed working in the dress shop. You've written letters to me, saying how fun it is to visit with ladies and how you love helping them with fashion." Julianne reached out to Baby Lil to prevent her from tumbling down the porch steps. "You're so good at that, Mother. Would you really give it all up to go back to housekeeping?"

"We have a housekeeper, Julianne. I mean to manage my home, just as I did when you were children. To plan menus, arrange flowers, entertain guests, that sort of thing. Surely, you know the difference. Didn't they teach homemaking skills in finishing school?"

Ignoring the question, Julianne bounced the baby on her knee.

"And what is that you're wearing?" Jane asked Julianne. "It looks as if it belongs in the rag bag."

"It's just an old school dress." Julianne shrugged. "Perfect for ranch life and helping with the children."

"Well, I hope to never see you wearing it in public."

"Oh, Mother," Delia scolded. "Don't be so hard on her."

Now Julianne took more notice of her mother's attire. Of course, it was quite stylish perfection. A dark purple ensemble, well-tailored but suitable for driving a buggy, and her gloves and boots and veiled hat all carefully chosen. As if jealous of Julianne's diverted attention, Lilly began to fuss, pounding on Julianne's skirt with her little fists. "She's probably wet," Julianne said, thinking it a good excuse to escape her mother. "Maybe I should go—"

"Here's your tea, ladies," Daisy announced as she came out with a loaded tray.

"Let me help." Delia got up to move the table in place.

"And I'll just take this young'un with me." Daisy picked up Lilly, balancing her on a hip. "Time for your morning nap, Baby Lil."

Delia thanked her and now it was just the three of them. As hard as it might be, Julianne knew this was her best chance to set her mother straight regarding her intentions, but she wasn't sure how to begin.

"I'm sorry I didn't let you and Father know about my change in traveling plans," she said carefully. "But everyone else was leaving the school and there seemed no reason to remain there one day longer than necessary, so I checked with the train station then simply arranged to leave a day earlier. I meant to wire you, but I was so busy getting ready, well, I just sort of forgot." Julianne felt her cheeks grow warm at her deceit.

"You forgot?" Her mother's pale blue eyes seemed to penetrate right through the lie. "Really? You expect me to believe that?"

"All right, Mother. I *chose* not to wire you. I wanted to come out here to Delia's ranch without a lot of fuss. To me, this place is home. And it's where I wanted to be. We even took a horse ride yesterday. And hopefully we'll do it again today. And Wyatt and Julius will be back from driving cows by suppertime, and I'm just so happy here. Surely you can understand."

"Happier here than with your own parents in your own home?"

"I've never even seen your new home, Mother. How can you call it my home?"

"Because it's our home, dear. And I've gotten it all ready for you. Your own sweet room and everything. I can't wait for you to see it. I've been so looking forward to your homecoming. And I've made wonderful plans, invited friends and all sorts of exciting things."

"I appreciate that, Mother. But I'm just not ready for all that. Not yet."

"Not yet?" Jane's tone grew cold. "When do you expect to be ready?"

"I don't really know. I wanted to stay here awhile, to help Delia and—"

"Delia has help. She has Ginger and Daisy and ranch hands. She does not need your help, Julianne."

"Ginger is getting old," Julianne protested. "It's hard for her to keep with the children and the housekeeping."

"And I would love Julianne's company out here," Delia added. "It can be lonely at times. Like when the men are off herding cattle. There's nothing like having a sister around."

"Like having a daughter around?" Jane locked eyes with Delia. "Is this the thanks a mother gets? Daughters paired off against her? And what about Julius? You have him living out here too. How can I compete with you, Delia?" She waved her arms. "With all this?"

"This isn't about competition," Delia said calmly. "Julius lives here because he wants to. He's full grown and capable of making his own decisions. He and Wyatt are as close as real brothers. And Julianne is a grown woman. All your children are fine responsible adults now. It's time to let them decide how and where they want to live."

Jane fished a lace-trimmed handkerchief from her bead-trimmed bag, using it to dab her eyes. "I am so disappointed. I have looked forward to your homecoming for so long, Julianne. And now this."

"I'm sorry." Julianne put a hand on her mother's shoulder. "And I'm happy to attend some of your social functions and whatnot. I'd love to see your new house and how your dress shop is doing. I just don't want to live there in town with you."

"You'll be amazed at how much town has grown in your absence," Delia said quickly, as if she knew the conversation needed to change course. "And it's not called Colorado City anymore. It's Colorado Springs now."

"I noticed that change when I got my train ticket." Julianne glanced nervously at her mother. "And I was surprised at how busy town looked yesterday. I can see it's grown a lot. You must like that, Mother. I imagine it's helped your dress shop business."

Jane nodded. "That's true. Did you know it's because of the hot springs, the ones over by Cheyenne Mountain?" Her voice grew more energized. "A real Prussian count has come here. His name is James Pourtales. Your father has actually met him socially. And Count Pourtales has purchased the old Wilcox dairy farm. It's a beautiful piece of property that just needs to be in the right hands. And we heard Count Pourtales has exciting plans for it. He's getting more investors and intends to turn it all into a showplace, with a casino and hotel and electric lights and telephones and everything. It'll be just like living in the big city again."

Julianne exchanged concerned glances with Delia but tried to sound enthused as she responded. "That must be wonderful for you, Mother. I know how much you've missed the East Coast and the big city and all that."

"Yes. It's exciting for your father too. He hopes to be involved with this development. He and his friend, Mr. Dayton, are attempting to establish some kind of partnership with the count. Can you imagine? Your father rubbing elbows with royalty?" She laughed. "In fact that's Mr. Dayton's first name. *Royal.* But, as Royal likes to say, he's not of royal lineage, just a royal name." Her eyes glittered brightly now—and not with tears.

The mention of Royal Dayton's name was unnerving to Julianne. "Well, it seems you and Father have a lot to occupy you these days," Julianne said quickly. "I should think you'd be glad not to have me under foot during all these exciting developments. But I would like to come visit sometime." She forced an overly bright smile.

"So you are set in your ways then?" Jane pursed her lips. "You plan to remain out here regardless of your parents' wishes?"

Julianne simply nodded.

"After all we've done for you?"

Julianne braced herself.

"The tuition to your finishing school was not inexpensive. I had to sell a lot of dresses to pay for that."

"That was your choice, Mother. If you remember, I was not in favor of going away to finishing school."

"No, you wanted to stay here. You were content to become a cowboy like your brother. I guess we'd call that a cowgirl." Her expression looked like she'd bitten into a sour lemon. "But your father and I had no intention of allowing that to happen. We didn't raise you to grovel in the dirt out on a farm with cows and pigs and sheep. And if you think your father will stand by and just watch you throwing yourself away out here, you've got another think coming."

Julianne was mad now. "Well, if you think you and my father can force me into a marriage with Royal Dayton—or even that Count whatever his name was—you've got another think coming too." She stood up as if to drive home her point. "And for you to insinuate that Delia's beautiful ranch is anything but wonderful is not just untrue, it's mean-spirited. I love it out here and I love my sister." She put her hand on Delia's shoulder. "And the things you just said make me want to live out here forever."

"Forever?" Jane stood too. "Taking care of your sister's children and animals? Is that how you'd live your life, Julianne? Truly?"

Julianne locked eyes with her. "Truly!"

"Well, I've said my piece. It's obvious you don't respect your parents the way the Bible instructs you to do. So I'll wash my hands of you, Julianne. But mark my words, young lady, your father will certainly have something to say about this."

"I'm sure he will, Mother. But you might as well tell him to save his breath because my mind is made up." Julianne planted her curled fists onto her hips. "And while you're at it, you might remind him that arranged marriages went out with hoop skirts."

Delia looked like she was about to laugh as she slipped an arm around their mother. "Oh, dear, I'm sure you will both make amends to each other in due time. Just let things cool down a bit first. You know that Julianne loves you, Mother. And I'm sure she respects you too. But you need to respect her rights as a grown woman to make up her own mind."

Julianne could tell by her mother's angry expression that Delia's words had gone over her head just like the fluffy white clouds floating across the bright blue sky.

"Good day, Mother," she said crisply, then, turning on her heel, marched straight into the house solidly closing the door. Let Delia have her. And despite Julianne's assurance earlier that she'd go visit her parents, she had no intention of doing so now. If she never had to speak to either of them again, it would be perfectly fine with her. She would rather grovel in the dirt for a lifetime than spend one single night in their over-priced fancy house in town.

4

Although her mother's visit had put a bit of a damper on Julianne's homecoming, everyone at the ranch still managed to have a celebration when Wyatt and Julius and the others got home that evening. After a delicious dinner and lively conversation, Julianne had put most of the disagreeable conversation with her mother behind her.

But as she got ready for bed, parts of it came back to taunt her. Particularly what her mother had said about respecting one's parents. Julianne knew that part of the Bible was from the Ten Commandments God had given to Moses—and they were supposed to be taken seriously. And, certainly, she had no intentions of murdering or stealing or any of those kinds of things. But how could she respect parents who seemed determined to ruin her life? And what about parents who broke other commandments by lying, cheating or stealing—all things she suspected her father had been guilty of doing? How could she respect him? And so, before going to bed, she asked God to help her with that particular commandment.

The next day, Julianne found herself continually bracing herself for her father's inevitable visit. She knew his attack on her would be more vicious and biting than her mother's, but she was determined to face him. Even if she didn't have Delia around to back her up. Just the same, she made sure to stay close to Delia and the children throughout the day. Just in case. But the day came and went with no sign of Father.

The next few days came and went as well. All without a single word from either of her parents. On one hand, it was a relief, almost as if they'd completely forgotten about her. On the other hand, she was suspicious. What might they be cooking up?

A full week passed and although Julianne was grateful for the reprieve, she was actually starting to feel a bit guilty. Had her words to Mother been so repulsive and hateful and unforgivable that the relationship was beyond repair? Finally, during a trail ride with Delia, during the children's naptime, Julianne raised the subject.

"I actually feel guilty," she confessed. "I know I hurt Mother's feelings. Do you think I should apologize?"

"I don't think it would hurt anything to say you're sorry for some of it. But I also think you should stand your ground on making your own choices in life."

"I just can't believe Father's made no effort to see me. I was certain he would storm the gates and try to drag me off by the hair to force me to marry that man."

Delia laughed. "Jefferson has his faults, but I don't think he'd go that far. It might damage his image and, according to Wyatt, he's got his eye on the upcoming election. We're not sure if it's for himself or in support of one of his friends."

"As unbelievable as that sounds, it gives me hope. I'd love for Father to be distracted with something like that and forget about me."

"Maybe that's what's happening."

"Maybe I should just enjoy it, but I keep thinking this might be the calm before the hurricane."

Delia laughed even louder. "Fortunately, we don't have hurricanes in Colorado. Now, I'll race you back to the house."

As they got closer to the house, Julianne noticed a carriage parked out front. "Are you expecting visitors?" she asked Delia as they stopped to leave their horses in the corral.

"No, but that looks a lot like Jefferson's rig."

"Oh, no." Julianne cringed. "I knew it was too good to be true and that my time of peace and quiet was about to run out."

"Now, don't get worried. It might be nothing." Delia waved over to where Wyatt was coming their way.

"Isn't that your stepfather's carriage?" he quietly asked her.

"Looks like it." She handed over her reins to Caleb.

"Yep, it's Jefferson all right," Caleb told them. "Got here just shortly after you ladies left."

"Is my mother with him?" she asked.

"Nope. Just him alone. I s'pect he's waiting in the house for you." He chuckled. "I thought if we all ignored him he might just go away."

"No luck with that," Julianne said drolly.

"Reckon you better go find out what he's here for." Caleb took Dolly's reins.

"Want me to come with you?" Wyatt asked. "I was just about to check on Julius and the fellas, but I could—"

"No, we can handle this," Delia assured him.

"He's probably just here to scold me for not going home," Julianne said lightly. "And I actually think I'm ready for it. I won't even make a fuss or argue, I'll just say no thanks, I'm staying put."

"Good girl." Wyatt patted her back.

Despite her attempt at nonchalance, Julianne felt a tightness inside of her, the same feeling she'd get before taking a test at school. But she could do this, she reminded herself. And if she wanted to be treated like a grown-up then she would act like one.

"Father," she said when she found him pacing in the living room.

"It's about time you got back," he said sharply.

"Well, it's good to see you too," she shot back.

"Hello, Jefferson," Delia said in a polite but firm tone. "I hope you've made yourself at home." She nodded to a coffee cup and what had probably been a plate of Daisy's delectable sugar cookies.

"I did not come here to be entertained," he said curtly. "I have bad news about your mother."

"What is it?" Delia said suddenly.

"Is she all right?" Julianne asked, fearful that something terrible might've happened while they were still amidst their disagreement.

"She had an accident in her buggy, lost control of the horse and—"

"Is she badly hurt?" Julianne asked.

"She has a broken leg," he said in an angry tone, as if Julianne was somehow personally responsible.

"I'm sorry to hear that." Delia sounded relieved. "But it could've been worse."

"Poor Mother." Julianne removed her gloves. "Is she in the hospital?"

"No, Dr. Muller prefers to treat her at home. And that's just the problem. Your poor mother needs help," he told Julianne. "She has begged me to bring you home to her. It's a daughter's place to help her mother at a time like this. Surely, you must understand."

Julianne looked at Delia for counsel.

"Maybe he's right," Delia said quietly. "I'd go help Mother, but there are the children and—"

"I'll go," Julianne said.

"Good." Jefferson reached for his hat. "Change your clothes and pack what you need for a day or two then we'll be on our way."

Without arguing or questioning, Julianne did as she was told. A part of her had been so frightened just now—what if the buggy accident had been worse? What if Mother had been killed? Julianne never would've forgiven herself for letting things between them end that way. Now she had a chance to make it all up to her mother, and she intended to do it. Somehow she would help Mother get well and hopefully help her to understand why Julianne needed to make her own choices for her own life.

Her father's countenance was like stone as he drove them to town. Even when she attempted small talk, he brushed her off. Clearly he was angry at her. Perhaps he even blamed her for Mother's accident. Or maybe it was simply her disinterest in being married off to his friend Royal Dayton that aggravated him.

Finally they were in town and driving through a new section of what looked like rather ornate homes. With turrets and trim and gingerbread and balconies, it almost seemed as if each house was competing against the next for attention. Even the colors seemed unusually bright. But according to her mother's letters, this was a popular trend. "So is this your neighborhood?" she asked.

He barely nodded without looking her way.

"The houses seem kind of fancy and frilly to me." She noticed his scowl grow deeper. Had she offended him? Did she care? "But that's probably what Mother wanted," she continued. "Although they do seem awfully close together. But maybe that's just compared to the Double W. Everything is so nicely spread out there."

She knew her father wouldn't appreciate that comment, but she was already missing the ranch, and questioning her decision to come to town. He finally stopped the carriage in front of a three-storied pink house with two turrets flanking its curved front porch. The white trim was frilly and curly and for some reason the house reminded her of a wedding cake, but she kept this opinion to herself.

"So this is your house?" She reached for the satchel that she'd packed with only enough things for a few days.

Again he just nodded and, since he wasn't offering to help her out, she jumped down on her own.

"Tell Jones to come tend the horses," he said gruffly.

"Jones?" she asked.

"Our houseman." He flicked the reins and continued on toward what looked like a carriage house, also painted pink with white trim.

Although this pink house wasn't a style she cared for, she thought that it seemed somewhat cheerful as she walked up to the porch. Hopefully the cheer would continue once she went inside. As she rang the bell, she fingered the fancy carvings on the front door, and tried to peek through an intricately beveled glass window.

"Hello?" A plain looking woman in a maid's uniform opened the door wider. "You must be Miss Blackstone."

"Yes, I'm Julianne." She smiled. "How do you do?"

"Fine, thank you. I'm Ellie. Come in, please."

"Nice to meet you, Ellie. I'm here to see my mother. And, oh yes, my father asked for Jones to go out and tend the horses."

"Thank you, Miss. I'll let him know. Your mother is in her room. Right this way." Ellie led her through the dimly lit house. Unlike the Double W ranch house, these rooms seemed small and crowded and dark. The windows had heavy drapes that were mostly drawn. "Here you go, Miss." Ellie tapped on the door, quietly calling out. "Your daughter is here to see you, Mrs. Blackstone."

Julianne heard her mother's weak response, saying to "send her in." Still clutching her satchel, Julianne timidly entered what seemed an even darker room. "Mother?" As her eyes adjusted she made out the bed and her mother in it. "It's so dark in here. May I draw the drapes?"

"If you like."

Julianne set down her satchel to open the heavy velvet drapes then turned to look at her mother. "I'm so sorry about your accident." She went closer and felt surprised to see her mother's messy hair and pale looking face. "Are you in much pain?"

"The doctor gave me some medicine." She groaned as she attempted to push herself up.

"Here, let me get you a pillow." Julianne hurried around to slip a pillow behind her mother, helping her to sit. "Is that better?"

"I suppose." Jane leaned back with a sigh.

"I'm so sorry," Julianne said again. "Not only for your accident, but also for the words I spoke to you last week. I hope you can forgive me, Mother."

"Yes, of course." She seemed to brighten slightly then it was as if a dark cloud came over her.

"Are you in pain?"

"It is painful to see you wearing such a sorry dress." Jane dramatically draped a hand over her eyes like a shield.

Julianne looked down at her plain brown dress. "I was in a hurry to get to you, Mother. I threw on the easiest thing."

"Well, do everyone a favor and put that horrid garment in Ellie's rag bag."

Julianne wanted to protest this suggestion but decided to change the subject. "So when did your accident occur?" Julianne pulled a chair close to the bed and sat.

"Yesterday."

"Father said your leg is broken. Any other injuries?"

She touched the side of her temple. "A blow to my head."

"How did it happen, Mother? Unless you're too tired to talk."

"I think it would be good to talk." Leaning her head back, she closed her eyes, and Julianne leaned in to listen. "Yesterday afternoon, I was delivering a dress to Mrs. Green. I wanted to take it myself. It was a lovely peach satin gown for her daughter's wedding on Saturday. At the crossroads, I reined my horse to the right, but he went the other way." Mother reached for her head again. "Or maybe I wanted to turn left, it's hard to remember."

"That's understandable. You've been through a trauma."

"I do recall troubling over something while driving…my memory is cloudy."

"What was troubling you?"

"Thinking of Mrs. Green and her daughter's wedding reminded me of you, Julianne, and how upset you'd made me." Her eyes were still closed, and her brow was creased, as if suffering severely.

"I'm so sorry." Julianne felt a wave of guilt. Was she partly to blame for her mother's accident? "But turning the wrong way caused your accident?"

"No, it was the fault of a reckless farmer with a tall wagonload of hay. He spooked my horse, causing my buggy to flip then ran into us." She opened her eyes and reached for her head again. "I probably still have straw in my hair."

"I don't see any, Mother, but what a terrible experience." Julianne reached for her mother's hand. "It must have been frightening."

"I'm still getting over the shock."

"And was the peach satin dress ruined?"

Jane almost smiled. "Now, that sounds like my daughter, the girl I used to know. Fortunately, for the Greens, the dress was untouched. Jones delivered it to them last night." She squeezed Julianne's hand. "Here is just one of the many reasons I need you, Julianne. To cheer me up like this. And help me get well. But perhaps most importantly, I need your help at the dress shop. I'm so worried it will all go to pieces in my absence." She peered up with a helpless almost childlike expression. "Can you please help me, dear?"

"Of course, Mother. That's why I came." She looked toward the foot of the bed. "Which leg is broken?"

"The right one. The doctor wrapped bandages around a splint."

"Not a plaster cast?"

"No, he said the splint was sufficient." Now she let out a moan. "Oh my, I'm in pain again." She pointed to a white bottle by her bedside. "Can you stir a teaspoon of that powder into water for me to drink? And then I must rest."

Julianne did as she was told, waiting for Mother to drink the chalky looking liquid. "Do you want me to close your drapes while you rest?"

"Yes. The light does hurt my eyes, dear. And, please, ask Ellie to show you to your room. You get all settled and make yourself at home. At noontime you can bring me my lunch and we'll talk again. I can explain what needs doing at the dress shop."

Julianne closed the drapes, picked up her satchel, then tiptoed out. As much as she appreciated her mother's invitation to make herself at home, she doubted she would ever feel much at home in this house. But she would do everything possible to help her mother get well…and everything necessary to avoid any interaction with her father.

5

Her parents' new house was, in many ways, much like their old one back in Pittsburgh. It didn't have the substantial feel of an older stone home, but it was definitely "showy" with all its frills and fine fabrics and tassels and useless decorative dust-collecting doodads. Her mother had always preferred the "finer things" as she liked to say, but in Julianne's opinion, finer seemed to have more to do with money than style. At least not her style. She preferred the Double W ranch house's simplicity and functionality. Even the front parlor had improved after Delia removed a lot of the fussy decorations put there by her stepmother.

Still, Julianne reminded herself as she unpacked her satchel, it was her parents' home. Not hers. And once Mother was on the mend, she intended to move straight back to the ranch. Already she missed it. She paused to study the room that her mother had made "specially" for her. Perhaps she would've liked it as a child, but she found it, like the rest of the house, overly done up and slightly suffocating. If she had to remain here more than a week or so, she might remove some of the cushions and heavy curtains. And she probably wouldn't wait that long to hide the pale porcelain figurines that reminded her of dead people.

She opened the closet then blinked in surprise. It looked like a miniature dress shop. Dresses, jackets, skirts, shirtwaists, hats, shoes, even petticoats—a complete wardrobe for a proper young lady. As if Mother thought she'd come home from school without a single stitch to wear. Granted, her dresses from school were not the height of fashion, as Mother was quick to remind her, but they were perfectly fine for ranch life. And she had no intention of putting this one in Ellie's rag bag.

Just the same, she was curious about these fine-looking clothes. And there once was a time—back in Pennsylvania—when clothing like this would've turned her head. But she'd changed since then. She carefully extracted a fluffy looking pink dress from the others. It was lavishly trimmed in ruffles and lace.

"My goodness!" she exclaimed out loud when she saw the puffy sleeves. They resembled balloons and were stuffed with tissue paper. Where would someone wear something like that? She carried the dress out into her room, holding it up to herself before the cheval mirror and had to admit that it wasn't as bad as she'd expected. But those sleeves.

Next she removed a pale blue silk dress that looked perfect for a summer evening, and to her relief had no puffy sleeves. Its short sleeves resembled loose tulip petals. And the relaxed neckline was flattering. She held it up and decided it was actually quite pretty and the shade of blue went nicely with her eyes.

Julianne examined some of the other garments and had to admit they were all well-made and, although she didn't appreciate the fussy ones, she could tell Mother had selected them with thought and care. Her mother had always been considered quite tasteful when it came to her personal appearance. She'd always relished the admiration it brought to her. One of the reasons Delia had suggested she open a dress shop several years ago. But Mother needed to understand that

Julianne wasn't a child anymore. She wasn't a doll to be dressed up and paraded about.

Still, she remembered how helpless Mother had looked in bed… and her pained request for Julianne to change her dress. Well, if it would help her recover sooner, it would be worth it. But first she would enjoy a nice relaxing bath. As she soaked in the lavender scented tub, she couldn't deny it was rather delightful to have her own private bathroom. At school, she'd shared the facility with twenty other girls in her dormitory. Even at Delia's, which had been an improvement, it was a shared bath. This was definitely luxurious. But she didn't want to get used to it.

She dressed in the most practical ensemble she could find in her fancy closet. A sky blue and white striped shirtwaist with overly large sleeves and a matching sky-blue skirt. She even took a bit of time pinning her hair up, hoping that would make Mother happy, then went back downstairs to see about serving her mother some lunch.

"There now," her mother said as Julianne entered her room, where the drapes had been drawn open again. "You look like a respectable young lady." She was propped up in bed and her messy hair had been smoothed and pinned, and she even had on a lacy pink bed jacket.

"You look better too." Julianne came closer. "You even have roses in your cheeks now."

Jane touched her cheek with a furrowed brow. "Hopefully I'm not feverish."

"Do you feel unwell?"

"I suppose I'm as well as I can be under the circumstances. I asked Ellie to bring our lunch in here so that you can keep me company. I hope you don't mind."

"Not at all. Maybe I should go help her."

"Nonsense. Sit down. Ellie can handle it."

Julianne sat down and smiled. "You really do look much better, Mother. I do believe you're on the mend."

Her mother's countenance seemed to darken as she reached up to touch her head. "I'm glad you think so."

"Oh, I know it'll take time for your leg to heal."

"And these headaches and dizzy spells." She pointed to the side table. "Perhaps I need more of that medicine. Do you mind?"

"It's only been a couple of hours," Julianne pointed out. "Is there any danger of taking too much?"

"No, no. The doctor said take it as needed for the pain."

Feeling uncertain, Julianne only put in half as much of the powder this time, but fortunately Mother didn't notice. "Here you go." She handed her the glass, watching as her mother sipped. "I appreciate all the fine clothes upstairs, but you really shouldn't have gone to so much trouble."

"Trouble?" Jane handed her the empty glass. "Having my daughter clothed like a stylish lady is no trouble. After all, as the owner of the most exclusive dress shop in Colorado Springs, I do have a reputation to maintain. I've even asked Delia to respect that when she and the children come into town. I understand wearing ranch clothes out in the country, but here in town, well, we like to keep up appearances."

"Right." Julianne ran her hand over the smooth fabric of her skirt. "I'll be interested to see your dress shop, Mother. You wrote to me of how you improved and enlarged it. I'm sure it's very nice."

"Yes, and that's exactly what I want to discuss with you today." Jane paused as Ellie carried in a large lunch tray, waiting for her to arrange it for them. After Ellie left, Jane continued to talk about the dress shop and how she wanted Julianne to spend time there. "I don't expect you to go in today, but if you could go tomorrow morning, I'd be most grateful." She sighed. "It's so distressful not knowing what might go on in my absence."

"I'm happy to go for you, Mother. I'll do whatever I can to help."

"And it's important that you arrive at the dress shop looking stylish and professional, Julianne. It will garner you more respect."

"I can understand that." Julianne dipped her spoon into the soup.

"I would suggest you wear the royal blue skirt and jacket with a white shirtwaist. It will make you appear older."

"Fine, I'll remember that."

As they ate lunch, Mother continued to instruct her as to what to do and how to behave tomorrow. Julianne had to bite her tongue a number of times, but she was determined to cooperate. And by the time they finished, Julianne felt heartened to see that Mother's appetite was good, and her coloring and energy much better than earlier. Still, Julianne felt determined not to mention Mother's physical condition since it seemed only to distress her. Plus she knew from experience that speaking of Mother's health often resulted in imaginations of the worst. Best to keep a positive focus.

After having breakfast with Mother, and receiving approval for her appearance, Julianne left for the dress shop. Since her parents' neighborhood was only a few blocks away, and it was a fine sunny morning, she declined her mother's offer of Jones to drive her in the carriage and opted to walk. To her relief, she and her father had not exchanged words since the silent ride from the ranch yesterday, but as she left the house he did bid her "good day."

Walking through town allowed her time to take in all the changes that had occurred during her time away at school. She'd heard about the recent mining boom that had brought lots of money and business to their town and, it was obvious, the population had increased considerably. But it was also obvious that some of the businesses on the edge of town had been thrown up quickly and cheaply. However, as she got toward the middle of town, the buildings became more substantial and attractive.

Her mother's shop, called *La Mode*, which was French for fashion, looked better than ever with its large plate glass windows and pretty displays of summery hats, scarves, and handbags. Very stylish.

The shop didn't open until nine and Julianne made sure she got there early enough to have a conversation with the employees.

Helena was the only one Julianne still knew and, according to Mother, the most experienced clerk, but not a managerial type. The other two clerks, Lizzie and Rowena, Mother described as capable and reliable, but little more than that. And the seamstresses who worked in back had no interest in sales. According to Mother, most of her shopgirls only remained long enough to get engaged and married and then they were gone. But Helena, with no interest in marriage, stayed on.

Thanks to Mother's telephone, Helena knew to expect Julianne this morning and was already unlocking the door. "Good morning," she said crisply. "Your mother warned me you were coming, but I really don't see the need of it. I have everything completely under control here. Both Lizzie and Rowena will be here today. Three clerks are more than plenty to run the shop adequately."

Julianne just smiled as she unpinned her hat. "I'm sure you're right, but it makes Mother feel much better to know that I'm here. I'll try not to get in your way."

"You can put your things in the backroom." Helena pointed toward the back with her feather duster.

"Everything looks bigger and better than I remember." Julianne slowly strolled through the enlarged shop. "Very impressive."

"Yes, La Mode is considered the finest women's apparel shop in the city." Helena dusted the top of a gleaming glass case of stylish gloves. "Your mother need not worry that it will change during her absence."

Julianne forced a smile. Clearly Helena didn't appreciate her presence, but there seemed little to do about it. So she simply went to the backroom and found a place to put her hat and gloves and handbag. Then checking her hair in the mirror, she smoothed the front of her tailored jacket and went back out.

Helena was letting a pair of attractive young women into the shop now. Introductions were made. The pretty brunette was Lizzie and the animated redhead Rowena. "Your mother has talked so much about you," Rowena said cheerfully as she removed her hat. "I feel like I know you."

"You look very sophisticated in that suit," Lizzie told her. "I encouraged your mother to get it for you."

"Thank you. It's very nice." Julianne smiled.

"How is Mrs. Blackstone feeling?" Rowena asked.

"As well as can be considering the circumstances."

"We sent her flowers," Lizzie said. "I hope she got them."

"Yes, the pink roses are lovely in her room," Julianne assured them.

"Enough chitchat," Helena announced. "It's almost time to open the store."

Rowena giggled then whispered, "Helena is all business, you know."

Helena cleared her throat. "Today Rowena will cover the accessories and Lizzie will assist with the foundations and lingerie. I will manage the ready-to-wear and fittings."

"What about Julianne?" Lizzie asked. "What will she do?"

"Since she knows little about working at the shop, I imagine she will just float around and observe." Helena frowned. "And, please, do not get in the way."

Julianne just nodded, but wondered, did Helena really think that selling women's clothing was as difficult as all that? Still, she was only here to placate her mother. Hopefully, after a few hours of observing and keeping out of everyone's way, she could go home and assure Mother that all was well here.

Despite not wanting to be in the dress shop, Julianne found herself pulled into it at times. And despite Helena's warning to stay out of the way, Julianne actually found herself helping customers from time to time. At least she hoped she was helping. It didn't take long to learn the lay of the store and pointing women in the right direction was simply good manners. And conversing with shoppers also helped pass the time. It seemed that none of them had heard of her mother's unfortunate accident and so, when they inquired as to her absence, Julianne informed them of her condition. And they all asked her to send their condolences.

By midafternoon, when Julianne's feet began to hurt from standing too long in her new shoes, she accepted Helena's suggestion to call it a day. "You've been here much longer than necessary," the older woman pointed out. "Just go home and assure your mother that we are doing perfectly fine in her absence."

"I'll do that," Julianne promised as she tugged on her gloves.

"And, really, there's no need for you to come back tomorrow." Helena opened the door for her. "If for some reason we do need extra help someday, I'll telephone your mother and let her know."

Julianne thanked her but suspected her mother would have more to say about that. Still, she was glad to leave. It was a nice enough store, but it felt stuffy in there and the smell of the perfume counter had given her a headache.

She got home just as a delivery boy was carrying up a box of what looked like candy. "For Mrs. Blackstone," he told her. She offered to take it in and gave him a small tip. Then, going quietly into the house, she went directly to her mother's room and was pleased to see her in a pretty dressing gown and sitting at her vanity.

"You're out of bed!" Julianne exclaimed.

Jane jumped in surprise. "Yes, well, your father helped me."

"That's wonderful." She handed her the box. "I think it's chocolates."

"Goodness, I've received all sorts of things." Jane waved to her dresser where several new bouquets and colorful cards were arranged. "My dear customers miss me."

"Yes. And everything is going like clockwork at your shop. No worries." Julianne sat down on the bed to loosen the laces of her shoe. "But my feet are aching from these pretty new shoes."

"Don't tell me about aches and pains." Jane reached for her head. "In fact, I think I feel a headache coming on. Can you go find your father and ask him to help me back into bed?"

"I'm sure I'm strong enough to help you," Julianne offered.

"No, I wouldn't feel safe. And when I'm dizzy, my balance is poor. Please, get your father. He's probably in his den."

"Yes, of course." Julianne stood.

"Then come back later, perhaps an hour or so, and bring me tea. Then we can talk."

Julianne agreed and hurried out. Finding her father in the den, she explained the situation, but instead of getting up, he continued reading his newspaper. "Mother seemed urgent," Julianne told him. "I offered to help, but she may be having a dizzy spell."

He carefully folded the paper then stood. "Yes, I'll go see to her." He paused to examine Julianne more closely. "You're looking very nice. Isn't it better to look like a young lady than a ranch hand?"

She wanted to tell him "not in the least," but knew that would only lead to a disagreement, and so she simply pursed her lips and nodded. But hearing his chuckle as he left grated on her. Of course, he assumed he'd gotten the upper hand on his daughter's behavior, but if he truly believed she would conform to his wishes, he was in for a very unhappy surprise.

6

The next few days fell into smooth albeit rather mundane routine. Julianne would dress carefully then breakfast with Mother. Then she would walk to La Mode where, despite Helena's objections, Julianne became more and more involved. Lizzie and Rowena appreciated her help, but Helena seemed increasingly irritated by it. Julianne usually went home by midafternoon, where she would report to Mother all the doings of the day over tea. And other than one uncomfortable evening sharing dinner with her father, Julianne would usually dine with her mother.

"It seems unnecessary for you to be confined to your bed all day," Julianne said after nearly a week. "Why don't we get you a wheeled chair and I can take you outside to enjoy the fresh air and sunshine and—"

"No, no, no! Just the thought of being wheeled around like that makes me feel sick. What if I had a dizzy spell and fell?"

"Oh, I hadn't considered that."

"Bed rest is best for now." Jane reached for her teacup. "Now, tell me about your day at the shop. Anything new?"

Julianne shared the comings and goings as best she could then finally got to the subject of Helena. Not wanting to upset her mother, she'd kept quiet on this subject. But after Helena had grabbed something out of her hands today and banished her to the backroom, Julianne felt something must be said.

"Helena seems to resent me being there, Mother."

Jane waved a hand. "Oh, I'm not surprised. She must see you as a threat, dear. I've made no secret that I'd love for you to run the shop for me. At least until you're married."

Julianne pressed her lips together, trying to think of a calm response.

"And it sounds as if you're handling it all very well, Julianne. And you look so pretty every day when you go into town. So stylish and respectable." She smiled brightly. "You truly make me proud."

"I'm glad I can be of help, Mother." Her words felt stiff.

"Your help is making me better too."

"Well, that's certainly good news."

"And I don't want you to worry about Helena. It's just her way. She is very jealous of her position and sees herself as indispensable."

"She does know how to run the shop efficiently."

"Yes, but the customers don't respond to her the way they do to me. Or the way I suspect they might do for you."

Julianne considered how already many of the shoppers seemed to prefer her to Helena. "I suppose I see what you're saying. Helena can be a little abrupt at times."

"I can't deny she's a good employee, but as you must've observed, she's not terribly stylish or attractive."

"But she has an excellent business head." Julianne remembered how quickly Helena had worked figures in her head today when she'd corrected Rowena's calculations on a rather large sale.

"That's true enough." Jane set her teacup down.

"And she's very committed to La Mode, Mother. I actually believe she'd make a good store manager for you—"

"No. I do not want to hear another word about that, Julianne."

She pressed her fingers to her temples. "Just thinking of that makes my head throb in pain."

"I'm sorry."

"Let's not speak of it anymore," Jane said firmly. "And I have other news to share. Delia sent me a note saying she and the children are coming to visit tomorrow. I sent a note back inviting them to stay for lunch, and I'd like you to join us."

"That's wonderful."

"And since you say everything is going so well at the shop, why don't you take the day off. Perhaps you can help Ellie set a nice table. We're having such mild weather, and I'd like to dine outside. Wouldn't that be festive?"

"And will you be able to join us?" Julianne asked.

"I'll have your father carry me out there."

Julianne considered suggesting a wheeled chair again, but her mother seemed so genuinely happy, she didn't want to upset her or do anything to dampen the cheery prospects of seeing Delia and the children tomorrow.

Delia would've gone to visit her ailing mother sooner, but the demands of moving plants from the greenhouse to the garden combined with a teething baby made delaying sound prudent. Still it was nearly a week and besides feeling compelled to see her mother, she was curious as to how Julianne was faring.

As usual, Caleb was glad to drive them to town and perform errands while she and the children visited. Although she looked forward to the day when she could drive her own carriage with her children, it was too precarious to balance a baby and rein in a four year old as well as a pair of strong horses. "Thanks, Caleb," she said as she and the children headed for the house.

"See you 'round two," he called back.

Billy was already trying to reach the doorbell and knocking on the door. She'd given him the usual speech about not touching the breakables and minding his manners, but for some reason he always seemed full of old nick when they came here. Ellie answered the door, warmly greeting them and leading them through the house. "The luncheon is set up outside," she explained. "Mrs. Blackstone thought the children would enjoy it."

"Mother is able to get outside?" Delia was surprised.

"Mr. Blackstone and my husband helped her out." Ellie opened the big glass doors and there, like the queen at the head of the table, sat her mother. Her leg propped on an ottoman, her back toward them.

"Delia!" Julianne set a vase of flowers on the side table. "And Billy Boy and Baby Lil!" She ran over to embrace all of them. "I'm so happy to see you!"

"How are you doing?" Delia asked quietly.

"I'm all right." Julianne reached for the baby to free Delia's hands.

"And Mother? Is she better?" Delia removed her hat.

"I think so," Julianne whispered, "but be careful if you ask about her health. It sometimes makes her—"

"Don't worry, I know all about that." Delia smiled as her mother turned her head to see what was transpiring behind her. "Hello, Mother," she called out. "My tribe has arrived."

"Come over here so I can see you," Jane called back.

"Go easy there, Billy," Delia warned as he charged toward his grandma. "Remember Gramma has a hurt leg."

Julianne carried Lilly over to the table. "And here is your darling granddaughter. Goodness, I think she's gotten bigger in just one week."

"Is she walking yet?" Jane asked.

"Almost." Delia sat down next to her mother. "Don't you look pretty, Mother. Such a lovely dressing gown. Do you carry those in your shop?"

"Of course." Jane reached over to tickle Lilly's chin. "Don't you look pretty in your little pink dress?"

"It's the one you got her for Christmas," Delia said. "It finally fits."

For the next hour, between eating lunch and playing with the children, Delia thought the five of them seemed more like a real family than ever. Having Julianne staying with Mother seemed to have worked some kind of magic.

"Have you been helping at the dress shop?" Delia asked Julianne.

"She's been a true Godsend," Jane answered for her.

"I wouldn't say that." Julianne waved a hand. "I do my best. But Helena probably enjoyed my absence today."

"How much longer do you plan to stay in town?" Delia asked.

"I'm not sure." Julianne glanced at their mother.

"The reason I ask is because it's almost time to drive the herd up to the highland and Julius hopes you'll join us. He made me promise to ask." Delia laughed. "I think he wants to show off his horseman skills. He thinks he can outride you now."

"I'd like to see that." Julianne grinned. "Tell him I'll be there with bells on."

Jane let out a little groan and Delia turned to look at her. "Are you all right, Mother?" She put a hand on her arm. "It's a pleasant surprise to see you're recovering so nicely."

Jane frowned then pressed her fingers to her temples. "I am recovering some, but I still get these horrid headaches and dizzy spells. And my leg aches something terrible right now." She sighed. "I'm afraid I have overdone it today."

"Oh, dear." Delia glanced at Julianne.

"Do you want me to get Jones and Father?" Julianne offered. "To carry you to your room?"

"Please, do." Jane sighed as Julianne hurried off. "I'm sorry to end the party like this, Delia, but I'm sure you understand."

"Of course. We didn't want to wear you out today. I know the children can be tiring. We shouldn't overstay our welcome."

"I do appreciate the visit. I hope you'll come again in a few days."

"Yes, as soon as we can."

For a moment, Jane just watched her grandchildren playing in the grass and neither of them spoke. Delia studied her mother, trying to determine if she truly felt unwell or if it was the conversation about the cattle drive that put her off. But she knew there was no point in asking, and besides, the men were here. Delia politely greeted her stepfather then bent down to kiss her mother's cheek. "Keep getting better, Mother. We love you."

"I love you too, dear." As the men lifted her, chair and all, Jane let out a loud groan as if in severe pain. But Delia couldn't help but notice, as they transported her into the house, her mother's face appeared serenely calm.

"Poor Mother," Julianne said. "First time out of her room. Perhaps it was too much for her."

"Perhaps." Delia grimaced. "Or perhaps she didn't like the sound of you going on the cattle drive."

Julianne nodded glumly. "I had similar thoughts."

"How long do you think you'll need to stay here?"

"I don't know. Every time I mention leaving, she seems to get worse."

"Right." Delia watched as Billy dragged his sister like a rag doll across the lawn. Lilly was giggling with glee, but her pretty pink dress would probably be grass stained. "What does her doctor say about how long it will take her to heal?"

"I haven't ever been here when he comes."

"What about using crutches or a wheelchair?"

"Her dizzy spells."

"Yes, of course." Delia checked her watch. "Well, it's about time for Caleb to come fetch us. Can I help you get the luncheon things back into the house?"

"No, Ellie and I can get it," Julianne said sullenly.

"Are you sad?"

"Not exactly. Just confused."

"Confused?"

"I want to go back to the ranch with you more than anything. And I really want to go on the cattle drive, but…"

"But?"

"I feel guilty about Mother."

"Guilty? You have no reason to feel guilty, Julianne. Goodness, here you've been slaving away to help her get better. If anyone should feel guilty, it's me."

"No, not like that." Now Julianne told her about how their mother was fretting over Julianne when she had her accident. "It's like I'm to blame."

Delia reached for her hand and looked into her eyes. "It wasn't your fault."

"But I'd said horrid things to her, Delia. And she was thinking about it."

"Nonsense. She's a grown woman. If she can't drive a buggy and think at the same time, well, she should be walking." Delia couldn't help but laugh. "Except that she obviously can't even do that now. But you are not to blame."

Julianne hugged her. "Thanks, I needed to hear that."

They said their good-byes and Caleb, who was already waiting for them, helped Delia and the children into the carriage. Although he whistled a cheery tune with Billy singing along, Delia felt a heaviness as they drove out of town. Something about their visit felt as off-key as Billy's singing. She disliked being suspicious of anyone, especially family, but she had the distinct impression Mother was manipulating Julianne. And she didn't like it—not one little bit. But what could she possibly do about it?

7

As badly as Julianne wanted to join in the cattle drive, which was just a week away, she was reluctant to broach the subject with Mother again. Instead, she poured all her energies into helping at the dress shop. Of course, Helena wasn't very appreciative of her efforts, but Julianne felt she'd found a place where she could be useful—in the office, where it seemed some things, including orders and correspondence, appeared to be neglected. "I think you need a type writing machine," she told Mother as they were finishing up breakfast.

"Whatever for?"

"The office work I was telling you about." Julianne finished her coffee. "It would be much more professional than handwritten letters. More modern."

"But who knows how to use such a machine?"

"I do," she said proudly. "I learned at finishing school and I'm rather good, if I do say so myself."

Her mother's eyes lit up. "Perhaps you are right. La Mode should be as up to date in the office as in the shop."

Julianne tried not to look surprised. "So you don't mind if I look for a type writing machine?"

"I think it's a good idea, but where would you find one?"

"I noticed a stationary store in town. Perhaps someone there can help me." Julianne dabbed her mouth with the napkin and stood, but Mother reached out for her hand, grasping it warmly.

"I just want to tell you, Julianne, how grateful I am to you for your help. I do not know what I would've done without my dear daughter during this time. Thank you."

"I'm glad I could be here for you." Julianne leaned down to kiss her cheek. As she left the house, she couldn't remember a time when she'd ever felt closer to her mother. Perhaps if this week continued to go well and Julianne continued to prove herself, Mother wouldn't balk at her participating in the cattle drive after all.

Seeing the stationary shop open, Julianne decided to stop in and inquire about typing machines.

"Sorry, Miss, we don't carry typewriters here. I can order you up one, but it will take a while to get here."

"How long is *awhile*?"

"Oh, I'd estimate about a month."

As she considered this, she noticed a tall fair-haired man looking at filing materials. Something about him seemed familiar—and then she remembered—*Levi Stanfield*. He was the young man who had so graciously danced with her at Delia and Wyatt's wedding. His father was Delia's lawyer. Julianne had only been twelve at the time, but she'd been starry-eyed over Levi Stanfield for some time. Whenever they went to town or any social event, she was always on the lookout for him. But she eventually learned he'd gone back East for college. She wasn't sure how old he was now, but supposed he'd be in his mid-twenties. She wondered if he was married.

"Hello," she said boldly as he approached the register with a cardboard box. "I'm sure you don't remember me, but I'm Delia Davis's sister and I met you long ago at her wedding." Julianne smiled brightly.

It took him a moment and then his eyes lit up. "Sure, I remember you. That was a fun day, and you were a good dancer…for a little girl."

"And you were kind enough to dance with me."

"I'm sorry, but I don't recall your name?"

"Julianne."

"That's right. Julianne." His smile seemed approving. "And all grown up now."

"I've been away at school and only back home for a short while."

"I was away at school too. I can hardly believe how much town has grown during my absence. But that's what a rush does to a place."

"Yes, I've been surprised at all the changes too."

"Well, it's a pleasure to see you again, Miss Williams."

"Williams?" She tilted her head to one side.

"I'm sorry. You're not a Williams?" He looked embarrassed. "Oh, are you married then?"

"No, no." She smiled as she realized his mistake. "You assumed I was a Williams because Delia's father was Winston Williams. But she's my half-sister. I'm Julianne Blackstone."

"Blackstone?" His brow creased.

She felt uneasy as she nodded. Something had changed at the mention of her last name.

"I see." He set his box on the counter. "Well, it's good to see you again, Miss Blackstone."

"Yes," she said primly. "You too, Mr. Stanfield." She turned back to the clerk. "I'll think about the typing machine," she said briskly. Then feeling a flush on her cheeks, she hurried out. But as she headed for the dress shop, she replayed their encounter. Levi Stanfield had grown noticeably chilly at the mention of her last name. Was her father's reputation really that bad? And if so, why exactly? Certainly, he had his faults, and she knew them well. But did everyone else in town know them too?

Levi regretted his disapproving reaction to Julianne Blackstone's last name. It wasn't her fault that her father's scruples were questionable, or that Jefferson Blackstone was currently involved with some disreputable opportunistic businessmen, including Royal Dayton. And it wasn't Julianne's fault that Levi was currently building a legal case to prevent these land-grabbing men from creating laws that would negatively impact all the other little towns popping up around Cripple Creek, not to mention the farms and ranches nearby.

Levi was well aware that a gold rush brought out the worst in some people or that innocent folks often suffered from their greed. But after all his years spent back East at Yale Law School, he was determined to do whatever he could to protect this beautiful part of the country. His father, now a sitting county judge, had taught Levi by example how to be a friend to farmers and ranchers and townsfolk, and how to treat people equally no matter what. So why had he been rude to Julianne Blackstone? Especially when, besides being friendly and pretty, she was a darn good dancer.

Determined to make it up to her, he spent the next two days trying to devise an excuse to bump into her again. Through a little research and observation, he discovered that the fancy dress shop called La Mode belonged to Julianne's mother and that Julianne was working there. Perhaps that was why she'd wanted a type writing machine. By midweek, he had a plan.

Admittedly, he felt a bit foolish walking into a women's dress shop during his midday lunch break, but he quickly made it clear he was there to purchase his mother a birthday gift. Her birthday wasn't until August, but the plain-faced woman helping needn't know that.

"What did you have in mind?" she asked.

"I'm not sure." He glanced around the shop, hoping to spy Julianne, but the only other person in the shop was a dark-haired young woman, watching him with avid interest. "Maybe I could look around a bit and see if something catches my eye."

"Yes, of course." The older woman stepped away, busying herself with a selection of rather flamboyant hats. Truth be told, he doubted if his conservative mother ever shopped in this place, but perhaps he could find something appropriate for her.

"What about a cashmere shawl?" The younger woman held out a crimson shawl with a long fringe, draping it over her shoulder for effect. "These are quite popular with our older customers."

"Yes, well, my mother already has a shawl she's quite fond of." He didn't add that his mother would never be caught dead wearing such a bright color.

"Perhaps a pair of kid leather gloves then?" She went over to the glass case. "They're soft and lightweight, but sturdy enough for driving a buggy. But perhaps your mother doesn't drive a buggy. Many older women don't care to." She leaned forward over the case, lowering her voice. "In fact, the owner of our store recently had an accident driving her buggy."

"Really?" His interest piqued. "Was that Mrs. Blackstone?"

She nodded, glancing around as if worried she might be overheard. "She was run down by a hay wagon and suffered a broken leg and a lump to the head."

"I am, uh, an acquaintance of her daughter, and I hadn't heard of her mother's accident. I hope she's recovering." He noticed the young woman's gaze dart toward the back of the store.

"Speaking of her daughter, there she is now," the woman said politely.

"Miss Blackstone," Levi said in a pleasant tone. "I'm pleased to see you. And I offer my condolences for your mother."

"Mr. Stanfield," she said in a cordial but cool tone. "What are you doing here?"

His smile felt uneasy. "I'm, uh, shopping for my mother's birthday gift."

"Perhaps you'd prefer Miss Blackstone's assistance," the brunette said crisply, and before he could answer, she went to greet a female customer just entering the shop.

"So, what can I help you with, Mr. Stanfield?" Julianne's smile was polite. "What sort of gift are you shopping for?"

"I'm not sure." He felt foolish now. "To be honest, I'm a bit out of my element here. Maybe this was a mistake."

"Oh, don't give up too easily." Her smile looked more genuine now. "We all make mistakes."

He relaxed some. "Well, my mother is a rather traditional woman. Although she has a nice brown shawl she's fond of, she might enjoy something a bit more cheerful. But not that bright red one the other clerk was showing me. Perhaps something in a more conservative color."

"Maybe she'd like something lighter weight, a shawl she could use on a summer evening." Julianne walked over to where the shawls were displayed. "What color are her eyes?"

He tried to remember as he stared into Julianne's sapphire blue eyes. "I, uh, I think they're the same color as mine. I've heard her say that before."

Julianne leaned forward to peer into his eyes. "Well, yours are blue too. Kind of a sky blue, I'd say."

"Yes, blue, of course." He felt stupid.

"Perhaps she'd like a blue shawl." She picked up a pale blue shawl with a shorter fringe on the edge. "Feel how soft this is." She held it out to him.

"It's very nice." He nodded. "That'll be perfect. Thank you."

"Wonderful." She smiled brightly. "Can we wrap it for you?"

"Yes. I'd appreciate that." He reached for his watch. "Is it all right if I pick it up later? I have an appointment at one."

"Certainly." She looped the shawl over her arm. "It will be ready for you before closing time at five."

"Is that when you go home?" He instantly regretted asking because he could see they were being watched by the older woman.

Julianne's cheeks turned a bit rosier. "I usually leave around three in order to have tea with my mother. But someone will be here to assist you."

"Thank you, Miss Blackstone. I'll pick it up later." Then, feeling self-conscious and ridiculous, he made a hasty exit. He was tempted to never show his face in the silly women's shop again but knew that would only draw more attention to himself. Perhaps he could arrange for someone else to fetch it for him.

By two-thirty, Julianne considered staying on later just to see if Levi Stanfield was really coming back. She'd already boxed and wrapped the blue shawl, and thought it made a thoughtful gift for his mother's birthday. But she could tell he'd been embarrassed when he left so abruptly. For that matter, she'd felt uncomfortable too. Would he really return?

Just minutes before three, Julianne began to rearrange the shawl counter. She was carefully refolding and laying them neatly out when Helena came over with a curious expression. "Is Mr. Stanfield your beau?" she asked bluntly. Fortunately, the shop was void of customers just then, but Lizzie stood attentively by.

"No, of course, not," Julianne replied lightly. "I barely know the man."

"Seemed like he knew you pretty well to me," Lizzie said with insinuation.

"We met years ago." Julianne carefully folded a rose-colored shawl. "But I haven't seen him in ages."

"Are you aware that his father is *Judge* Stanfield?" Helena pressed.

"I know his father was my sister's lawyer at one time." Julianne stepped away from the shawl counter, keeping her eyes away from the front door. "And now that it's almost three, I'll get ready to go home."

Eager to escape their curious looks, she went to the backroom. There, she took her time to wash her hands. Then she carefully pinned her hat into place, checking it in the mirror. She slowly pulled on and buttoned her gloves. By the time she checked the clock again, it was ten minutes past three. No more dillydallying, she told herself, as she reached for her handbag. Time to go home.

As she came back into the shop, she could hear a male voice saying, "thank you," and knew it was Levi. Composing herself, she casually walked out and, seeing that he was done paying Helena for his purchase, she went over to the counter to say hello.

"I hope your mother has a very pleasant birthday," she told him then proceeded to the door. She was only a few doors down when he caught up with her.

"Wait," he said. "I wanted to thank you."

"Thank *me*?" She turned to look up at him, noticing how his eyes looked even bluer out here with the Colorado sky behind him.

"Yes." He held up the pretty box. "You did a very nice job wrapping this for me. Well, I assume you did it."

"La Mode likes to serve its customers."

"And for that, I thank you. May I walk with you a bit?"

"Of course." She nodded, trying to suppress the flutter of excitement rushing through her. Perhaps it was no coincidence he'd come to La Mode today.

"I have a confession to make," he said quietly.

"What's that?" She looked curiously at him.

"It's not really my mother's birthday. That's not until August."

"Oh, well, you'll be prepared then," she said lightly.

"The rest of my confession is that I came to the shop today just to see you."

"Oh?" She pursed her lips, weighing her words. "I got the impression you didn't approve of me the other day when we met at the stationary store."

"That was my mistake. To be honest, I was caught off guard by your last name."

"I noticed." She stopped walking to look intently at him. "I've been away at school a few years, but since coming home, I've observed that a number of people react quite negatively to the name Blackstone. I can only assume that's because of my father?"

"So you're not aware of your father's politics? Or his associations?"

"The truth is, although I'm currently living under my parents' roof I rarely see my father. We are not on the best of terms. I'm only here in town to aid in my mother's recovery and to help at her dress store. As soon as she's well enough I plan to return to my sister's ranch."

"I see." He sounded relieved but looked slightly puzzled.

She nodded toward the busy street she needed to cross. "I'm going that direction."

He waited for a wagon and carriage to pass by then offered his arm as they crossed the street together. "This town just gets busier and busier."

"It's not nearly as big and busy as Pittsburgh, where I spent my childhood, but it's certainly growing fast. I have to admit I was disappointed to see how much it's changed when I came back a few weeks ago."

"I felt exactly the same when I came home last year."

"So you've been back for a year, Mr. Stanfield?"

"That's right, but please, call me Levi."

"Only if you will call me Julianne."

His eyes twinkled. "I'd be glad to."

As they strolled toward her neighborhood, they made pleasant small talk about the town and recent changes and modernizations. She told him about her schooling and about how much she'd missed the cattle ranch and riding with Delia every day. "I'm hoping to join them on a cattle drive next week."

"A cattle drive?" His brows arched with interest. "Isn't that a little rough for a lady?"

"I've done it before," she shot back. "My twin brother Julius and I used to go with them every year. It's hard work, but a lot of fun."

"You must be quite a horsewoman."

"I can hold my own."

"I'm impressed," he said. "And to be honest, I'm a little bit jealous."

"Do you ride?"

"Yes, but I've never been on a cattle drive. We have a small farm just outside of town, but the only cattle we have are a couple of jersey milk cows."

"I didn't expect a lawyer and judge to live on a farm," she confessed. "Did you miss that when you were at law school?"

Levi admitted he had, and then told her a bit about Yale. Although he wasn't bragging, she could tell that he must've been fairly brilliant to pass his law exams at a young age, and already he'd been practicing for a year.

"When Dad was made judge, he had to let his practice go, but his dream was always that I could pick up where he left off."

"Sounds like you've done that."

"I'm trying. But Dad was a truly great lawyer. And I guess that's what makes him such a good judge." He sounded proud as he told her about his father's career and some landmark cases. But not the kind of pride she'd witnessed so often by her father. This was the genuine admiration of a loving son who truly respected his dad.

To her relief, Levi didn't mention her father again. Although she was curious as to how her father had earned himself what she could only assume was a disreputable reputation, she didn't care to hear the details. Especially from Levi. She knew her father well enough to imagine there was just reason for people to question his name. And good reason for her to distance herself from him. The sooner she got moved back to the Double W, the happier she'd be. Except for one thing. That would put more distance between her and Levi as well, and she wasn't ready for that.

8

During her time spent with Mother, Julianne began to realize that she actually wielded some control over her mother's previously unpredictable moodiness. As it turned out, when Julianne was in good spirits, her mother was likewise. And after her pleasant time in Levi's company today, Julianne was in a very positive frame of mind. Naturally, she wasn't eager for her mother to know of her acquaintance with the handsome young lawyer. Especially since it was obvious Levi didn't approve of her father. But just thinking about Levi Stanfield put a smile on Julianne's face. Subsequently, Mother was happy too.

"I've been considering your suggestion of a wheeled chair," Mother told her as they shared dinner in her room again. "I'm tired of being confined."

"That's wonderful. Would you like me to see about getting you one?"

"I've already asked your father to look into it."

Julianne was tempted to inquire about her mother's dizzy spells, but worried that might unravel this new idea, said nothing. "I think getting out of this room will help you get well sooner, Mother. Fresh air and sunshine are good medicine."

"You are good medicine too, Julianne. I don't know what I'd do without you. Now give me a full report of your day."

Julianne filled her in about the dress shop without mentioning a word about the highlight of her day—Levi Stanfield. She even remained after dinner, sitting with Mother as she tediously perused the most recent issue of *Harper's Bazaar*, patiently listening to all her mother's commentary on what ladies were wearing in Paris and London and how she wanted to import the same styles here.

"You are very missed at La Mode," Julianne said as they came to the last page of the periodical. "Your sense of style is greatly appreciated by your customers, Mother."

"And I do believe that working at La Mode has been good for you," Mother said as she closed the magazine. "I'm so pleased. Very pleased!"

Julianne kissed her mother good night, then, seeing her father sitting alone in the den with his newspaper, she even popped her head in to tell him good night as well. He looked up with a surprised expression, then actually smiled. "Good night, dear daughter."

She felt unusually lighthearted as she went upstairs. Not just about Levi, but her parents as well. Perhaps people had misjudged her father. She was well aware of how his arrogance and pride were off-putting. As for his "politics," she knew he'd stepped on some toes, but wasn't that the way it went with politics? People never agreed on everything. Even if she was wrong, even if there was more to it than that, she just didn't want to think about it right now. She would rather think about a certain young lawyer.

Julianne took even greater care with her appearance the next morning. She knew it was because Levi had inquired about walking her home again someday. He hadn't said which day, but she wanted to be prepared just in case. Her mother seemed pleased with her appearance at breakfast, commenting that Julianne looked "prettier than ever." And even her father paid her an unexpected compliment as she was preparing to leave the house.

She thanked him and asked about the wheeled chair for her mother.

He assured her he would see to it. "And I have a favor to ask of you," he said in an unusually kind voice.

"What's that?" Using the foyer mirror, she carefully pinned her hat.

"Your mother has suggested I invite you to accompany me to the Mayor's Picnic on Saturday. As you know this festivity launches the upcoming Fourth of July celebrations and the city's birthday at the end of the month."

"Oh?" She turned to look at him.

"I would be greatly honored if you'd be my guest, Julianne. All the city officials and businessmen, and townspeople will be there. There will be music and a picnic luncheon and lots of fun activities."

Julianne pursed her lips.

"Please, don't say no." His dark eyes looked sad. "I realize I've made a lot of mistakes with my children and my family, but don't I deserve a second chance?"

"Of course, you do. It's just that Delia and Wyatt are heading out for their cattle drive this weekend. And Julius too. I hoped to go with them."

"You would turn down your father to go chasing after a bunch of dusty old cows?" He looked genuinely hurt now.

Julianne suddenly remembered Levi. Surely he'd be at the Mayor's Picnic too. It would be her chance to see him again. "All right, Father. I will go with you to the picnic."

"Thank you, Julianne. I'm sure you won't regret it." He extended his arms to embrace her. It was a stiff hug and uncharacteristic of him, but she thought perhaps he truly was trying to change his ways. And, as a daughter, perhaps it was her responsibility to help him. Maybe this was God's way of showing her how to respect her parents.

They said good-bye and Julianne headed for town. Delia would be disappointed to hear Julianne wasn't joining them, but she would understand. She'd always encouraged Julianne to forgive and forget and to mend her fences with her parents. Julianne would send Delia a note from the dress shop explaining the situation. And Delia would surely respect Julianne's choice to give her father another chance. Naturally, Julianne wouldn't mention anything about Levi Stanfield yet. Or that he might've had anything to do with her decision to remain in town. It was too soon for that.

Julianne didn't have to wait until three o'clock to see Levi. He showed up at the dress shop shortly before noon. "If you're not busy, I have something to show you." He tipped his hat to Helena. "Something that might be useful for your business here."

"Really?"

"Are you free to come with me?"

"Of course." She nodded firmly. "I'm not an employee. I can come and go as I please. I'll get my hat and things." She glanced at Helena and the clerks, who were all staring, then turned back to Levi. "Meet me outside."

Without explaining what she herself didn't know was happening, she told Helena that she would be back later. Although Helena gave her what was clearly a look of disapproval, Julianne held her head high and made her exit.

"I hope I didn't put you in an awkward position," Levi said as he led her toward the center of town. "I just wanted to surprise you with something."

"Helena will get over it," she assured him. "But you've got me curious. Where are you taking me?"

"To the courthouse."

"Goodness, I hope I'm not in trouble."

He laughed. "No worries. It's just that I got this idea, and I asked my father and he agreed."

"Now you've got me bursting with curiosity. What on earth are you—"

"No more questions about that."

"Fine. Then I'll ask about your mother's birthday gift. Did you hide it away or did you give it to her?"

He laughed. "I actually forgot it in my office, but I decided to take it home and give it to her early."

"That's nice. She can enjoy it during the summer months." They were at the courthouse now.

"First, we'll take a look at what's going on in my father's courtroom." He led her up the steps. "He's hearing a big case today."

"What sort of case?"

"A claim-jumper hearing," he said quietly as they entered the building. "A lot of it has been going around lately. This one a few months ago, at the first mine that struck gold. It involves a lot of money. I was watching earlier, but they took a short recess. The miner who alleges his claim was stolen will be taking the stand."

"Sounds interesting."

He held up a forefinger for quiet as he led her through a set of heavy wooden doors, and, directing her into a back bench of the crowded courtroom, he slid in after her. The court was already in session, with Levi's father presiding. Julianne was surprised by how judge-like and respectful Orville Stanfield looked in his black robe and somber expression. In the witness stand sat a bearded elderly man in a rumpled suit. He was being questioned by a well-dressed attorney who was obviously not on his side.

"That's the plaintiff, the miner fighting for his claim," Levi whispered in her ear.

She just nodded, but the way the lawyer was grilling the miner filled Julianne with indignant pity. The questions felt misleading, as if designed to make the miner look bad instead of getting to the truth. Even when the old man tried to explain more fully, he was cut off in midsentence. It seemed very unfair.

The miner's attorney looked to be quite elderly too, but at least he called out a few objections, which Judge Stanfield sustained. Still, it seemed the claim-jumper's attorney had the upper hand. Julianne looked at Levi, curious as to his take on this since he was an attorney. But his expression was impossible to read. He'd probably be a good poker player.

Eventually the miner was excused from the stand and since it was well past noon, Judge Stanfield called for a lunchtime recess. "Come on," Levi told her. "Let's get out." He led her from the courtroom but remained in the courthouse. "This way." He took her down a hallway and then let himself into what appeared to be a private office.

"This is my father's chambers," he told her. Now he took her over to a tall cabinet and, opening it up, pointed to a dusty looking typing machine. "This model is a little outdated, but I think it still works," he explained. "I asked my father if he wanted to keep it, and he said he'd rather have the space it was using. He offered it to me awhile back, but I have a newer model. So I asked if I could give it to you."

"I can gladly pay you for it," she said. "My mother allowed me—"

"No, it's a gift. My father suggested it. That way if the machine doesn't work right, or needs repairs, we won't feel responsible. Because you can't look a gift horse in the mouth." His eyes twinkled. "What do you think?"

She fingered the keys, testing to see how easily they moved. "It appears to be in good shape to me."

"You never know." He looked closely at her. "So do you really know how to use it? Are you an able type writer?"

She nodded eagerly. "I'm pretty fast and I don't make many mistakes. This is so exciting. I can put this right to use at La Mode, typing letters and orders and things. I really don't enjoy working out front in the dress shop. To be honest, I'm not all that interested in fashion and not much good at sales. This will give me an excuse to remain in back doing office work."

"Then you can have it on one agreement."

"What's that?"

"If you ever quit your mother's shop, and you need another form of employment, you must come be a type writer for me."

"You're seeking a type writer?"

"Most definitely. Right now I do my own typing, and there is plenty of it. But I'm painfully slow and make lots of mistakes. I prefer longhand, but my handwriting is a bit difficult to read. And legal documents are best type written."

"So why haven't you hired a type writer?"

"I haven't been able to find a good one."

She smiled and stuck out her hand. "Then I agree, if I ever stop working for Mother, I will gladly come and type for you. To be honest, working in a law office sounds far more interesting than a dress shop."

He shook her hand. "I'll have this delivered to La Mode by the end of the day."

"Thank you!" She was so happy, she had to control herself from hugging him.

"Now I'll walk you back to your dress shop," he offered. "That is unless you'd like a quick tour of the courthouse."

"I'd love one."

By the time he finished showing her every crook and cranny of the courthouse, the hearing against the claim-jumper had started up again. Seeing that Levi was eager to watch it, Julianne insisted on parting ways. As she strolled back to La Mode, she wondered about Levi's offer of a typing job. Was it really sincere, or was he just being kind? Of course, her mother would be hurt if Julianne left La Mode but working in a law office sounded far more interesting. In fact, she was suddenly quite curious to hear how the claim-jumping dispute was going.

Levi remained at the hearing until the end of the day. Not only because it was compelling, but because his dad wanted him there. It was the first of a number of cases very similar to this one, some that Levi himself would be representing. And like all courtroom hearings and trials, there was always something to be learned by listening to someone else's case.

Although Levi was trying to remain impartial, like his father was doing, his sympathies lay with Horace Crawley. The old miner's gold claim had been allegedly stolen by Thomas Martin and a questionable surveyor. Martin and a few other smooth talkers had tricked a lot of miners out of claims, but Crawley was the first one to stand up to him in court.

Unfortunately, old Crawley seemed to have gotten the short end of the prosecution stick. His attorney, Jack Leonard, in his eighties and hard of hearing, was being entirely too complacent. Pitted against the Denver defense attorney representing Martin, a wiry short man, given to repetitive questioning and long-winded speeches, Jack Leonard was like the mouse going after the lion. At times it was hard for Levi to just sit quietly by and listen.

Levi hoped his father would rule in favor of Horace Crawley, but with Martin's lawyer introducing more evidence tomorrow, it was hard to say. Despite personal opinions, a judge had to rule according to the evidence and testimony, and according to law. No one could predict how this would end. But one thing Levi could predict, at the end of the day, Dad would be tired.

That was why Levi was staying quiet on their trip home to their farm just outside of town. He drove the horses and Dad just leaned back and relaxed. Sometimes he smoked his pipe. But not today. As tempted as Levi was to discuss the case, he knew how much Dad appreciated the silence after a long day like this had been. They were almost home before either of them spoke.

"Days like today make me grateful we don't live in town," Orville Stanfield finally said. "Sometimes your mother talks about moving back, but I'm not ready for it. Not yet."

Levi had turned down his parents' offer to live in the little house they'd owned for as long as he could remember. Partly because, like Dad, he liked living out in the country, and partly because he knew his parents were getting older and needed a little extra help around their small farm. "It is good to live away from all the noise and hustle-bustle. Especially with the way town keeps growing."

"Not only that, but I enjoy the peaceful ride through the countryside every day. Gives me time to clear my head. Your mother should appreciate that too. Makes me a nicer man at the supper table." He chuckled.

"You had a pretty long day, Dad. I'm sure you're worn out."

"I've no doubt you have opinions on today's case, son, and I'll be curious to hear them when it's over, but I appreciate you keeping your thoughts to yourself for now."

Levi just nodded.

"Say, I saw you with that pretty girl in my courtroom this morning. Is that the one you thought might like my old type writing machine?"

"Yes, I gave it to her today. And she was most appreciative."

"Tell me more about this young lady. All I know is her name is Julianne and she was nice looking. How did you meet her?"

"You've actually met her before, Dad. Her sister is Delia Davis of the Double W Ranch."

"Oh, yes, Winston Williams's daughter Delia. And I know Delia had that stepsister Miranda from Winston's second marriage, the stepdaughter who contested Winston's will and lost." His eyes lit up. "Now I do recall that Delia had a young brother and sister too. Weren't they twins?"

"That's right. Her brother works out on the ranch. Julianne just finished schooling back East and now works for her mother in town."

"Works for her mother? What sort of business? Is she a secretary?"

"Her mother owns that fancy women's dress shop, La Mode."

Levi noticed his dad's brows draw together. "That business is owned by the Blackstone family, and I believe Mrs. Blackstone runs it." He nodded. "Yes, now I remember. Jane Blackstone is Delia Davis's mother. It's hard to believe. Two completely different sort of women." He glanced at Levi. "Now what sort of young lady is this Julianne. I know she's not Winston's child so I assume her last name is Blackstone?"

Levi cleared his throat. "That's right."

"Julianne Blackstone." His dad rubbed his chin.

"From what I can see, Julianne is more like her sister Delia than her parents. Julianne and Delia are very close and if her mother hadn't gotten injured, Julianne would be living out on the Double W right now."

"Her mother got injured?"

Levi explained about the buggy accident.

"An accident like that should've been reported at the courthouse. Never heard a word about it. And you say it was a serious injury? Surprised Jefferson Blackstone isn't suing someone. From what I hear, he's that sort of man."

"I had similar thoughts." Levi reined the horses to turn onto their property.

"Interesting."

Neither spoke as they drove up to the house, but Levi suspected his father was chewing on all this. Levi's mother waved from the front porch and the dog raced out to meet them. Levi grinned to think of the surprise he'd brought home for his mom. She'd question such a nice gift for no special occasion, but he planned to tell her it was simply because he loved her. Oh, he knew it would probably make her cry, but that was all right. After all, she was the one who often said that "sometimes a good woman just needs a good cry."

Still, as he handed the pretty box to his mother, his mind remained on Julianne. Or more precisely, *her* mother. It did seem odd that Jefferson Blackstone hadn't reported the buggy accident to the courthouse. Especially since it sounded as if the farmer's hay wagon had toppled Mrs. Blackstone's rig. Of course, that was just one side of the story and Levi knew there were always at least two. Perhaps Mrs. Blackstone had been at fault and the family was embarrassed to come forward and own up to it. And since it seemed she was the only one injured, it probably didn't matter.

9

On Friday, Levi was loitering outside the dress shop when Julianne left La Mode around three o'clock. He acted nonchalant when he greeted her, as if their meeting was purely coincidental, but after a few steps, he confessed.

"A quarter to three I thought of you. In my defense, I spent most of the afternoon drafting a very drawn out and detailed last will and testament and was in dire need of some fresh air and exercise. So I took myself for a walk." He grinned. "And decided to pause here."

"I'm glad you did because I wanted to personally say thank you for the typing machine. It's been wonderful."

"So it really works?"

"It needed a little cleaning and oil and a new ink ribbon. But after that, it's been a dream. I've been typing most of the day."

"Too bad you can't type out that long will for me."

"Why don't I?"

"Oh, that was only wishful thinking."

"But I could type it for you. I got so much done at the dress shop today. I'm afraid I won't have enough office work to keep me busy next week. Please, let me do it for you, Levi, it can be my way of really thanking you for the typing machine."

"I'll think about it." His mouth twisted to one side. "Although you'd have to agree to confidentiality if you did any legal typing for me. I might even need to draw up a contract for you."

"That would be fine. Speaking of legal things, how did the claim-jumping case turn out or is it still going on? I keep feeling sorry for that old miner. I hope he gets a fair shake."

"My father ruled in his favor this morning, and in my opinion rightly so, but Martin's attorney plans to appeal to a higher court. I heard he already wired the Colorado Supreme Court in Denver."

"What does that mean?"

"It means Thomas Martin and his attorney plan to contest my dad's ruling. They will fight long and hard to hold on to that claim. It involves a lot of money that they don't mean to let go. Not only that, but if Thomas Martin were to lose to old Horace Crawley in Denver, a lot more disgruntled miners will crawl out of the woodwork and file suits against Martin as well. There's already a line of upcoming trials on the docket. Not only against Martin, but a few other players as well."

"So claim-jumping is rather common?"

"Unfortunately, there are a lot of greedy fellows that see uneducated miners as fair game. What we're hoping for is that the Colorado Supreme Court upholds my dad's findings. Of course, Martin and his lawyer will hate that, and it'd probably bankrupt Thomas Martin. But this whole region will be better off for it."

"Why is that?"

"Fellows like Martin reinvest their ill-gotten funds in things like saloons, casinos, and lots of other get-rich-quick schemes to empty the miners' pockets."

"That's too bad. So these other miners, ones that might be suing to get their claims back, would you consider helping them—as their attorney?"

He grinned. "I already have several clients like old Crawley and after today, I suspect I'll get a few more. I like Jack Leonard well enough, but I don't think he's up to it. Not at the top of his game."

"Leonard? Is that the elderly lawyer working for Crawley?"

"Yes. He's a good man, and he's been practicing law forever, but he should probably retire."

"He did seem a little slow. Especially against Mr. Martin's fast-talking lawyer."

"You got that right." He nodded. "But enough about the law. Tell me, Julianne, how's your mother doing? Is her health improving?"

"Some days are better than others. She has a wheeled chair now, so she can get around a little."

"That's good news."

"And I've learned to be careful about what I say to her."

"Why's that?"

"Well, if I inquire about her health, she seems to get worse."

"I see."

"And if I mention something like moving back to the ranch or going on the cattle drive, she acts like she's dying."

"Speaking of the cattle drive, when is that?"

"They always go the week before Independence Day. Then there's a big barbecue at the Double W on July Fourth. It's lots of fun." She imagined how much more fun if she and Levi were there together.

"Do they need any more hands for the cattle drive?"

She took in his dark blue waistcoat and shiny black boots. "You? You'd actually go on a cattle drive?"

"Why not?" He grinned. "Sounds exciting."

"It is." She sighed. "Unfortunately, my parents had a fit about it, so I promised not to go. Not this time."

"That's too bad."

"But I do plan to go up at the end of summer."

"You mean if your mother will allow it?" His tone had a slight teasing edge to it.

"My mother will be fully recovered by then," she declared, although she wasn't fully convinced herself.

"Are you sure of that?"

They were only a few houses away from her house now, and she turned to study him. "What are you insinuating, Levi?"

"I don't know your mother, and I probably shouldn't say this, but it almost sounds as if she's controlling you with her health conditions."

Julianne suddenly felt defensive. "You're right, you *don't* know her."

"All I'm saying is what if she never gets well? Will you remain at her beck and call for the rest of your life?"

"Of course not. She will get well. I know she will." Still, she wondered…what if Levi was right? She started to walk again, hoping their conversation would change course.

"So what does her doctor say, Julianne?"

"Her doctor?"

"Surely the doctor visits to check on her injuries. To see how her leg is mending, and the headaches and dizziness. Have you been with your mother when he visits?"

"No."

"Maybe you should be."

"I offered once, but she's a very private woman. She doesn't want me there when the doctor comes."

"Since you are helping with her care, perhaps you should speak to her doctor on your own. Do you even *know* who her doctor is?"

Julianne felt slightly indignant now, as if he was questioning her judgment. "Yes, I do." She stood up straighter. "It's Dr. Edwin Muller. I know because I heard my father mention getting the wheeled chair from him. Not that this is any of your business." She slightly regretted her last snippet, but why was he questioning her on this?

"Please, understand me, Julianne, I don't doubt your devotion to your mother's recovery." He spoke gently. "I just don't like to see anyone take advantage of you."

"No one is taking advantage of me," she answered sharply. "I'm a grown woman, Levi, and I'm helping my mother because it's a daughter's duty. When she is better, I will go my own way."

"I hope she is better soon." He stopped walking since they were in front of her house.

Julianne made a stiff smile. "I would invite you in, but with my ailing mother, I don't feel it's appropriate."

"I understand. Give her my regards."

Julianne considered this request. So far she had not even mentioned Levi to her mother. And the thought of inviting him into the house was a bit frightening. Partly because she felt sure Mother would not approve, but even more so because she suspected Levi would want nothing to do with her if he spent any time in the company of her parents. Particularly her father. So she thanked Levi for escorting her home and told him a rather curt good-bye.

As she marched up to the front door she felt angry. Not at Levi exactly, although he had definitely triggered something inside of her. But mostly she was angry at herself...angry for feeling embarrassed by her parents.

Levi felt confused as he walked back to town. He hadn't meant to offend Julianne, although he clearly had done so. But he was worried about her, concerned for the way her parents seemed to be controlling her—and not necessarily for her own good either. He strongly suspected they had their own agendas in mind. And for some reason he felt strangely protective of Julianne. Oh, he knew she was a strong young woman and probably able to take care of herself—except, it seemed, when it came to her mother. And maybe her father too.

He knew he shouldn't interfere, but Dr. Edwin Muller's office was downstairs from the law office, and they often exchanged pleasantries. Why not do so today? He still had a few things to wrap up before joining his father on the trip home, but he had time for a quick little visit with the good doctor. And seeing Dr. Muller opening his office door, to let out a young mother and a baby carriage, provided the perfect opportunity.

"Good afternoon." Levi tipped his hat to them. "Beautiful day for a walk."

"Hello, young lawyer," Dr. Muller called out as the mother wheeled her infant down the street. "I heard the good news about old Crawley winning his court case."

"It's kind of a mixed bag of news." Levi explained about Martin's appeal.

"That's too bad." Dr. Muller stepped out into the sunshine. "But I'm glad your father made a fair ruling. From what I hear, Thomas Martin has taken advantage of a lot of good folks. And getting richer and richer doing it. Have you heard he and his cronies want to put a casino right here in town?"

"They'd have to jump through some legal hoops to do that, and as long as my dad's on the bench, I don't see it happening."

"That's why we like having your dad on the bench." He slapped Levi's back. "I bet you'll be doing the same thing someday. I keep hearing good things about you."

"Thanks, but that'll be a long ways down the road." He peered down the busy street. "I still can't get used to all this coming and going here in town. The street's so busy it's becoming dangerous."

"Downright dangerous. I treated a young boy just this morning. On his way to school, and he got trampled by a horse that broke out of its harness."

"Is he all right?"

"A broken arm and shaken up some, but he couldn't wait to go show off his plaster cast to his friends. He'll be fine."

"I heard about Mrs. Blackstone's buggy accident. How's her recovery coming?"

"Mrs. Blackstone?"

"Yes, she had a broken leg and head injury."

Dr. Muller twisted the edge of his mustache with a frown. "Hmm, she must've been treated by a different physician. I haven't seen her."

"Oh? Well, you're not the only doctor in town these days."

"That's true." He shook his head. "But I don't like losing patients to them."

"Don't worry, with this boom, you should be plenty busy."

He smiled. "That's true. I was just telling myself to enjoy what little free time I have right now. I'll probably get some emergency calls during the weekend. I usually do."

Levi tipped his hat again then headed up the stairs. So Dr. Muller wasn't treating Mrs. Blackstone…and no one had reported an accident to the courthouse. Halfway to his office, he had another thought. If Mrs. Blackstone's carriage had overturned it would likely be damaged. And Levi's good friend Joe Brandt just happened to run the only carriage repair shop in town. Perhaps he'd go pay him a visit.

10

JULIANNE GOT THE SENSE THAT SOMETHING WAS GOING ON AS SOON as she went into the house. For one thing, the drapes in the front parlor were pulled open, which brought some welcome light and life into the room. Besides that she smelled food cooking. That wasn't so unusual, but when she peeked in the kitchen, she found Ellie up to her elbows in pots and pans.

"Looks like you're pretty busy in here," Julianne observed.

"We're having guests for dinner. Can I do something for you?"

"No, you're the one who appears to need help."

Ellie wiped the back of her hand across her forehead. "Thank you, but I'm fine, Miss. Just got a lot going at the moment. Dinner will be at seven."

"Then I won't disturb you."

As Julianne passed through the dining room, she noticed the big table was already partially set with six places. With her father and mother and her, it appeared they would be having three guests. She considered this. Could it possibly be Delia and Wyatt and Julius? It wouldn't be unusual for Delia to leave the children with Ginger since it would be their bedtime anyway. Oh, what a fun evening this could be!

She removed her hat and gloves then went to seek out her mother. Since getting her wheeled chair, she was on the move more. Julianne wasn't surprised not to find her in her room. And her father was not in his den. And the front room was vacant too. However, the drapes were drawn there, and a large bouquet of roses graced the marble top table.

Julianne considered searching outside, thinking they might've taken a stroll through the garden, but decided to recluse to her own room instead. After her busy day at work, a little quiet time alone sounded most welcome. Especially since they were having guests tonight. Hopefully it would be her beloved family.

Julianne had so much to tell Delia. But she'd have to get her alone since it was mostly about Levi. And she would swear her sister to secrecy. By now she had decided that Levi's persistent questioning about Mother was simply his way of saying he cared about Julianne. And if he cared that much, well, perhaps he felt like she did. Oh, she knew it was too soon to really know such things—one of the reasons she was eager to talk to Delia and ask lots of questions—but Julianne felt fairly certain she was in love.

After a relaxing bath and time spent reading a book she'd found downstairs, a book that just happened to be about law, Julianne got dressed. She chose the pale blue silk dress, feeling certain Mother must've had it made especially for her. It really was lovely, and she told herself to remember to thank Mother for her thoughtfulness. In fact, since Ellie was busy with dinner, she wondered if Mother might need help dressing. So around six, she went down to see.

To her surprise, Mother was actually standing in front of her dressing table when Julianne peeked through the cracked open door to check on her. Fully dressed in a flowing dark blue gown that showed off her figure, she was pinning up her hair. For an older woman, Jane Blackstone had maintained her looks. Fascinated, Julianne watched for a moment as her mother pinned an ornate comb on top. She was reluctant to speak out and frighten her mother, especially since her dizzy spells could hinder her balance. And so she tapped lightly on the partially opened door.

"Just a minute," Jane called out. And to Julianne's surprise, her mother made it quite agilely back into her wheeled chair.

"I just wanted to see if you need help dressing." Julianne opened the door fully now, stepping into the room. "But I see you're already dressed."

"Yes, well, your father helped me." Jane's smile looked nervous.

"You look beautiful." Julianne went closer. "No one would even guess you'd had a bad accident."

"Yes, well, thank you. I hope I haven't overdone it. I'm not used to such exertions, and you know we're entertaining tonight."

"So I've heard."

"Oh, Julianne!" she exclaimed as if just seeing her. "Turn around and let me see you in that gorgeous gown."

Julianne complied, slowly turning.

"You look like a goddess." Mother sighed. "But you need help with your hair. Bring me my brush set, and some pins, and sit down on my vanity bench."

"I don't want to wear you out."

"Do as I say, dear daughter. Arranging your hair will not wear me out in the least."

As Mother fussed with Julianne's hair, pinning the curls up even higher, she talked happily about how well she was feeling and how delightful it would be to have guests. But when Julianne inquired as to who was coming, Mother was coy. "It's a surprise, dear. But I assure you, we will have a delightful evening. Now get me my jewelry box. I have just the thing for you."

She brought the box over and Mother searched out a pair of glittering earrings with diamonds dangling on the ends of the delicate gold chains. "Aren't these just lovely?"

"Yes, but they're far too fancy for me. Are those real diamonds?"

"Of course."

"But what if I lose one?"

"If you'll sit down so we can get them on properly, you won't lose one."

"I wish I'd brought my things from the ranch. Then I could've worn my sapphire earrings, the ones Delia gave me back in Pittsburgh. They would look nice with this gown." She didn't want to admit she would prefer those to these fancier ones.

"I think these ones look beautiful with the gown. You look like a princess, Julianne."

"Well, if I'm a princess, you must be the queen." They both laughed. But then Julianne remembered how Ginger used to call Mother *the queen*, but not as a compliment. Ginger hadn't liked being bossed around when the Blackstones first came to the ranch. But Mother had softened up a lot since then. Running the dress shop had probably helped with that, and perhaps the buggy accident had softened her too.

Julianne was tempted to ask Mother about how she'd been able to stand by herself earlier but knew talking of such a thing just now could make problems for their evening. So she decided to just keep it to herself. But if she got any time with Delia tonight, she'd tell her about it.

"I hear voices," Mother said. "Could you be good enough to wheel me out?"

"Of course." Julianne smiled. "Aren't you glad you agreed to this chair, Mother. It allows you to participate in life again. And no one would even guess there was a broken leg under there." She pointed to the long dark blue skirt of her mother's gown.

"Precisely what I'm hoping. I'd hate to be regarded as an invalid. It sounds as if they're in the front room. I'm sure your father is playing the perfect host."

As Julianne wheeled her mother out, she could tell the voices did not belong to Delia, Wyatt, or Julius. The conversation sounded too formal to be family.

"It's a delightful pleasure to meet both of you," her father was saying in a fancy tone. "Mr. Dayton has spoken so fondly of you both. Welcome to our humble home."

Pleasantries were being exchanged as Julianne wheeled her mother into the front room. "And there they are," Jefferson announced, "the women of the house." He began to introduce everyone, starting with the couple who appeared to be her parents' age, Mr. and Mrs. Bronson. "They've recently relocated here from New York," Jefferson told them.

"New York by way of Denver," Mr. Bronson said. "And we prefer Colorado Springs to Denver. Much more potential here."

"And, please, disperse of Mr. and Mrs.," the woman said to Mother. "I'm Evelyn and my husband is Darnel."

"Pleased to meet you, I'm Jane." Mother pointed down to her lap. "And as you can see I'm a bit laid up. It's only a broken leg and hopefully I won't be trapped in this torturous chair for too long." She waved to Julianne. "This is my daughter Julianne. I don't know what I'd do without her. She's truly an angel sent from God during my recovery."

"And a beautiful angel she is." Evelyn grasped Julianne's hand. "I'm pleased to meet you, dear."

"And I'd like you to know Mr. Dayton." Father directed this introduction to Julianne. "He's a good friend and business associate of mine. Your mother has already made his acquaintance. Mr. Dayton, this is my lovely daughter."

"I've heard so much about you, Miss Blackstone." The strikingly handsome man reached for Julianne's hand. "It's a pleasure to finally meet you."

"Oh, please, do call her Julianne," Mother told Mr. Dayton. "No need for such formalities here among friends."

His dark eyes gleamed in a way that suggested he liked what he was seeing. "Only if Julianne will call me Royal."

The name set off an alarm in Julianne's head. This was the man her parents had wanted her to marry. What was he doing here? Still, she reminded herself, she'd made her position clear to her parents. They knew she would not budge on this. *Just be polite and get through this.*

"I'm pleased to meet you," she said stiffly, aware that he was still grasping her hand.

"Your father tells me you're helping out in your mother's dress shop." He bowed slightly then released her hand.

"That's right." She clasped both her hands in front of her.

"I visited La Mode today and the little shop is absolutely divine," Evelyn exclaimed. "I almost felt I was on the continent for a moment. What a delightful selection of women's apparel. I saw nothing like your shop in Denver, Jane." She turned to Julianne. "But I didn't see you there, dear."

"I've been doing office work. In the back of the store," Julianne explained.

"Can you believe our daughter learned to be a typist at finishing school of all places," Jefferson said lightly. "Not exactly why we sent her back East."

"She learned lots of other refinements there too, Jefferson. Don't go on so, you'll make her feel bad."

But he had moved on, pouring the gentlemen drinks. Mother suggested the ladies move to the parlor until dinner was served. "The gentlemen probably wish to talk business without us."

"Oh, but to lose such loveliness, even for a few minutes." Royal's eyes were still fixed on Julianne. "I can't say that I agree with this plan, dear hostess."

Mother just laughed. "Don't worry, we will reconvene at the dinner table very shortly."

"I'll only agree if I can arrange the seating at the table." He chuckled, but still watched Julianne. Almost as if she were a tasty morsel about to be served on tonight's menu.

In the parlor, Evelyn Bronson sat next to Julianne on the divan. Reaching for Julianne's hand, she began to speak of all the exotic sounding places she'd been around the world. "And you, my dear child, should visit all these places too. I just have a feeling that is your destiny. You're such a beautiful and sophisticated child, you deserve such lovely experiences."

Julianne didn't know what to say. On one hand, she was slightly flattered, but something else in her felt like running in the opposite direction. "Thank you for such kind words," she managed to say with some dignity. "I'll admit that your description of Paris and Rome and Vienna sounds intriguing, but I doubt I'll ever have real occasion to travel so far."

"Oh, I beg your pardon, dear, but I think you will." Evelyn gave a winking smile to Mother. "Don't you think so too, Jane? Can't you just imagine your elegant daughter gracing these romantic destinations?"

Mother looked slightly stunned. "I'm sure I don't know about that. But all things are possible nowadays. If Julianne desires such adventures, I'm sure she shall have them."

Julianne felt irked at this. "Mother. I can't imagine you'd allow me to venture so far from you. After not wanting me away on the cattle drive this weekend, and that adventure was much closer to home."

Evelyn's eyes grew wide. "A *cattle* drive? With *real* cows? You cannot be serious."

"My girl jests with you, Evelyn." Mother's smile looked stiff. "You see, my older daughter Delia owns a large cattle ranch outside of town. And my son Julius, who is Julianne's twin, works with her there. When the twins were children, they used to ride the horses and play like cowboys."

"It wasn't just play, Mother. It was hard work driving cattle up to the grasslands. But it was fun too." She turned to Evelyn. "My brother in law has increased the herd and the cattle drive promises to be quite exciting this year."

"My goodness." Evelyn laughed. "And are there real cowboys too?"

"Of course." Julianne tried not to laugh. "The ranch hands are very experienced. They rope and ride and brand and everything. Even my brother has turned into a pretty decent cowboy."

"I would love to see such a thing," Evelyn declared.

"I'd be happy to take you there any time you like."

"Now that does sound like an adventure." Evelyn clapped her hands. "I will definitely take you up on that offer."

Julianne was tempted to press Mother on the upcoming cattle drive again, but Father was announcing dinner. And the gentlemen all insisted on offering an arm to the ladies, which meant Julianne was stuck with Royal.

"I hear your father is escorting you to the festivities tomorrow," he told her as they all paraded toward the dining room. "It promises to be a fun day. Have you heard about all the activities?" Without waiting for her answer, he continued to list all the goings on planned for the celebration. "Here you go." He pulled out her chair, waiting for her to sit. And, despite her determination to treat him with cool disdain, she had to admit he was a likeable man.

As he sat beside her, she tried to guess his age. His full head of wavy brown hair suggested he wasn't as old as Wyatt had assumed, but probably in his early to mid-thirties. And while they ate dinner, he was always quick to jump in when the conversation lulled, he was complimentary and gracious to everyone, and his manners were impeccable. All in all, Julianne decided that she liked him. Oh, she didn't care to marry the man, but he was nothing like the horrid ogre she'd imagined. And she couldn't even fault her parents for trying to make a match for her with him. Except that she preferred Levi.

After dinner, Royal insisted on strolling the garden, with Julianne as his guide. As they walked, he continued to visit congenially, paying her far more compliments than she was accustomed to or deserved. It was flattering, but disturbing. She had no doubt that he still considered her marriageable. Of course, she knew no one could force her into it, but she had no doubts her father would like to.

"Tell me about the town you've named after yourself," she said as they headed back for the house.

"So you've heard about Dayton Springs?"

"My sister mentioned it. And I've been curious."

He chuckled. "It wasn't my idea to call it that. A friend suggested the name and it just seemed to stick. It's only a small mining town, but like everything else around here, it's growing rapidly." He opened the door for her.

"There you are." Father came over to place a hand on Royal's shoulder. "Darnel was just sharing a rather interesting proposition that I think you'll want to hear." His smile to Julianne felt condescending, but that wasn't unusual. "And the ladies are waiting for you in the parlor."

Glad to escape Royal's attentions, she hurried to the parlor where her mother asked her to go fetch tea. "Ellie was supposed to bring it to us, but she seems to be sidetracked."

"I'll get it." Julianne took the back route to the kitchen to find the tea tray nearly ready, and a kitchen full of dirty dishes. "Let me take it for you, Ellie. Looks like you've got your hands full."

"Thank you." Ellie nodded. "Jones promised to help with clean-up, but I ain't seen hide nor hair of him."

"I'll come help after the guests leave," Julianne suggested.

"Oh, no, Miss. Your mother wouldn't hear of it."

As she took the tray, Julianne wasn't sure she cared if it would upset Mother. Something about seeing her standing by herself earlier just didn't sit well with her. She went down the hall past the den this time. She knew the men were drinking brandy and from the smell of the air, enjoying some cigars too. She paused as the sound of a familiar name—Thomas Martin. They were talking about the man accused of claim-jumping.

"Thomas Martin? We can't count on him now. He's thrown a great big wrench into the works," Royal said angrily.

"That's right," Father declared. "His funds will be tied up until his case against Horace Crawley is resolved in Denver."

"Thanks to Judge Stanfield. And there's no guarantee it will be resolved," Royal said. "Now there are other claim-jumping cases lining up. Including some with my name on them. If it all goes the same way, we'll have trouble funding this project."

"Are you saying the project is in danger?" Darnel asked them.

"Not if we can get it settled fast. We get the wheels rolling and there's no stopping it," Father told him. "We'll all have more money than we know what to do with."

"Speed is of the essence," Royal said.

"You've heard the Daniels's case is on the docket for Monday," Father told them. "If Judge Stanfield continues these rulings, we can't move fast enough on the development."

"I tried to convince the mayor yesterday," Royal said. "Despite his interest and support, he says Judge Stanfield won't budge on the city ordinance."

"A casino in town is not going to work," Father agreed. "That's why we go to Plan B. And why I took Darnel to meet with Lionel Edwards today."

Julianne knew it was wrong to eavesdrop but couldn't seem to stop herself. Especially hearing how smug her father sounded. What were they up to?

"Ah, the Edwards's farm," Royal said with interest. "Is it even for sale?"

"Not for the general public, but for the right price, Lionel has agreed to sell off twenty acres," Father informed him.

"And I just happen to have the right price," Darnel declared.

"That property abuts town and the acreage we'll purchase runs right along the south side border," Father's voice oozed with enthusiasm. "It's like having our cake and eating it too. Our casino will be so nearby, it's like having it in town. In time, no one will know the difference."

"Perfect!" Royal exclaimed. "I can already see it in my mind's eye. We'll place a big hotel and nice restaurant right on the border of town. It will play a buffer to help get townsfolk on board. Shortly thereafter we'll add a big saloon with dance hall girls and the works. Then we'll build the biggest best fanciest casino this side of the Mississippi. I'll talk to my architect friend and get him working on it Monday. Jefferson, you get your surveyors to plat it out for us as soon as the deed is written. We will run a road straight into town and design the whole works in such a way that no one will even realize it's not part of the Springs."

"And no city taxes," Father chimed in.

"I'm liking this more and more," Darnel declared. "You can definitely count me in. Just don't tell my wife all the details just yet."

Julianne heard footsteps coming toward the cracked open door and, balancing the tea tray, she moved quickly down the hallway. But what she'd overheard was more than a little concerning. These men were planning a development that would greatly impact the town. And their association with Thomas Martin, and other claim-jumpers…well, it was all very troubling. She wondered what Levi would make of it.

11

JULIANNE'S ONLY HOPE FOR THE MAYOR'S PICNIC TODAY WAS THAT Levi might be there—and perhaps he would rescue her with a smile or, better yet, his companionship. She was very eager to talk to him. And since she'd already promised Father she'd go with him, despite her misgivings, she had decided to comply. Even to the point of wearing the "picnic" dress suggested by Mother.

But as they strolled toward town, she wished she'd chosen a more conservative ensemble, something more reflective of her mood. This fluffy pink fabric with its ruffles and lace seemed to suggest frivolity and lightness. And yet she felt heavy and dark. At least she'd had the wherewithal to refuse the silly pink parasol.

As they approached the city park, where today's activities would take place, she noticed others making their way there. Visiting and laughing, with an air of expectation, as if everyone anticipated a fun, lighthearted day. And perhaps she was overreacting to what she'd overheard last night. Eavesdroppers often got their facts mixed up. What if she had misunderstood their real intentions?

At the park's entrance, her father greeted an elderly couple, pausing to introduce them to Julianne. And their smiles and cheeriness seem to rub off on her as she exchanged pleasantries with them. But as they entered the town park, she was taken aback by a poster for the upcoming election. She stopped to stare. "Royal Dayton for US Senate?" she read the words aloud.

"Yes, didn't you know about that?" her father asked as he tipped his hat to a young couple wheeling a baby buggy.

She shook her head then suddenly remembered Delia saying something about the political aspirations of both her father and Royal.

"I'm Royal's campaign manager." Father waved to someone in the park. "We think he has a good chance of winning too. He'll be making a speech later today."

She had no response to that.

He lowered his voice. "And if Royal wins the race, I will win a good position." Smiling pleasantly, he linked his arm with hers and led her toward the bandstand where people were already gathered for the opening ceremony. Taking her past people, who were standing behind the chairs lined around the bandstand, he led her to the front, where dignitaries were being seated. Off to the opposite side, she noticed Judge Stanfield and a gray-haired woman she assumed to be Levi's mother, and there on the end was Levi. And he was looking directly at her.

"Ah, there you are." Royal stepped up to take her hand. "I've been waiting for you." He smiled. "And you were definitely worth waiting for. You look lovely, Julianne."

She was too surprised to say anything.

"I've saved you seats." He nodded to where Mr. and Mrs. Bronson, festively dressed, were already seated. "Hello, Julianne," Evelyn called out. "Come and sit next to me, dear girl. I want to hear more about your sister's ranch and those cowboys." She laughed merrily. "When I told Darnel about it last night, he didn't quite believe me."

Not knowing what else to do, Julianne took the chair next to

Evelyn, awkwardly greeting her. "I assumed these seats were for dignitaries," she whispered to her.

"Just the usual riffraff." Evelyn chuckled. "Dignitaries, politicians, and millionaires." She lowered her voice and nodded in the direction where Levi and his family were sitting. "That bearded man, just a few chairs down, is Count Pourtales. And the couple beside him—the white-haired gentleman and the woman in the purple dress—are millionaires from Denver."

Julianne glanced that direction just in time to see Levi staring back at her. His expression, like in the courtroom that day, was hard to read, but she thought she saw a flash of something in those sky-blue eyes. Was it anger, jealousy, concern, disgust? She didn't know, but it made her turn away in time to see Royal taking his place in the chair next to her. Smiling boldly, he even took the liberty of placing a hand on her shoulder after he sat, acting as if they had some sort of prearranged agreement. And then her father sat next to him.

Feeling trapped and conspicuous, Julianne stared down at her lap and tugging at the edges of her lacy gloves, tried to think of a way to escape this most awkward situation. But the mayor was already taking his place behind the podium, raising his hands to quiet the crowd, and then starting his welcome speech.

Levi didn't know what to make of Julianne today. It was as if she had turned into someone else—overnight—someone he had no desire to know. He suspected his father had noticed her with Royal Dayton too. And he was probably as confused as Levi about it. Fortunately, Mother was unaware that he'd had interests in that girl, or any girl for that matter. As for his hopes to casually run into Julianne at the picnic and introduce them to her today—that wouldn't be happening.

It was hard to focus on the welcome speech. Mayor Redding was relatively new to Colorado Springs but seemed to be well liked. Still, Levi questioned whether the man was as naïve as he sometimes sounded. Or, even worse, had he been paid off by someone to look the other way? Perhaps it might even be someone sitting in the illustrious front row of this gathering. A lot of money was represented here, and some of it was from disreputable people with money-making schemes to line their own pockets.

Just last night, Levi's father had confided in him about how Thomas Martin had offered a payoff if his claim-jump case had gone in his favor. Of course, that never happened. Levi's dad was not for sale. But what about the mayor? Was he just being overly optimistic or had someone paid him off? Maybe even Julianne's charming companion, a certain Mr. Royal Dayton. Levi didn't like feeling like this, but something inside him was twisted tight at the moment.

He turned his attention back to Mayor Redding. He now boasted of unprecedented growth and the modern improvements that would make everyone's life better. He continued to ramble, proudly proclaiming the bright future for the whole region. Everything was coming up roses, life was a bowl of cherries, and the streets would probably be paved with gold before long.

Was the mayor that oblivious to the dark storm clouds gathered around their fair city? Or was Levi's foul mood over Julianne's friends just souring this whole celebration? He glanced her direction again. Everyone around her looked gratified by the speech, almost smug. And why not? If everything the mayor projected was true, they had every reason to be pleased.

The mayor failed to mention how every time a new mine came through, unscrupulous fortune-hunters slithered in right behind them. These self-serving entrepreneurs would throw together glittery saloons and casinos and fill them with painted up dance hall girls—anything sparkling enough to lure the gold from the miners' pockets. And if that didn't fatten their bank accounts quickly enough they could always resort to various forms of claim-jumping.

Levi knew from several lawsuits he was working on, there was a growing number of clever ways to steal a mine these days. Many usurpers were attempting to steal claims "within the limits of the law" by hiring sleazy attorneys or crooked surveyors. Just like Thomas Martin had done.

By now, Levi knew that case fairly well. Martin's surveyors had created a false land plat to illegally entitle him to old Horace Crawley's gold mine. Of course, Levi's father had seen through it. What happened when the Colorado Supreme Court heard the case remained to be seen, but as soon as Martin's appeal was filed, Crawley's mine would be shut down and his funds, including his gold, would be frozen.

These were the concerning sort of things Levi and his dad discussed around the dinner table almost every evening. Whether Mayor Redding cared to admit it or not, some of these affluent opportunistic newcomers weren't going to win any citizenship awards. Unfortunately, Julianne's father and his friends were all part of that element. But Levi had never imagined Julianne willingly socializing with them. Hadn't she claimed that she and her father weren't even on speaking terms? What was going on?

Julianne never got the chance to say as much as a hello to Levi at the celebration picnic. His parents remained, but Levi had quickly disappeared after the mayor's speech. Although she seemed fairly hemmed in by her father and Royal and their gregarious friends, she finally managed to slip away and, feeling strangely emboldened, she approached Levi's father at the dessert table.

"Good afternoon, Judge Stanfield."

He turned to her with a surprised look then smiled. "Good afternoon, young lady."

"We haven't met, but I am—"

"You are a friend of my son's." He set down his piece of apple pie to shake her hand. "Julianne Blackstone. Levi has spoken of you."

"Oh?" She blinked. "Well, I just wanted to say thank you for the typing machine you so graciously gave to me."

"That old machine was just taking up space and gathering dust. I'm glad you could make use of it. Levi told me you got it working and were pleased with it."

"It's a wonderful machine." She picked up a plate with a slice of yellow cake on it. "I, uh, I'm sorry Levi isn't here today."

"He was here but left early." He picked up his pie plate. "I think something may have been troubling him."

"Oh?"

"I probably shouldn't mention this, but because it concerns me, and because I believe Levi is concerned as well, I will speak my piece." He glanced around as if to see if anyone was near enough to overhear him.

"What is it you wish to say?"

"I suspect Levi is troubled by your companions."

"You mean my *father's* friends?" She grimaced to see that Thomas Martin had just sat down with her father and Royal and the others at their table. Standing here with the respectable judge really did make them seem like a bunch of crooks dressed up in fine clothing. Was that how he viewed them?

"Perhaps the question should be, are your father's friends your friends too, Miss Blackstone?" He looked into her eyes. "Because some of those friends may not be the best influence for a decent young lady."

"Believe me, Judge Stanfield, I have similar concerns." She bit her lip, wondering how much to say and yet she intuitively trusted this man. "But it can be complicated and confusing. Sometimes it's hard to balance respecting one's parents and doing what you feel is right. I'm not sure that anyone really understands my dilemma." She peered curiously at him, wondering if he had any idea what she was up against.

"I think I get your meaning." He slowly nodded.

She didn't know what to say and suddenly felt awkward.

"And I must say you appear to be a sensible young woman to me.

I can understand why Levi values your friendship." Judge Stanfield's smile felt warm and fatherly. "I hope you'll consider me your friend too."

"Thank you, I'd like that." She couldn't even explain why, but she suddenly felt tears in her eyes. "I should probably get back to my—"

"I'd be pleased if you would allow me to introduce you to my wife, Miss Blackstone." He nodded toward the table he'd left. "I'm sure her curiosity has piqued at witnessing me conversing with such an attractive young lady. May I take you to meet her?"

"I would love to meet her."

As Julianne followed the judge to his table, she felt eyes on her. She didn't even need to look over to see it was her father and Royal and their colorful friends. They probably had all kinds of questions for her. Hopefully, she could come up with some satisfying answers by the time she rejoined them. Or perhaps she should simply bid her father good day and make a swift exit.

The judge politely introduced her to his wife. Mrs. Stanfield was cordial but naturally inquisitive. "Julianne Blackstone?" she repeated. "That must be your mother who owns that exclusive dress shop."

"Yes. I've been working for her while she recovers from a buggy accident." Even as she said this, Julianne wondered how badly her mother had actually been hurt.

"So you must be the one who helped Levi choose this pretty shawl for me." Mrs. Stanfield patted her shoulder. "It's perfect for summer."

"And it looks lovely on you," Julianne told her.

"Miss Blackstone is a good friend of Levi's," the judge told his wife. "In fact, Levi gifted her with my old worn out typing machine. And I hear she's got it in working order again."

Mrs. Stanfield looked surprised. "And do you know how to type write?"

Julianne explained how she'd learned at finishing school. "To be honest, it wasn't a course they offered, but I helped in the office.

And typing was far more interesting to me than fancy needlework or French cuisine."

Mrs. Stanfield laughed. "You're a practical modern young woman."

"I wish Levi had stayed around for the picnic." The judge gazed around the park. "I think he'll be sorry he missed you, Miss Blackstone."

"Please give him my regards." She smiled at Mrs. Stanfield. "It's been a pleasure to meet you, ma'am. But I should probably return to my father." Her smile faded and she exchanged glances with the judge.

"May I have another private word with you, Miss Blackstone?" He glanced at his wife who nodded as if she approved.

"Yes, of course." Julianne followed him over to stand beneath the shade of some aspen trees.

"There is something I think you should know about." His tone was serious.

"What's that?"

"Levi and I couldn't understand a few details regarding your mother's recent accident and, since he was concerned for you, he did some checking."

"Checking?"

"I'm sorry to report some things just don't measure up." He paused as a couple of kids playing tag darted past before he continued. "First of all, there was no report of a buggy accident involving your mother reported at the courthouse. Now that in itself isn't so unusual, although word of mouth usually gets these stories circulating like wildfire, or at the very least they wind up in the newspaper. But I never heard a word about this one. Next of all, Levi's law office is directly above Dr. Muller's office, and in passing, Levi made a casual inquiry as to your mother's recovery. Dr. Muller knew nothing of such an accident."

"But I'm sure he's her doctor. His name's on her prescription bottle." Julianne felt heat rise up the back of her neck.

"It's possible that your mother has another doctor treating her injuries. Have you ever seen her doctor visit?"

She just shook her head.

"And finally, Levi asked his friend Joe Brandt, a good man who owns the only carriage repair shop in town, about your mother's damaged buggy. Joe has repaired a carriage for your father in the past but has never touched your mother's buggy. It's possible that it needed no repairs after the accident, but that seems unlikely if it was run down by a hay wagon and overturned."

Julianne tried to tame a rush of conflicting emotions. When the judge first began, she'd felt violated to think Levi would check on her mother's credibility like that. But as he'd continued, she grew suspicious because what he said made sense. Finally, she felt angry to imagine her mother had deceived her.

"Now, it's possible that these are all just coincidental, Miss Blackstone."

"That seems unlikely, doesn't it?" She sighed. "And to be honest, I've wondered about a few questionable things myself." She remembered seeing her mother standing alone last night. "Thank you for telling me about this."

"I know Levi wanted to say something, but he was worried about offending you."

"It's not easy to hear, but I'd rather not be in the dark about it." Julianne nodded, knowing what she needed to do next. "After learning certain things, I've decided it's prudent that I leave my parents' home. I plan to go live with my sister on her ranch. That's where I've wanted to be the whole time anyway. I just need to think of the best way to accomplish this." She didn't care what her father said, but she hated to imagine the tantrum Mother would throw when she heard this news. "Please let Levi know that I'm going home. I mean home to be with my sister. That's the place I really consider home."

Somehow just saying those words aloud filled her with a new confidence as she strode back over to her father's table. She could feel all of them watching her. She knew they wanted to know what business she had with Judge Stanfield and his wife. And she had a story ready for them.

"Father," she said directly to him. "I've had more than enough celebrations and sunshine for the day." She adjusted the wide brim of her hat. "I think I shall go home to check on Mother. Please, excuse me."

"Then I suppose I should escort you home," Father offered without enthusiasm.

"No, no. I'm perfectly fine on my own."

"Then let me escort you." Royal was already standing.

"That's not necessary," she told him.

"I say it is necessary." He beamed at her. "We can't let a beautiful girl like you walk home alone. What peril might befall such a lovely maid?" He made a mock bow and his friends laughed. "I insist."

"Well, I—"

"And I insist on knowing what you were discussing with Judge Stanfield," her father said. Although he was smiling, there was a chilly edge to his voice.

"We're all curious about that," Evelyn told her with twinkling eyes. "Although I'm always suitably impressed with a young woman able to make friends with folks in high places. I've found it's helpful to know people with influence."

"Influence?" Thomas Martin scowled. "Judge Stanfield might think he has influence here, but he's a small potato compared to the Colorado Supreme Court. When I win my case there, Judge Stanfield will probably lose his seat here." He laughed. "Good riddance."

Julianne knew she should keep quiet, but something in her refused. "Judge Stanfield is an honorable respectable judge and I suspect the Colorado Supreme Court will uphold his ruling."

Everyone at the table looked surprised, but her father and Mr. Martin looked angry.

"For a little lady, your daughter uses some pretty big words," Mr. Martin said to her father.

Royal linked his arm with hers. "That's because she's an intelligent young woman. And I intend to escort her safely home and, during that time, I hope to hear what other intelligent things she has on her mind." He looked at her. "Do you mind if I walk with you?"

Suddenly feeling Royal Dayton might be the safest of the group, she agreed. At least it got her away from her father. And as soon as she got home, she planned to start packing and get herself off to the Double W. Maybe in time for the trail ride too.

12

NEITHER SPOKE UNTIL THEY WERE WELL BEYOND THE CITY PARK AND that's when Julianne decided to make herself crystal clear. "I appreciate your willingness to walk me home, Mr. Dayton, but I'd prefer to go on my own, thank you."

"What is with this Mr. Dayton business?" He sounded slightly hurt. "I thought we were on a first name basis, dear Julianne. What's changed?"

"I'm sorry. But, please, Royal, I would rather walk home alone if you don't mind." She kept her tone crisp and cool.

"But I'd hoped to speak to you, Julianne. Intelligently. I appreciated how you stood up to everyone just now. It shows you have spirit and brains and are unafraid of your own opinions. Very admirable."

"I suppose I should say thank you." She stopped walking to look squarely at him. "But I would prefer to say good-bye."

"Oh, now, you're just being harsh. Please, Julianne. I listened to your opinion of Judge Stanfield, it's only fair you should hear mine."

"Why is that?" She continued walking, but at a faster pace.

"Because you've only been in town a short while. Tell me honestly, when did you first meet the judge?"

"I only met him today, but I observed him in his courtroom once."

"Then, let's be fair. How well can you possibly know the man?"

"Well enough to know he's honest and respectable."

"I don't disagree with you. Judge Stanfield is an upstanding man, and a good lawyer. If I were in trouble, I would like him to represent me."

She felt almost pleasantly surprised but continued her quick pace. The sooner she was away from him the better.

"The only thing I have against Orville Stanfield is he's not progressive."

"What does that mean?"

"He opposes development."

"How is that?"

"He's like a giant blockade against progress, Julianne. He's of the old-fashioned point of view that bigger is not better. He wants Colorado Springs to stay in the Dark Ages. I suspect he'd like to change the town's name back to Colorado City and remove the telephone lines and electricity."

"I know that can't be true."

"For all we know, he might do away with our modern hotel, the railroad lines, and the hospital. Before long we'd all be wearing animal skins, carrying big clubs, and howling at the moon."

"Now, you're just being ridiculous."

"Maybe, but he's made his position clear, Julianne. He questions progress over and over, again and again. He opposes changes in law and—"

"Why shouldn't he oppose changes in law?"

"Because the way our government is supposed to work is by having our laws formed and transformed by the people and for the people. A republic is constantly subject to change and revision and improvement."

"But only if they are good changes," she argued. "And not everyone agrees on the same kind of changes. You should know that."

"Judge Stanfield opposes *all* change. He is against *all* development. That's not good government, Julianne. Surely, you must understand how a narrow-minded judge can be harmful to the justice system. Judge Stanfield isn't good for the people or the town. He might be a nice old fellow, but he should be removed from the bench. The people deserve better."

In front of her house, she turned to lock eyes with him. "And is sneaking a casino and saloon and all sorts of other prohibited businesses right on the edge of town *better* for the people? Or is it simply a profitable scheme for you and my father and your selfish friends to get rich quick?"

His eyes flashed with what looked like anger, but his lips were a solid tight line, and he said nothing.

"Thank you for getting me home safely, Mr. Dayton, but don't you have a campaign speech to deliver this afternoon, or did you just waste it on me?"

"As a matter of fact, I do have a speech to give." He tipped his hat, but his dark eyes were hard as granite. "Good day, Miss Blackstone."

She knew he was through with her. And that was fine because she was more than finished with him. Royal Dayton might have a smooth talking, handsome veneer that hoodwinked some folks, but she could see straight through him. He was a wolf in sheep's clothing, and hopefully the voters in their region would figure that out before the election in November. If she had anything to say about it, they would.

Instead of going in the front door, Julianne went around the side of the house and let herself into the carriage house. Behind Father's carriage, she spied Mother's smaller buggy and, upon opening the doors wide to allow the sunshine in, she could see that the shiny black buggy was without a scratch.

"What're you doing in there?" Jones's shadow appeared behind her.

"Good afternoon, Mr. Jones. Father asked me to drive Mother's buggy to pick him up." She didn't like telling a lie, but it was the first explanation that came to her, because she knew Jones was more used to Father's orders than anyone's. "Could you please get it ready for me while I go inside?"

He nodded. "Sure thing, Miss."

She smiled. "Thank you." And hurrying into the house, she hoped her father planned to remain at the park during the speeches and other festivities. She knew she needed to work fast.

"Julianne!" Mother exclaimed. She was standing in front of the kitchen table, but quickly sank down in her wheeled chair with a guilty expression. "What are you doing home? And sneaking through the back door like that?" Already she was wheeling herself away, heading toward her bedroom.

"Sorry to startle you." Julianne followed her down the hallway. "But I don't see why you don't just walk. It would be easier."

"Don't be ridiculous." Inside her bedroom, she turned the chair to stare at Julianne. "What has gotten into you?"

"Just the truth. You don't need that chair, do you, Mother?"

"What on earth are you saying?" She held out the leg wrapped in the splint.

"I'm saying I know that you're not really hurt."

"Just because I'm getting better doesn't mean—"

"You were never in a buggy accident, Mother. I know this for a fact. Dr. Muller has not been treating you. Your buggy doesn't have a scratch on it. There's no record of your accident at the courthouse." Julianne went closer, pulling up the dressing gown hiding the supposedly broken leg. "And that splint looks rather sloppy, Mother. You must've been in a hurry when you wrapped it this morning."

"Julianne!"

"The game is over." Julianne glared at her. "I trusted you, Mother, but you have deceived me and used me, and I'm going back to the Double W right now."

"Please, don't go, darling. I need you here with me."

"I'm going. You don't need me, Mother. You're just using me. I thought things had changed. I thought you had changed. I almost enjoyed being your daughter." Julianne had tears in her eyes as she backed away. "But you tricked me."

"It was your father's idea." Mother actually stood now, walking toward her. The guise was over. "Please, don't leave like this, dear. We can fix this. I can explain everything to you. If you'll only listen."

"Nothing you can say will change anything, Mother. I'm leaving." She ran upstairs to her room and, grabbing her satchel, she stuffed a few things in it. She wanted to change out of the silly pink dress but knew that time was of the essence.

Mother was waiting at the foot of the steps and, despite the tears in her eyes, Julianne felt no pity. "I'm taking your buggy," she informed her. "I'll ask someone at the ranch to return it to you."

"That's fine." Mother just nodded. "I deserve this treatment, Julianne. I'm sorry for tricking you. Your father thought it was the only way to get you married to Royal. He thought if you got to know Royal, you'd see what a good upstanding man he is. And you two did seem to get along last night. We were hopeful."

"Royal Dayton is a trickster, a wolf in sheep's clothing. Maybe he's made you believe he's not, but I know what he and Father are up to, and I have no respect for them, or any of Father's friends."

"What are you saying? What are they up to? Please, tell me what you know."

"Why don't you ask your husband to explain it?" She looked up at the grandfather clock. "I have to go now."

"Julianne." Her voice choked. "Please, don't leave."

"Nothing can stop me, Mother."

"Then please try to forgive me for deceiving you. I'm really sorry. I know it was wrong. But I just wanted you here with me. I wanted my daughter." She started to sob.

"Maybe we can patch this thing up someday." Julianne softened. "But not today, Mother. There's just too much at stake here."

"What will I tell your father?" Mother followed Julianne to the front door.

"Tell him the truth." Julianne had an idea. "Tell him I'm driving cattle with my sister and brother." She couldn't help but feel satisfaction to imagine how angry that would make him. Then, despite her resolve to leave her mother in pain, she turned to face her. "Hopefully, we'll get past this someday." She leaned over to kiss her mother's cheek. "Just not today." As she opened the door, she heard the telephone ringing. "Better get that, Mother. Now that you can walk again."

As Julianne got into the buggy that was waiting in front of the house, she thought about what she'd said about the cattle drive. She'd only thrown that out there to inflict a bit more pain on her parents, but realized that if she hurried, she might actually be able to make it to their camp before sundown. The first day was always slow going, keeping the cows on the trail, moving them up into the hills. And the trail was easy to follow.

Yes, she decided as she got on the road leading away from town. That's exactly what she would do. She urged the horse to a trot and was impressed with how fast Mother's buggy could move. Going on the cattle drive sounded like just what she needed. Tonight, around the campfire, she'd have time to talk to Delia and Julius and Wyatt, to explain to them all that had gone on with her parents, and to get their advice. The ride up there would give her time to clear her head. She needed that. And when they returned to the ranch in a few days, she could start to pick up the pieces of her life again.

Caleb was surprised to see her emerge from the buggy. Calling out to him, she explained her plan to catch up with the cattle drive. "I need to hurry!"

"Well, you might want to change out of that pretty dress first," he teased as he took the lead to the horse. "And you don't need to hurry as much as you think. They got a late start. I s'pect you'll easily catch up to 'em before they make camp." He tipped his head to the buggy. "What about this?"

"Maybe someone can return it to my parents, or just wait and my father will probably send someone to get it."

Caleb nodded. "While you're gettin' changed, I'll saddle up Dolly for you."

She thanked him then hurried into the house where she found Ginger and Daisy getting the children ready for afternoon naptime. "What in tarnation are you doing here?" Ginger asked as Billy ran down the stairs to greet her.

"I'm going on the cattle drive." Julianne grasped Billy's hand, leading him back upstairs. "I heard they got a late start. Is everything all right?"

"We thought Billy Boy here was sick," Ginger explained.

"I was real sick, Aunt Julianne." He made a sad face.

"Well, not *real* sick," Ginger clarified. "He got into a jar of my sweet pickle preserves and ate the whole thing then wound up with a big ol' tummy ache that scared his poor mama and daddy."

"I didn't eat the whole thing, Ginger." He held up a finger. "There was one pickle left in the jar."

Ginger reached for his hand. "Yes, but when you upchucked, it looked more like you ate *three* jars of pickles."

He grinned. "I sure won't do that again, Ginger. I promise."

Julianne smiled, running her fingers through her nephew's hair. "Looks like you're the man in the house now, Billy. You better be good for Ginger while we're out driving those cows."

He stood straighter. "I'm gonna go on a cattle drive too someday. Daddy promised to show me how to rope a calf when he gets back."

"Only if you're a good boy." Ginger winked at Julianne. "Now, you better get out of that party dress and on your way. They headed out late, but you still gotta get a move on if you want to catch 'em."

Julianne kissed Billy's forehead. "See you later, Billy Boy." She hurried to her room and quickly changed into riding clothes. By the time she got back downstairs, Ginger had already put together some provisions.

"You might get hungry before you catch up with the others." Ginger handed her the bag. "You be safe out there."

She thanked her then headed out to the stables to find that Caleb not only had Dolly saddled and tacked up, but a bedroll and some other supplies were already strapped on her. Julianne shoved a few things into a saddlebag then thanked him. "I'm so glad I get to do this."

"I'm glad for you too." He watched her swing up into the saddle. "Your family will be mighty glad too." He patted Dolly's rump. "You two gals have fun out there." Now he frowned. "You ain't packing heat, Miss."

"I'm probably safer without a firearm." She reassured him with a smile. "I'm not very good with a gun."

"Well, then watch out for critters," he warned. "And don't worry too much, I s'pect the drivers probably scared most anything dangerous away by now."

She thanked him again, then reining Dolly around, she nudged her with her boot heels, and they were on their way. Dolly seemed happy to kick up her heels and they made good time following the trail that started on the edge of the cow pasture. The cattle trail was plainly visible, and Dolly seemed to understand their destination, so Julianne just relaxed in the saddle, giving the horse her head.

Soaking up the sun and the natural beauty around her, Julianne tried to purge out all the mixed emotions still surging through her. There was nothing she could do about any of it out here anyway.

Well, besides praying. That couldn't hurt. And she'd heard Delia say, more than once, that it was always easier to pray on the back of a good horse. As she rode—and prayed—Julianne realized her sister, as usual, was right.

13

Levi left his law office to pick up his parents following the Mayor's Picnic. They hadn't cared to sit through the speech making or partake in the music and dancing later, so he'd promised to get them promptly at two. He knew they were disappointed that he didn't stick around for the "food and fun," but seeing Julianne surrounded by a bunch of wealthy self-serving crooks had erased his appetite. He knew that even the tastiest fried chicken would sit like a lump of lead in his stomach if he had to watch Julianne hobnobbing with that crowd.

As he drove down Main Street, he remembered the walks he'd enjoyed with Julianne, the conversations they'd had, the laughter they'd shared. And he didn't really believe she was like her father and his disreputable friends, or that she even enjoyed the company she was keeping. But why was she keeping it? She was a grown woman with what seemed a fairly strong will. Why didn't she stand up to her parents if she thought they were in the wrong?

As he drove his father's carriage to the city park where other carriages were stopping to pick up passengers, he wondered what it would feel like to have parents like Julianne's. Perhaps he was being too critical of her. After all, his parents were good decent folks. People he was proud to be associated with. And he knew Julianne was embarrassed by her father's reputation. She didn't even like to speak of him. Maybe Levi had been too hasty to run out on the festivities today. Maybe he should've stuck around and spent some time with her.

As he pulled to a stop by the park's entrance, he noticed a lot of folks were leaving. Like him and his parents, they had better things to do than listen to the political candidates' speeches. He already had a fairly good idea of the candidates' platforms and what they would say. There was a great rift in this boom town. Those who seemed hellbent to grow the Springs into another Denver—and profit from it. And those who wanted to move more slowly and carefully, like his father. The speeches would go back and forth this afternoon.

And gifted speakers like Royal Dayton, with his uncanny ability to hold his listeners spellbound even if he was feeding them a bunch of hogwash, would probably be the highlight of the afternoon. He'd heard the man before and could never understand how others could listen to his long-winded pontificating with such patient interest. It always reminded Levi of the proverb that said a multitude of words concealed a lying heart, or something to that effect.

During the course of the afternoon speeches, it was possible that a spontaneous debate would break out between two opposing candidates. And sometimes that led to hoots and calls from the audience, that could possibly erupt into a fight. One of the reasons his parents chose to go home early. But seeing the marshal and some of his deputies posted about, Levi didn't expect there'd be any serious trouble today.

After spotting his parents making their way to him, he scanned the thinning crowd for Julianne. She should be easy to spot in her ruffled pink dress. But although he observed her father and Royal and their crooked cronies gathered around the bandstand, Levi didn't see Julianne. And that was a relief. He waved to his parents, waiting for his dad to help Mother into the backseat of the open carriage.

"Go ahead and sit with Mother," Levi called as he urged the team forward to make way for the wagon behind him. "I'm sure you're both tired and it's more comfortable back there."

"Don't mind if I do," Dad told him. "Thanks, son."

"Did you get anything to eat?" Mother asked.

"I wasn't too hungry. I can get something at home."

"I saved you a molasses cookie. It's here in my handbag."

He laughed. "Of course you did, Mother."

She reached over to hand the sweet to him. "I know how you like them."

He thanked her, munching on the cookie as he turned to go out of town.

"I wish you'd stayed," Dad said. "I had an interesting conversation with a friend of yours."

"Oh?" He took another bite. "Who was that?"

"A very pretty and intelligent young lady."

Levi chewed slowly, waiting.

"A Miss Julianne Blackstone."

"I see." Levi tried to conceal his curiosity.

"She wondered what had happened to you."

"How did you happen to have a conversation with her?" Levi asked.

"She wanted to thank me for the typing machine." Dad seemed to be trailing this out for some reason.

"I got to meet her too, son," Mother said cheerfully. "She seems like a very sweet girl. Not at all like I'd imagine a child of Jefferson Blackstone to be like."

Levi cleared his throat. "She's a nice enough girl, but I did find it incongruent to see her so entrenched in her father's company."

"I don't think it was by choice," Dad told him. "I think young Julianne is caught between a rock and a hard place."

"How so?" Levi asked.

"She's trying to balance respecting her parents against questioning their ethics. At least that's the impression she gave me."

"That sounds about right," Levi agreed.

"Poor girl." Mother made a tsk-tsk sound. "That is a difficult position."

"So I thought perhaps I could help her out," Dad said slowly. "I informed her about the investigation you've been doing on her mother's alleged buggy accident."

"Oh, Dad, you didn't!" Levi looked back at his father.

"Sorry, son, but I think she deserves to know the truth."

"But we don't know if it is the truth. What if my suspicions are wrong?"

"I told her nothing was for sure or for certain, Levi, just that she might want to be aware and check these things out for herself."

"How did she react?" he asked.

"Frankly, she didn't seem too surprised."

Levi wasn't sure what to think. He didn't like the idea of Dad disclosing Levi's sleuthing activities, but at the same time felt relieved that Julianne was apprised.

"I didn't know about any of this," Mother said with concern. "But it worries me to think you put that poor girl at such odds against her parents. What is she going to do now?"

"She said she was going to move out to her sister's ranch," Dad told her.

"That would be Delia Davis." Mother sounded better now. "She's a very nice woman. And I like her husband too. I still find it hard to believe either Delia or Julianne are related to Jefferson Blackstone. Just doesn't seem right."

"Julianne's sister Delia isn't related to Mr. Blackstone," Levi clarified.

"Yes, yes, that's right. She was Winston's daughter. I always liked

Winston too. Such an innovative farmer. Delia told me that she's carrying on with a lot of his techniques."

"Well, Julianne will sure be better off with her sister than with her parents," Levi admitted.

"I feel sorry for her," Mother said. "Julianne seems to be caught in a—"

Her words were cut off by two loud bangs in close sequence. Levi tightened the reins as his mother gasped and then screamed. "What's going—"

"Stop, stop, Levi! Something's wrong with your father. Oh, dear God, he's been shot! He's bleeding!"

"Whoa!" Levi reined the team to a stop then jerked around to see Dad slumped against Mother. His forehead was bleeding, and he was clutching his chest. Trying to think fast, Levi looked all around then fixed his eyes on a ridge not far ahead. In the same instant he noticed a dust cloud and a single horse and rider making a getaway.

"The shots must've come from there." He snapped the reins, turning the team around. "I'm taking us back to town. To the hospital. Hold on to him, Mother. I'm going to go fast."

As Levi drove the team in a full run toward town, he could hear his mother talking and praying and sobbing all at the same time. "Please, Lord, don't take him," she cried. "Hold on, Orville, hold on! Go faster, Levi—faster!"

"I'm trying, Mother!"

"Oh, please, spare him, sweet Jesus, *please*, *please*, *spare him*," she prayed over and over. "It's going to be all right, Orville dear. Levi will get us to the hospital. Just hold on. Hold on!"

Despite the speed of the horses and the fact they were only a few miles out of town, the ride back seemed to take forever. Like his mother, Levi was praying too. Silently pleading with God to spare his father—and to curse the lowdown varmint who'd shot him. Even when they got into town, Levi continued to gallop the horse, hollering for folks to clear the way, that it was an emergency.

With the hospital in sight, Levi yelled out to a bystander at the foot of the steps. "Judge Stanfield's been shot! Get help from the hospital!" The man looked shocked then took off up the hospital steps as Levi reined the team to a stop. He jerked on the carriage brake then jumped out to help with Dad. Both his parents were covered in blood. "Mother, are you hurt?" he asked.

"No," she sobbed. "Just your father."

"Let me get him." Levi slid an arm around his father, but already a pair of men had stepped up to help, with one of the sisters standing nearby. Before long, Dad was on a stretcher being taken into the hospital.

"Oh, Levi," Mother sobbed into his shoulder.

Supporting her with one arm, Levi walked her up the steps where another sister rushed over to help. "She's not wounded," he explained.

"Not physically," the sister said. "But she needs help."

He nodded. "Thank you."

Another sister came over to assist Levi, leading him to a washroom where he could clean off some of his father's blood. As he washed his face, he wondered who had done this? *And why?* Then he threw down the towel and went out to telephone the marshal's office, briefly telling him the situation.

"Marshal Rivers is still at the Mayor's Picnic, but I'll be right over," the man on the other end promised.

In a few minutes, Deputy Garson showed up and, meeting in a private office, Levi told him everything he could recall about the shooting. "I only saw one man. He must've been positioned on that rim on the west side of the road, about halfway between our farm and town. I couldn't see what he was wearing. Mostly brown. But he was riding a paint. Black and white paint. I couldn't see the man too well, and it all happened so fast, but he had the look of a cowhand or drifter. I'd guess medium build and height. That's about all I know. He was a ways off." He tried to remember. "Maybe two hundred yards, so he must've used a rifle."

"We'll find out after the doctor removes the bullets." Deputy Garson frowned. "How's your father? Still alive?"

"He was alive." Levi sighed. "But a head wound and chest wound."

"Doesn't sound good."

Levi stood. "I better check on my mother."

"I'll fetch the marshal. I'm sure he'll have some questions."

As Levi went to find his mother, he kept asking himself who the shooter was and why he'd done it. He felt certain it wasn't an accidental shooting or hunting accident. Someone had planned the whole thing out, figured that Judge Stanfield would be coming home on that road about that time of day, laid in wait, then attempted to murder him. It could be an act of vengeance, or an act of prevention, or even both. Plenty of folks had it out for the judge, but how many would go to such lengths to kill him?

Usually a crime like this meant the stakes were high. There was something to be gained monetarily. Money, gold, land. And the tough guy Levi had spotted from the road didn't appear to be a high-roller. More likely, he was a hired gun. But who was paying him?

"Levi." Mother waved to him and, seeing her looking so sad and forlorn, blood stains still on her shawl and dress, he hurried over, and holding her in his arms, he just let her cry. She pulled out a damp handkerchief and wiped her eyes and, stepping back, she let out a raspy sigh.

"Why did this happen?" she asked him in a meek voice. "Why?"

"I don't know."

"Have you heard anything yet?" she asked. "About your father?"

"No. Have you?"

"Just that he's in surgery."

Levi put an arm around her, leading her over to the waiting area. "I'm guessing no news is good news, Mother. They must still be working on him."

"Thank God for this hospital," she said as she sat. "And the sisters here are so kind. They even offered me one of their nun uniforms, but I just couldn't bear to wear a black dress." She choked back a sob. "Not yet."

He tried to comfort her, reminding her that Dad was always a good one to recover from anything, whether an illness or like the broken thumb he had last winter. "He's a tough old codger." Seeing Marshal John Rivers coming into the hospital, Levi waved him over.

"I'm so sorry to hear about the shooting," Marshal Rivers told them. "How's he doing?"

"We don't know." Levi explained he was still in surgery.

"You look worn out, Mrs. Stanfield." Marshal Rivers put a hand on her shoulder. "I told Gwendolyn you might like to go up to the house for a spell and she promised to get a room ready for you."

"That's very kind, but I can't leave here until I know Orville is out of the woods and…" Her voice trailed off as Deputy Garson came over to join them.

"The offer's good for as long as you need it," Marshal Rivers said. He turned to Levi. "Let's go find someplace private to talk. You too, Garson."

The three men returned to the room where Levi and Garson had talked, and Marshal Rivers began to go over the details of the crime. "I sent a pair of deputies to check out the rim where you say the shooting came from. To get hoofprints and footprints and anything else that might help."

"I suspect the shooter's a hired killer," Levi said.

"You're probably right." Marshal Rivers nodded. "Question is who's behind it?"

"I've been listing the possibilities in my head," Levi admitted.

"Why don't we put them down on paper?"

While the deputy wrote, Levi began to list the most likely suspects. "There's the obvious. Like a disgruntled Thomas Martin, furious about losing his claim in court. And there's Bart Vincent's outrage about his son getting locked up for twenty years, even though he probably deserved more. Not to mention some mine claims that will be pending soon."

"These development schemers probably have the most money at stake," Deputy Garson suggested. "I heard there was some complaining when their casino plans got shot down last week after Judge Stanfield interpreted the City Charter for them."

"Maybe so." Marshal Rivers rubbed his chin. "But I can't see them hiring a gunman to shoot down the judge for that. Doesn't change the City Charter to kill a judge."

"My thoughts too," Levi agreed. "And Thomas Martin doesn't have much to gain by having my dad shot. His case still has to play by the Colorado Supreme Court."

"And Bart Vincent might be mad about the judge locking up Edgar, but I can't see him hiring a gunman to shoot him."

"Although Bart probably has friends who'd do it for free," Marshal Rivers added.

"There are a number of claim-jumping hearings on my dad's upcoming docket," Levi told them. "If some of the jumpers saw how Martin's hearing turned out, could be they're worried."

"It would definitely be in their interest to put the judge out of commission, or at least off of their cases. Everyone knows Judge Stanfield doesn't roll over for anyone."

Levi wanted to add *like Judge Barrows might do*. It was no secret he leaned toward progressive influencers and smooth-talking investors, even if they were bending the law to suit their purposes.

"And we all know that any claim-jumpers headed for a hearing would prefer Barrows's court to Stanfield's." Marshal Rivers looked at Levi. "Can you find me a list of the upcoming cases?"

"Sure. I've been going over a lot of them with my dad. I could probably list them for you right here."

"You know, this gives me an idea." Marshal Rivers tapped the side of his head. "What if we had a judge who thought like Orville fill the bench? Just until Orville is back on his feet." He frowned. "Hoping that happens."

"What do you mean?" Garson asked.

"What if we had a Judge Stanfield to replace Judge Stanfield?"

They both looked at Levi.

"You can't be serious." Levi shook his head. "I'm flattered, but a little young for the bench."

"It would just be temporary. Everyone knows you're smart, Levi. Finishing law school as fast as you did, head of your class. Your dad's done plenty of bragging about you when you're not around."

"But this is—"

"A really good idea," Garson finished. "What a great way to keep those claim-jumpers from getting the upper hand."

"Except for one thing." Marshal Rivers frowned. "We could be putting Levi in danger."

"I'm not worried about that," Levi told them. "I'd be happy to do this for my father's sake, but I just don't think folks would respect someone as young as me on the bench."

"Respect is earned, son." Marshal Rivers stood. "Anyway, we don't need to resolve this now. Tomorrow's Sunday. You just give it some thought."

Levi promised he would, but as he went back to check on his mother, he still thought it seemed a foolish plan. They'd probably laugh him right out of the courtroom.

14

Julianne had been on the cattle drive trail for less than an hour when she heard the sound of hooves. Was she already catching up with the herd? She paused to listen, trying to determine if they were up ahead or off in the rough. Maybe someone was rounding up strays. Maybe she could help.She reached for her rope then called out a friendly "Hello?"

But instead of an answer, she heard fast hooves pounding up from behind her. Turning her horse to see, and hoping it was Julius sneaking up to surprise her, she felt something hit her from behind—hard. She tumbled sideways right out of the saddle and hit the ground.

Scrambling to her feet, and furious at Julius, she was ready to fight. If this really was a prank, it was not funny. Her doubled fist held up, she spun around. But in the same instant, she was jumped from behind, and flattened to the ground. Facedown in the dirt, she struggled to regain her breath then yelled. "What the devil is—"

A dirty hand slapped across her mouth. "Shut up or you'll be sorry," a voice hissed in her ear. Still kicking and struggling to escape, she felt something hard jab into her ribs. "I mean it, girl. Keep still or I shoot."

Seeing the glint of metal, she knew it was a revolver and her attacker was serious. She quit fighting him and decided to try reasoning. "If you're robbing me," she said quietly, "I have nothing of value. You might as well let me go."

"You're more valuable than you think." Still holding her facedown, he pressed his knee into her back, pinning her painfully into the uneven ground. Another set of horse hooves were approaching. If only it were Julius or Wyatt or one of the ranch hands.

"I got 'er, Beau." Her assailant's voice had a grating squeaky edge to it.

"Shut up, fool," the other man growled.

The other man—Beau?—dismounted. With her head on the ground, all she could see was worn dusty boots walking toward her.

"Gag and blindfold her," Beau said gruffly. "And tie her hands in front."

"I'm on it," Squeaky voice replied, then snickering like this was some sort of game, he wrapped and tied a foul-smelling blue bandana over her mouth. Another went over her eyes, tied so tightly she felt she might be blind by the time it was removed. If it were removed.

"Hurry up," Beau told him. "Those trail drivers might double back and we gotta get her outta here."

Squeaky flipped her onto her back and, using what felt like rough twine, bound her hands tightly together. "There." Squeaky pulled her to her feet.

"Let's get her on her horse."

"And then we skedaddle? And meet up with Danner?"

"Come on, help me." Together they hoisted her into the saddle. "Say, Julianne's not half bad looking." Beau patted her leg. "She's a pretty little cowgirl."

"You know her name?" Squeaky asked.

"Shut up," Beau snapped. "Just tie her in and don't ask questions."

Squeaky used more twine to tie her hands to the saddle horn, but there was a little give in the binding. With her feet still dangling by her sides, she wondered if she could slide her tied hands over the slick surface of the saddle horn and jump down. But then what?

"Get your feet in them stirrups unless you wanna be drug." Beau patted her leg again. "Might mess up that pretty face."

Hot tears burned beneath the blindfold as she fumbled her boots into the stirrups. Determined not to cry as the horses started to move in the opposite direction of the cattle drive, she tried to think of an escape, but nothing came to mind. The only thing she knew to do was pray. And blocking out everything but the movement of her horse and three simple words, she did pray. *God help me*, she prayed with each step of Dolly's hooves. Over and over she prayed those same three words. *God help me, God help me, God help me.*

Maybe it was riding dependable, even-tempered Dolly or maybe it was God's grace, but an unexplainable calmness came over her as they rode. For a while they traveled in the cooling shadows, cluing her that they were southbound on the east side of a mountain. Her family from the Double W would be on the other side of it. After a while they made a sharp left turn, and it wasn't long before she felt the late afternoon sunshine on her back. They were traveling east.

She tried to recall what might be out in this part of desolate country. Besides a couple of large cattle ranches spread miles apart, it was just open range. Her kidnappers probably felt safe moving their hostage in these parts. No one would be around to see them. But where were they headed? And more importantly, why? What could possibly be their purpose in taking her? A ransom seemed unlikely, although Squeaky had insinuated she was valuable. But valuable to whom? Not her father. And Delia and Wyatt were comfortable, but not wealthy. Everything they had went right back into the ranch.

She decided to line up what little facts she knew. One of the guys was named Beau. But she didn't know anyone by that name. She'd also heard the name Danner, and it sounded as if he was the one behind her abduction. But she knew no one named Danner. They obviously knew who she was since they'd called her by name more than once. So this wasn't just random outlaws out to kidnap someone for the fun of it, they had a specific plan and purpose. But what was it?

It seemed clear these men must've received specific knowledge of her whereabouts from someone. Otherwise they couldn't have been lying in wait for her. But how many people had known she'd be out here today, trying to catch up with the cattle drive? That could narrow her list down considerably.

But besides Caleb, Ginger, and Daisy—trusted ranch friends—the only one who knew she was going on the cattle drive was her mother. And, despite her hurt feelings toward Mother, she didn't believe she could be behind this. Mother might not be completely trustworthy, but Julianne knew she loved her children. This could not possibly be related to Mother.

Of course, Mother would've surely told Father. Hadn't Julianne suggested as much? Just to taunt him. So Father would know all about her plans by now. But what would be his motive for something this extreme? And, really, would her father allow his only daughter to be treated in such a manner? He might be a selfish unscrupulous man, but to endanger one of his own children…it seemed highly unlikely.

And yet she had crossed him by rejecting his hopes for an arranged marriage with Royal Dayton. But as badly as he wanted her wed to Royal, Father wasn't a stupid man. A foolish scheme like kidnapping his own daughter would not improve his prospects of having Royal for his son-in-law. That was perfectly ridiculous.

Still, there was no denying Father was in cahoots with Royal Dayton. And not just as his campaign manager either. She remembered eavesdropping on their suspicious scheme—was that only last night? She'd heard how they planned to sneak a big casino and some other sleazy enterprises right alongside town. And how they planned to act fast.

She knew their only motivation was money. They didn't care that their corrupt plans might be a detriment to the town. They only wanted to line their own pockets at the expense of others. Although she hadn't heard all the details, she'd been eager to share this information with Levi today. She'd wanted to hear his legal opinion about their intent to purchase the farmland adjacent to town in order to build the casino that had been disallowed within the city limits. But she never got the chance. She'd considered telling his father at the picnic, but then he'd taken her to meet his sweet wife and it had just felt inappropriate.

Suddenly she recalled what she'd said to Royal in front of her parents' house. She'd angrily spouted off to him, revealing that she had knowledge of what they wanted kept secret. But was that reason to have her kidnapped? Like her father, Royal was not a stupid man either. And yet Royal had much at stake. Not just money. Royal hoped to win a US senate seat. If word of his corrupt dealings got out, he might lose the bid and his reputation. He could not afford that.

Still, would he really resort to kidnapping? Just to keep her quiet? Didn't he realize he'd be in serious trouble when the law found out? If the law found out…and that remained to be seen. What if she was never found? She realized the horses had stopped.

"There's the line shack," Beau said.

"You sure?" Squeaky asked. "Don't look right to me."

"How do you know what's right or what ain't?" Beau sounded irritated as the horses stopped. "Why you gotta question every dang thing, little brother?"

"Maybe cuz I wanna know what's going on," Squeaky answered. "Maybe I don't trust you. Maybe things ain't linin' up quite right."

"Aw, shut your trap," Beau growled. "I'll get her in there. You hide the horses in that stand of trees. Danner said there's a pond for watering 'em."

Julianne felt Beau's hand grip her arm and she was suddenly jerked down from her horse. Losing her balance, she tumbled to the ground, but not wanting those grubby hands on her, she struggled to her feet.

Beau grabbed the back of her neck, pulling her so close she could smell his sour breath. "Sure do like yellow-haired girls," he said into her ear. "Even all dirty in your cowgirl outfit, you're still mighty pretty."

Bracing herself for the worst, she silently prayed for God's help.

"Walk," he commanded. Moving one foot in front of the other until she heard the sound of a rusty door hinge and a clunk. Now he gave her a rough shove, thrusting into a musty smelling space. Even with her blindfold still in place, she could tell it was dark in here. She stood, silently praying, trying not to sob in fear.

After some shuffling she heard the door slam shut and what sounded like a bolt jammed into place, and she knew she was alone. Crumpling to the floor, she curled up in a ball, and just sobbed. She was still in that position when she heard the two men arguing again.

"I said put that bandana on!" Beau yelled.

"Why?" Squeaky demanded. "It ain't like we're outlaws, Beau."

"We want her to think we are," Beau said more quietly.

"Why?"

"Cuz that's how Danner wants it. Remember when we used to play like we was Billy the Kid when we were kids?"

"Yeah."

"So just do that now."

"Why?" Squeaky asked again.

"Dang you and your dang questions. I ain't telling ya again. You put that bandana on or you'll know the reason why!" Beau yelled.

Still curled up in a ball, she heard the door open again; she waited without moving, hoping they'd think she was asleep—or dead—and just leave her alone.

"I brung your bedroll and a few things." Squeaky sounded almost apologetic. He dropped something to the wooden floor, and she still didn't move.

"I can take your gag off if you promise not to scream."

Wanting the nasty rag removed, she sat up and nodded, sitting still as he untied it.

"Thank you." Her voice sounded raspy.

"I reckon I can take off your blindfold too."

She thanked him again, waiting as he fumbled to loosen and remove it. She blinked, adjusting her eyes to the bright slats of late afternoon sunlight coming between the boards of the shack. She looked up to see his face concealed by a bandana and his hat pulled down low. For some reason Beau was protecting their identity and that gave her hope. Maybe they didn't intend to kill her after all.

"Can you untie my hands?" she asked meekly. "The twine is so tight, it really hurts."

"I'll cut you loose for now, but I'll have to ask my broth, uh—I mean my friend, if that's all right." He opened a pocket knife and sliced off the twine to reveal red lines that had cut into her skin.

"Thank you." She rubbed her wrists.

"I went through your belongings." He gave her saddlebag a kick with the toe of his boot. "Had to make sure you ain't got no gun or nothing like that. Saw you had some food and there's water in your canteen, so I reckon you're good for the night."

Again she thanked him. It was strange to be thanking her abductor, but she hoped she might be able to soften him up a little. He seemed the better of the two brothers and, even if he refused to help her escape, he might be her only hope for the time being.

He stood there for a moment, just watching her. Then he opened the door so the late afternoon light poured in. "Now I'm warning you, Miss, you better not make no fuss or noise in here. That is unless you want real trouble."

She nodded mutely. Wasn't she already in real trouble?

15

It was early evening by the time Levi and his mother were finally reassured by the doctor that Dad's injuries, though serious, were not life threatening.

"The gunshot to his head was only a flesh wound," Dr. Muller explained. "A lot of blood, but nothing concerning. It was the chest wound that worried me, but the judge is a lucky man—or God was watching out for him. The bullet missed his heart by less than two inches."

Mother gasped, covering her mouth. "But he's really all right?"

"Yes. He's recovering from surgery now."

"May we see him?"

Dr. Muller rubbed his chin. "He's been through a lot and resting quietly. I hate to disturb him. He's got two attentive sisters watching over him, they'll sit with him all night. I'd rather you wait until morning, Mrs. Stanfield."

She simply nodded, but Levi saw tears glistening in her eyes.

"So you got the bullet out?" Levi asked.

"Yes." Dr. Muller produced a rifle bullet.

"I promised to get it to Marshal Rivers as soon as possible."

The doctor gave Levi the bullet. "It was a tricky procedure and took longer than expected. The judge lost a lot of blood and there's still risk of infection, but I expect him to recover. In time." His smile was reassuring but weary.

"How much time?" Levi pocketed the bullet.

"Depends. Right now he's weak and needs to rest quietly."

"But I can see him in the morning?" Mother asked.

"Yes, of course." Dr. Muller peered curiously at her. "You, good lady, need to go home and get a good night's sleep."

"She doesn't want to go home," Levi explained. "But maybe we can convince her to stay the night at the marshal's house. His wife has offered her a room."

"Then as your physician, I recommend you take it," Dr. Muller told her.

To Levi's relief, Mother agreed to stay at the Rivers's, and he got her there just as Mrs. Rivers was setting the table. "I put out places for both of you," she told them, "and I'm not taking no for an answer." She looked at Mother then hugged her. "You poor thing. You've been through so much. Let's get you up to the guest room where you can clean up for dinner. We're about the same size, I'll loan you one of my dresses."

While Mother and Mrs. Rivers went upstairs, Levi found Marshal Rivers going over some paperwork in his den. After giving him the update on his father's condition, he handed him the bullet. "Doc Muller said it barely missed his heart."

The marshal examined the bullet. "I think this was fired from a Springfield 1880. Not that many of those around."

"So it should help then?"

"Hopefully." He patted Levi's back. "I've been thinking about our plan to put you on the bench, Levi. It might be our best shot at catching whoever tried to kill your father. But there's no denying it's dangerous."

"I've been thinking about it too. I want that killer caught. I'm willing to risk it."

"My men will be in the courtroom to protect you," he promised. "Armed but in plain clothes. And we'll have to keep a close watch outside the courtroom too. You good with that?"

"If it catches this killer, it'll be worth it."

"And for the time being, let's spread the rumor that the judge is incapacitated or perhaps even dead. Just in case the killer thinks he can sneak into the hospital to finish him off."

"I noticed you kept one of your men on duty there. Thanks."

"Yep. Not taking this lightly."

"I appreciate that." Levi checked the time. "I know your wife's getting ready to serve dinner, but I need to get out to the farm to feed the animals and check on things."

"I don't want you going out there by yourself." Marshal Rivers reached for his gun holster. "And I don't want you staying out there alone. Not until we get this thing figured out. We'll go see to your animals, get you and your mother some things, and come back to town. I'll ask Gwendolyn to keep our supper warm while we're gone."

Levi was grateful for the marshal's help but didn't like the idea of leaving his parents' farm unattended or staying in town for more than one night.

Julianne was grateful for her bedroll as the evening air grew cooler. Wrapped up in her blanket, she sat in the middle of the floor and tried to think of an escape plan. No one had returned to check on her and, heeding Squeaky's warning, she had been quiet. Quiet as a mouse, although the critters scampering around the edges of the little shack, which she assumed were mice, were not that quiet.

She was also thankful for her canteen, but only allowed herself tiny sips for fear she could run dry and still be stuck in here. And Ginger's provisions, which she was most grateful for, but rationing likewise, she kept close to her under the blanket. She didn't want the mice to smell them and come looking.

She could hear the men outside. They'd made a campfire and it smelled like they were cooking meat. Glad she had her own food to eat, at least for now, she hoped they wouldn't come back here and try to share something with her. The less she saw of them, particularly Beau, the better. She was tempted to go peek through one of the cracks in the shack's walls, maybe get a look at them without their bandana masks, but she didn't want them to hear her moving about and come investigate. Beau's comments about her pretty yellow hair already had her worried enough.

As the evening wore on, she could tell they'd been imbibing in "celebratory" whiskey because Squeaky kept insisting that he wasn't getting his fair share of the "hooch" as he called it. She also knew, based on the argument that was brewing, they were not in agreement on how their earnings from her kidnapping should be divided.

It started when Beau bragged about the thousand dollars Danner was paying him. It seemed his tongue got loosened up after he'd "hogged all the hooch." That made Squeaky angry, because it seemed he'd agreed to help his brother for a lot less. Naturally, he felt cheated.

"Why we ain't doin' a fifty-fifty split?" he loudly demanded.

"Because I'm the one who set it up with Danner. Not you."

"Yeah, but I did most of the work," Squeaky argued.

"Most of the work? I planned the whole blasted thing and you know it."

"I'm the one who jumped her and tied her up!" Squeaky yelled back at him. "While you just stood around doing nothing."

"I was keeping a watch out for the Double W ranch boys and you know it."

The brothers obviously no longer cared if anyone was listening as their voices got louder and louder. And who was there to hear them out here? Well, besides Julianne? Hopefully they assumed she was sleeping.

"I offered you two hundred dollars yesterday," Beau growled back at him. "You were glad enough about it then."

"That was then, this is now."

"You ain't gonna go changing things on me, Red. This was my deal. You can take your two hundred or nothing."

"And let you take the whole thousand?"

"If you don't shut up about this, I'm gonna wail the tar outta you," Beau threatened.

Now Squeaky swore at his brother and the sound of crashing glass made her think it was the whiskey bottle thrown into the fire. Were they about to resort to fisticuffs? "You know what, you can just keep the whole thousand, Beau. Finish this yourself. I'm done with you. I'm going back to town."

There was a brief lull and then Beau spoke in a much calmer tone.

"Maybe you're right, Red. Maybe I ain't being fair. Sleep on it. Tomorrow we'll talk."

"And if you ain't reasonable tomorrow, I'll light on outta here."

"G'night, Red."

"G'night, Beau."

She listened to the sounds of someone throwing more wood on their fire and the rustlings that sounded like bedrolls being arranged and then it was quiet…and finally, snoring.

Julianne got up and quietly walked around the dark space, feeling the walls to find if there was a weak spot somewhere or boarded-up window that might have a loose board. But it all felt fairly solid, and she found nothing on the floor that she could use to pry anything off. Even the door felt securely latched from the outside.

She went back to the center of the room to rearrange her bedroll and provisions. Trying to make herself comfortable, she prayed again. "God deliver me from my captors," she whispered quietly and then she tried to go to sleep.

But her mind wouldn't stop racing. She kept going over the events of the last couple of days, trying to line things up and make sense. By now she felt sure that Royal was behind this. And perhaps her father, although that was painful to imagine. He could be a scoundrel, but to subject his own daughter to this? That seemed too much. But Royal had much to lose if she leaked word out about his devious investment plans. For that matter, so did her father.

By now she knew someone named Danner had paid the brothers, Beau and Red, a thousand dollars to kidnap her. It was possible they just wanted to get her out of the way for a while—long enough to seal their land deal with the farmer and start building their fancy casino property. But what then? If she were let go, wouldn't Danner and Royal and whoever else was involved be worried she would talk? And she *would* talk, wouldn't she? Or would she be too afraid by then? She couldn't deny that this whole ordeal was terrifying. If only she could just sleep. Praying for rest and for God's help, she finally slipped into a fitful slumber.

On Sunday morning, after Levi and Mother visited Dad in the hospital, and after they felt reassured that he was going to make a full recovery, Mother encouraged Levi to pay Julianne a visit.

"I can't explain why, but I'm worried about that girl," she told Levi as they stood in the hallway outside the judge's secured and private room. "I think you should go check on her."

"Check on her?"

"There's something I didn't mention yesterday, Levi. On our ride home, we were talking about meeting her at the Mayor's Picnic. Remember, just before your father got shot?"

"Yes, I remember."

"Well, your father didn't notice this because his back was facing to her."

"To Julianne?"

"Yes. I was watching her. After talking to us, she went back to the table where she'd been sitting with her father and Royal Dayton and a few of their friends. And it appeared that Julianne was about to leave. She was talking to her father and his companions, probably saying her good-byes. But I'm sure she was attempting to excuse herself. And suddenly Royal Dayton stood up and linked arms with her."

Mother put her hand on his forearm and looked intently into his eyes. "Now, this is what troubled me, son. Poor Julianne didn't look the least bit pleased by it. Her father just smiled as if he was happy about it. And, although it seemed Julianne was trying to get out of it, it appeared that Mr. Dayton escorted her home."

Levi didn't feel terribly surprised. "I'm sure Julianne's father thinks Dayton a good match for his daughter."

"But something about it seemed wrong. I could tell by her expression. She was not comfortable with that man. And I'm worried she might still be in her parents' home, and her father might still be pressuring her. Oh, I'm probably just overly nervous because of your father's condition but, Levi, I do wish you'd check on her."

Since the Blackstone house was just a short distance from the hospital, he agreed to go. For Mother's sake he acted nonchalant, but after hearing her concern, he couldn't help but feel worried too. Not only that, but the last time they'd spoken, he knew he'd offended her by questioning her mother's accident. Then he completely ignored her at the picnic. He owed it to her to straighten things out. He felt uncomfortable standing on her porch, waiting for someone to come to the door. When the maid answered, he explained he was there to speak to Julianne.

"Miss Blackstone is not here. Would you like to speak to her mother?"

He considered this. "Yes, thank you."

The maid led him to a parlor and told him to make himself comfortable. Without sitting, he looked around the fussy room and wondered how anyone made themselves comfortable in here.

"Hello?" An older woman in a stylish dark blue dress came into the room. "Can I help you?"

"Are you Mrs. Blackstone?" he asked.

"That's right." She narrowed her eyes.

"I'm Levi Stanfield. A friend of Julianne's." He wanted to ask what happened to her wheeled chair and broken leg but knew better.

"Oh, yes. The lawyer who gave her the typing machine." The woman's smile looked uneasy. "What can I do for you?"

"I came to see Julianne, but I was told she's not here. Does that mean she no longer lives here, or has she stepped out?"

"Who is here?" a man's voice said. Now Julianne's father stepped into the room. Although they had never been formally introduced, Levi recognized him.

"This is Julianne's friend, Mr. Stanfield."

Mr. Blackstone's dark brows arched. "Judge Stanfield's son?"

"That's right." Levi forced a polite smile.

"I'm sorry to hear about your father."

"What is it you've heard?" Levi voided his tone and face of expression.

"That he was, well, wasn't he shot?"

"Where did you hear that?" Levi looked evenly at him. Was he nervous?

"These things get around town. Friends talk. You went to school back East; you know how small towns can be." Mr. Blackstone shrugged. "I was just hoping your father wasn't seriously injured."

"Speaking of injuries." Levi turned the attention to Mrs. Blackstone. "I see you've made a complete recovery from your buggy accident."

Her hand went to her mouth, but she simply nodded.

Levi kept his eyes on her. "But you didn't answer my question, Mrs. Blackstone. Does Julianne still reside here, or has she gone to live with her sister?"

"I, uh, I don't—"

"She's on the cattle drive," Mr. Blackstone blurted out.

"Oh?" Levi nodded. "I know she was hoping to do that."

There was a long pause and Levi studied this very unusual couple, trying to figure them out then wondering if there was any point to it. And was it any wonder Julianne wanted to live elsewhere?

"So, tell us, Mr. Stanfield, how is your father?" Mr. Blackstone asked in what he probably thought was a sympathetic tone. "Will he survive the gunshot wound?"

Levi looked evenly at him. "Perhaps you should ask around town? Inquire from your friends." He turned to Mrs. Blackstone. "Good day, ma'am." And without another word, he left. But as he made his way to the front door, he noticed a shadow crossing the front room. Taking a quick look, he saw it was Royal Dayton. *Birds of a feather.*

Without addressing Mr. Dayton, Levi took his leave. But as he walked back to the hospital, he had questions. A lot of questions. Not about Julianne's mother. That was not surprising. But the fact Jefferson Blackstone assumed to know of Dad's shooting even though Marshal Rivers had told everyone to keep quiet about it.

Of course, Levi knew how little it took to get a rumor circulating. Perhaps someone at the hospital, although the sisters were trustworthy and reliable. Maybe a deputy's wife, but that seemed unlikely. Still, someone had let the cat out of the bag and if Jefferson Blackstone knew, a lot of others probably did too. He would have to speak to Marshal Rivers about this. But at least he could rest assured that Julianne got to go on the cattle drive. Or did she?

Suddenly he remembered her saying that the cattle drive conflicted with the Mayor's Picnic. And she'd been forced to attend the picnic—he'd seen her with his own eyes. So why would her father claim she was on the cattle drive? Did he think she could be in two places at once? Or did he have something to hide?

Levi didn't trust Jefferson Blackstone. Especially after seeing Royal Dayton lurking in the shadows of his house. And yet Levi couldn't make sense of why Jefferson should lie about where his daughter might be. Unless there was something really sinister going on. And after seeing his father shot yesterday, Levi felt anything was possible.

Whatever the case, something about Julianne's whereabouts just didn't add up, and Levi felt compelled to get to the bottom of it. He had two choices. He could return to her parents' house and demand a thorough search for her. But that was silly. Besides knowing they'd refuse, he couldn't imagine she'd been locked in the attic. Her mother might not be fully trustworthy, but she wouldn't allow her daughter to be treated like that.

That left the Double W Ranch. It's possible she was just staying out there until her sister and the others came home. But he wanted to know for sure. Plus he felt he needed to see her. To explain things. To apologize.

Knowing his dad was in good hands at the hospital, with one of the marshal's best men guarding him, and the sisters carefully tending to him, Levi left a message with his mother, informing her that he was going to check on the animals at the farm. She would be relieved to hear it. She loved her dog and her chickens and milk cow.

16

Knowing that Marshal Rivers wanted to keep track of him, Levi stopped by his office to let him know his plans. And being that no one was aware that Levi would be sitting on his father's bench by tomorrow, like a "sitting duck" as Levi was imagining it, the marshal agreed to let him go unaccompanied.

"You'll probably see some deputies out that way. We already combed the rim where you spotted the shooter. I sent them out to cover the area around there. Hoping they'll find a trail and track the culprit down. That would solve everything."

Levi told him about his conversation with Jefferson Blackstone. "Seems odd that he knew about the shooting since you were keeping it quiet. But it was his interest in whether Dad was alive or dead that got my attention."

"That's why I'm staying in town. I got a few things I want to check out." Marshal Rivers put on his hat. "You keep a watchful eye too, Levi. And let me know if you notice anything worth my attention."

Levi promised to do so then headed out. Instead of taking the carriage like he'd done last night with the marshal, he rode his saddle horse that they'd ponied back with them last night. He wanted the freedom of fast hooves beneath him if he needed it.

But out on the open road with the sun overhead and the intense blue sky behind the white-topped mountains, he didn't feel unsafe. Still, he heeded the marshal's warning and kept a watchful eye. His plan was to go directly to the Double W. Hopefully he'd find Julianne and they could spend some time together. Then he'd stop by his family's farm on the way home and see to the animals.

When he reached the Double W, an old ranch hand came out to greet him, introducing himself simply as Caleb.

"I'm Levi Stanfield." He got off his horse and extended his hand.

"Judge Stanfield's boy?" Caleb smiled as they shook.

"That's right. I heard Julianne might be out here and I wanted to pay her a visit."

Caleb nodded toward the hills. "She's on a cattle drive with her sister and family."

Levi frowned. "I thought she missed out on that. I understood she stayed in town when they all headed out?"

"She right near missed out. But Delia and Wyatt and the rest got a late start. They thought their young'un was sick. Seems little Billy got a tummy ache from too many sweet pickles." He chuckled.

"So Julianne got to go after all." Levi grinned. "Glad to hear it. She really had hoped to go with them."

"Yep. I'll bet they were pleased as punch when she caught up with 'em that first night. Her brother Julius had been hopin' to show off his ropin' skills. I'm sure they're having a right good time."

"When will they be back?"

"Wednesday. Midday most likely. But you never know till ya see the whites of their eyes."

Levi visited with the old man for a while, then seeing the sun high in the sky excused himself. "I better head for home. Need to help with our animals." He gazed across the pasture of sheep. "Not nearly as many as you have here, but they still need tending too."

"You give my regards to your pa." Caleb smiled. "Tell him I hope he's comin' out here for our big barbecue on the Fourth. He's a doggone good horseshoe thrower, and I'd like him for my partner this year."

Levi nodded, keeping the truth about Dad to himself. "I'll be sure and let him know."

"And you better come too." Caleb had a knowing grin. "Miss Julianne would probably like that."

Levi went to visit the hospital early Monday morning. Mother had told him that Dad wanted to see him. "He's very weak," she'd warned. "But he wants to talk to you."

"Does he know I'm going to be sworn in? That I'm replacing him on the bench just until he's well?"

"Marshal Rivers explained it to him." She frowned. "Can't say your father was pleased, but he understands." She kissed Levi's cheek. "Good luck to you today, son. Let your father know I'm going to help Gwendolyn with some chores, then I'll be in to visit around ten."

He promised to do that then waited for Marshal Rivers to come downstairs, and the two of them walked to the hospital together. "Are you nervous?" the marshal asked as they strolled down Main Street.

"Not yet. But I might be after news spreads that I'm hearing my father's cases."

"We've tried to keep the lid on things, but you never know. Also we started spreading the rumor that Judge Stanfield isn't long for this world. Your mother knows and is playing along too."

"Dad will be safer that way. Until you get this case solved and we get the responsible parties incarcerated."

"I'm hoping we'll wrap it up soon. My men followed what they believe was the shooter's trail, tracked it for a fair ways. I wanted to tell you about it last night, but I had that meeting in town with the mayor and council, getting everyone on board for swearing you in today. Lasted until almost midnight."

"I'm curious how that went, but first I want to hear about the trail. Where did it lead?"

"Interestingly, it seemed to cut right into the Double W Ranch."

"Are you sure of that?" Levi felt a surge of alarm. Was it possible one of the Double W men were involved?

"One of my best trackers was on it, and he seemed fairly certain. The rider of the first horse, which we believe belongs to the shooter, cut through unfenced property on Double W land. And he shortly thereafter met up with a second horse."

"Still on the ranch land?"

"Yep. The two traveled together until they joined the cattle drive trail. Of course, it was impossible to track after that. Too torn up. Might be why they did it."

Levi was working the timeline in his head. "Did your tracker think they continued on up with the cattle drive?"

"He couldn't say, but it did make me wonder if they could be Double W ranch hands. How was your visit there yesterday? Did you talk to Miss Blackstone?"

"She was away on the cattle drive." Levi fiddled with his pocket watch, still trying to work out the timeline of Saturday's events. "Julianne got there too late to head out with them, but a ranch hand told me they'd gotten a late start, so Julianne set out to catch up with them. I didn't ask him exactly what time that was, but it seems to me it was pretty close to the same time my dad was shot."

"What are you suggesting? You don't think Miss Blackstone has anything to do with your father's shooting."

"No, of course not. But it worries me that she was in the vicinity." Levi reminded him of his conversation with Jefferson yesterday, and how Royal had been lurking in the shadows listening. "Something about that whole visit felt off to me."

"The fellow you spoke to at the ranch? Did you get his name? Was he a reputable character?"

"Absolutely. Old Caleb. I've met him before. He's a friend of Dad's."

"I know who you mean. A good dependable man. Think I'll send my men out there to talk to him. Then they can do some more tracking along that cattle drive trail. I'd go too, but I'd rather stick close to you for the time being."

They were nearly to the hospital now, and despite Levi's concerns for Julianne, he was relieved to know the marshal would be following this up. "About that other thing?" he asked as they paused on the steps. "Last night's meeting. Was it pretty rough?"

Marshal Rivers's half-smile was an answer in itself. "There was some disagreeing. But we talked it out and I made them understand the goal was justice. I also promised we'd be looking for a judge to replace you as soon as possible. I couldn't mention we hoped to have your father back on the bench. Don't want the word leaked out that he'll recover. In fact, it helped our case to make it look like he wasn't going to make it. The pity factor."

"I see."

"I planned to go in and speak to your father, but I want to get some deputies headed out to the Double W. Hopefully they can find that outlaw's trail again, maybe even better." He tipped his head. "Give the judge my best and I'll meet you at the courthouse at nine."

Levi promised to do that then hurried up to see his dad. Deputy Garson, posted by the door, just nodded, and Levi let himself in. To his pleased surprise, Dad was sitting up in bed. His color looked good, and he smiled to see Levi. One of the sister's was just removing his breakfast tray, and based on the empty dishes, it looked like his appetite was healthy.

"You're looking good." Levi shook his hand, noticing even his grip was improved.

"Had a good night, and almost feel like myself again." Dad studied Levi. "You look mighty good yourself. That your good Sunday suit?"

"Mother insisted." Levi shrugged. "Just this morning, she and I were saying how you're always a quick one to recover, Dad. But I hope you'll go easy. That chest wound will take some time to heal."

He nodded. "I know you're right, but it does feel good to feel better. Do you have time to sit?"

Levi pulled a chair close to the bed. "Mother asked me to tell you she'll be here around ten."

"That's good." Dad peered closely at Levi. "How're you doing, son? Ready to take the oath and sit on the bench?"

"It seems a little premature, considering my age. But all things considered, I guess I'm ready. Just glad it's temporary. And seeing you looking so much better, I'm not so concerned."

Dad's brow creased. "Well, I hope you're a little concerned. Marshal Rivers assures me you'll be well protected, but watch your back, Levi."

"I will. Any advice you have for me? I stayed up late last night going over this week's cases again. They look fairly straightforward."

"You know law better than I do, son. Better than any man in this town. But you're still green. So take it slow and easy. Don't let them rush you or get you rattled. I know they'll try. Take your time and be firm." He smiled. "And keep using that poker face. I swear you must've got that from your mother's side of the family. Never wanted to play a hand of cards with her dad."

Levi laughed.

"You're going to make a fine judge, son. Hopefully for just a short while, at least for now. Later on, after you get some gray hairs on you, you'll make a *great* judge. I have no doubts."

"I'll report to you at the end of the day, to get your advice. If you're up for it."

"I'd appreciate that." His father sighed. "Wish I could watch you being sworn in. The youngest judge in these parts. Maybe the whole country."

"Don't forget, it's just a short-term thing."

"For now it is."

"Next time, you'll be there to see me sworn in." Levi reached for Dad's hand again. "You just keep getting well. And don't overdo it." He glanced at the sister sitting quietly in the nearby chair, and she solemnly nodded, as if to assure she would keep his father in line while he recovered.

As he walked through the town that was just starting to come to life, Levi felt conspicuous. He wasn't sure why since only a handful of city officials knew about his appointment today. Perhaps it was his good suit, or the fact some people had heard his father was dead or dying. Maybe they thought he was on his way to the funeral. Whatever it was, he was relieved to see Marshal Rivers waiting on the courthouse steps.

"Nervous yet?" the marshal asked quietly.

Keeping his poker face, he nodded. "A little."

"Well, no one would know to look at you. Keep it up, Levi. Or should I say Judge Stanfield?"

"Dad was looking better," Levi quietly told him as they went inside. "I think he's going to make a fast recovery."

"We'll keep that under our hats."

A court aid came over to greet them, directing them to the meeting room that would be used to swear in Levi. "As usual, we've opened it to the public," he told them as he opened the door. "I doubt there will be many present since this has happened so quickly. I'm sure word hasn't gotten around yet."

Even as the aid said this, Levi noticed a familiar figure in the audience. Obviously, Royal Dayton had heard about it, as well as a couple of his friends. For some unexplainable reason, Levi felt relieved that Julianne's father wasn't one of them. Still, as the marshal and he proceeded to the front of the room, he kept his poker face on and his back rigid. Not that he truly expected a bullet to go into it, but he was bracing himself.

17

After another uncomfortable sleepless night, Julianne woke to the sound of male voices quietly talking. It took her a moment to remember where she was, and that the voices belonged to the two brothers holding her captive. It was her third day in the shack, and she felt more desperate than ever. The brothers had spent the previous day playing cards, eating, drinking, and fighting. The issue of how they'd split their payoff money was still unresolved.

Strangely enough, she felt like she'd gotten to know them while spying on them through the cracks in the shack. Beau, the older brother, was definitely the boss. Acting as if he was smarter than Red, he called the shots and didn't like to be questioned. He wore a fringed leather jacket and walked with a swagger. With his dark wavy hair and strong facial features, he was more attractive than his skinny younger brother. But he was more troubling too, and it didn't help that he seemed to idolize Billy the Kid. Didn't he understand how that outlaw was shot down at about the same age as Beau? Didn't he care?

Despite Red's greasy carrot-red hair, freckles, and that squeaky voice, she liked him better. He was the kinder of the two. And he seemed her best hope for getting out of here. If only she could win him over somehow.

Curious as to why they were bickering now, Julianne got up to peer through the biggest slit between the boards. The brothers were standing on opposite sides of their campfire. Beau with feet spread and hands on his hips, looked ready to fight. Red was pacing back and forth, clearly agitated.

"You know we need supplies," Beau declared hotly.

"How long are we gonna be stuck out here?" Red demanded. "This ain't how you told me things would go."

"I don't know how long! I just know I gotta go to town. Just do like I say, Red, and stop questioning every doggone thing."

"Wha'd'ya gonna use for money?" Red protested. "You said we were broke."

"I gotta meet with Danner. He'll give me money."

"You mean he's gonna pay you off?" Red pulled off his hat, slapping it against his leg. "You're probably gonna light out and—"

"I never said that!"

"You're gonna leave me here stuck with the girl!"

"Don't be ignorant, Red. That ain't how the plan works." Beau's tone softened slightly. "You're my brother. You think I'd leave you holdin' the bag?"

"I dunno." Red ran his hands through his hair as he paced. "But I don't like you knowing the whole plan, Beau, and you keeping me in the dark. You ain't been honest with me about—"

"I already told you I don't know the whole plan. Quit questioning everything."

"It ain't fair. You make me do the dirty work then ya take most the money." He pointed his hat at Beau. "What's to make me stay here and guard the girl while you go runnin' around?"

"Because I'm payin' you, Red."

"Not enough. This was s'posed to be a two-day job and then we turn her over. And now we're outta food and—"

"That's why I'm goin' to town, stupid!"

"You ain't goin' nowhere." Red stepped up to face off his brother. "Not until you promise me one thing." He swung his finger in front of Beau. "Swear that you're—"

"I swear I'm coming back, Red. Honest, we won't get paid if I don't. You gotta trust me, brother."

"That's not what I meant. You gotta promise me a fair split. Do you swear you'll—"

"I already told you I'll do you right." Beau's tone softened. "I'm your brother."

Red was still in Beau's face. "You *better* make it right, brother. And one more thing, if you're not back by noon, I'm gonna let the girl go free."

"No!" Beau raised a fist. "I can't promise ya I'll get back that quick. You know I gotta meet with Danner. And go to the store for supplies. And I wanna check on Ma. That'll take some time."

"Then ya better get a move on."

Now Beau was in Red's face. "You don't let her go, Red. I mean it! You let her go and we get nothin'. You understand? Nothin'!"

Red stepped back. "I'll give you till late afternoon, but I swear, you ain't here by then and the girl and me are gone."

"I swear I'll be back, Red. I'll bring lots of good vittles and hooch and a new deck of cards and all sorts of good stuff. I promise. You and me will have us a real good time out here. We stick together till Danner pays us off. Then we'll split, fair an' square. No more fightin'."

Red seemed appeased as he shoved his hat back on his head. "And bring back s'more blankets. I got real cold last night."

"Right. And you get more firewood. And check on the horses. And whatever you do, keep a good watch on that girl."

Red assured him he would then Beau headed toward the trees where the horses were being kept. After a minute or two, she saw Beau ride out. He was on a black and white paint, and it looked like he took Red's warning seriously because he urged the horse into a fast gallop.

Red squatted down, poking the campfire coals with a stick then shaking a cast-iron pan. He really wasn't much more than a kid. Probably younger than her. And, although part of her despised both these fellows, she felt sad to think a young man like Red had already been tempted into a life of crime. What would happen when he got caught? Or if he didn't get caught?

With Beau gone, Julianne decided to poke around the shack a bit more. No longer as concerned about making noise or drawing attention, she tugged and pulled and even kicked the walls and the door, but the shack was sturdier than it looked.

"Whatcha doing in there?" Red demanded.

"Just moving around," she called back. "Trying to get warm."

"Yeah, it was cold last night."

"Yes, and you have a fire to warm up on." She hoped he'd take a hint and let her out. What then? She didn't know. But it would get her one step closer to freedom. She didn't think she'd have the nerve to steal his gun and shoot him, but perhaps she could threaten him with it before making a run for her horse. But both brothers kept their pistols holstered. Although, it looked like Beau had left his rifle behind. Even if she could get her hands on it, Red would have the advantage with his pistol.

She'd remembered the cast-iron frying pan, imagining herself grabbing it up and whacking him on the head when his back was turned. She didn't want to kill him, but she wouldn't mind knocking him out. But how would she get out and sneak up on him like that?

"Are ya hungry?" he yelled. "Outta food?"

"Yes," she called back. She still had one biscuit and a piece of jerky left over from Ginger's provisions, but he didn't need to know that. Besides, it wouldn't last long—and she was hungry. Hopefully it would get him to open the door and let her out, and maybe she could attempt an escape. She stood by the door, hoping this was her chance, but unsure of what to do. Suddenly the door cracked open.

"No fast moves," he said firmly. "I got my gun and I know how to use it." He pushed the door open a little wider. "Get back against the wall, Julianne. Now!"

Hearing the serious tone of his voice, she slowly backed away.

"I got some leftover bacon ya can have. I'm gonna set it on the floor real easy. So don't try nothin'."

With her back to the wall, she folded her arms in front of her and waited. Red opened the door about a foot wide then slid a metal dish across the floor. "Only reason I'm giving ya this is cuz Beau's getting more food today." Then he quickly closed and latched the door.

She called out a thank you, then went to pick up the dish. There were three strips of bacon. She sniffed to see it actually smelled good. Feeling grateful, she sat down and picked up a piece. As she ate, she wondered if there was another way to persuade Red to let her out. They'd already given her a bucket to use for a toilet so that excuse wouldn't work. And when she asked for water, they simply took her canteen and refilled it.

But with Beau away, this felt like her best chance. She had to think of something. Her best hope seemed to be to soften Red up. He was definitely more compassionate than Beau. And yet he had helped kidnap her. But why had he? For the money. And now he was unhappy with his lesser cut. Maybe that was the way to reach him.

What if she offered him more cash than his brother? Would that work? After finishing her bacon, she called out to Red again, but hearing no response, she peeked through the crack to see he was just going into the aspen trees where the horses were kept. He wouldn't be able to hear her from here. Assuming he wouldn't be gone long, she decided to use this time to put together a tempting proposition. And hopefully she'd get him to agree to it, and help her out of here, long before his brother returned.

Every few minutes, she went over to peer out, but there was no sign of him. What on earth was taking him so long? For the second time, she decided to try pounding the walls and door, hoping to find a weak spot. Around and around she went, testing each board and the boarded-up windows and door. Nothing seemed to be budging.

Finally, worn out from kicking and beating the walls, she sank down onto her bedroll to wait. That's when she noticed the tin pan Red had brought with the bacon. Had he forgotten it? She peeked out again, and still didn't see him. So now she began to pound and stomp the tin plate, trying to create a tool she could use to pry out nails, or loosen up a board. Finally she got it bent into something that resembled a spade and went to work on the boards. She managed to loosen a nail and mangle some wood, but then she cut her hand on the sharp metal edge. Bleeding profusely, she had to stop and tear strips of cloth to bandage it up.

She didn't know how much time had passed since Beau had left, but hearing footsteps and scuffling noises outside, she worried he might already be back. But when she got to her peeping crack, she saw it was only Red. He had an armload of wood that he was neatly stacking next to the campfire. Knowing her time of opportunity was shrinking, she called out to him again.

"Wha'd'ya want?" he yelled back as he finished with the wood.

"Can we talk a minute?"

"I dunno." He stood up, brushing wood scraps from his pants.

"It's just that I'm lonely," she called out in what she hoped was an appealing tone.

"Well, no tricks now." He cautiously approached the shack. "Whatcha need?"

"Honest, I just want to talk to someone."

"Whatcha wanna talk about?"

"I just feel confused. I wish I knew why you guys kidnapped me," she began gently, hoping to win his trust. "I mean if it's for money,

I'm sure my family will pay you. And there's no reason to wait. Just let them know you have me and ask them to pay. I know they will. My parents aren't rich, but they're fairly well off. My mother owns that fancy dress shop in town. La Mode. I work in the office there and I know there's lots of cash in the safe. I bet my mother could easily pull together three or four thousand dollars." Of course, that wasn't true, but did kidnappers deserve the truth?

"Three or four thousand dollars?" He let out a low whistle.

"Sure. And my father could get even more from his bank. And there's my sister and her husband. They own the Double W Ranch. They're really rich. I bet they would pay ten thousand to get me back. All together you could probably get about twenty thousand dollars."

"Twenty thousand dollars?" He sounded incredulous.

"I'm sure, between them, they have that much."

"That's a heck-of-a lot of money. Ya really think they'd pay it?"

"My family loves me. I'm sure they—"

"Shush. That's Beau. Back from town already. That was quick."

She watched as he hurried away from the shack, going over to talk to Beau. Suddenly the two were arguing again. Then Beau smacked Red right in the face with his fist. Red tumbled backward to the ground, holding his chin with his hand.

"Ya ain't changing the plan!" Beau yelled. "That girl is flat-out lying, Red! Are you too stupid to see it?" He reached out a hand to help his brother to his feet. "Sorry, I had to hit you, but someone's gotta knock some sense into ya. That girl's playing you for the fool while I'm gone, and you're too ignorant to know."

"But she said *twenty thousand dollars*, Beau. That's ten for you and ten for me. We'd be rich!"

"Ain't nobody got that much money. Besides that, ya know what'd happen to us if we changed the plan?"

Red still looked doubtful. She knew he wanted that money. But maybe she'd exaggerated too much. Beau was smarter than Red.

Maybe she should be honest with both of them. Surely she could offer more than what this Danner fellow was paying. She wondered how much her parents would actually pay. What if they refused to pay? But her mother would pay. She knew it.

"Maybe you're right, Beau. Twenty thousand is a lot. But her ma owns that fancy dress shop, and her sister owns the Double W. Don't you think folks like that got plenty of money. I bet they'd give us at least five thousand. That's more'n Danner's payin'."

"Look, Red." Beau put his face inches from his brother's. "You don't seem to get this. If we don't do this Danner's way, we could end up dead. Do you understand me? *Dead*."

"Why would he kill us?" Red looked scared now.

"That's how he works. He's killed others. And he'd probably kill Ma too."

"He'd kill Ma?" Red's Adam's apple went up and down.

"So, don't think ya can go changin' the plan." Beau thumped him in the chest. "Now help me unload my horse."

Julianne knew her plan had failed. Red probably wouldn't be tempted by any amount of money if it meant their lives were on the line. And their mother's too. Who could blame him?

The brothers were unloading Beau's saddlebags now. Beau had brightened up and was talking about his trip to town. "Ma is fine," he told Red. "She even sent us a pie. She thinks we're hunting jack-rabbits for a rancher. Asked me to be sure and bring home some meat."

"That's cuz ya brought Pa's rifle." Red sniffed a paper parcel. "Good, ya got coffee."

"And sugar too." Beau tossed a sack to Red.

"Danner gave you the money for all this?" Red sounded suspicious. "Did he already pay ya off the thousand too? Ya holding out on me?"

"Nah. I told you, we don't get paid till we're done. But I met with him, and he gave me cash for supplies. Said we might need to hold her out here longer now."

"Last night, you said a few days." Red scowled.

"Things changed."

"Ya keep telling me don't change the plan, but Danner keeps changing it."

"It's his plan so he calls the shots. Ya wanna get paid or not? Besides, I told him more days would make it cost more. And he agreed."

"How much longer is it gonna be?" Red's voice grew squeakier than usual.

"Dunno for sure." Beau held up what looked like two bottles of whiskey. "But I got us some hooch to help pass the time." He handed one to Red and set the other on a stump. "And some playin' cards too."

"Thanks." Red opened it, took a swig then handed it back. "So what's new in town? Did ya see anyone besides Ma and Danner?"

"Saw Geraldine Hopkins in the store." Beau poked Red in the chest with a chuckle. "She was asking about you."

"What'd Geraldine say?" Red took another swig.

"Just wanted to know when you'd be comin' to town."

"Wha'd'ya tell her?"

"That you and I were on a job and that we're getting paid nicely. She liked that."

Red nodded. "I like that too. Anything else new?" He held the bottle out to Beau.

Beau took a slow swig and wiped his mouth with the back of his hand. "And, oh yeah, Judge Stanfield got shot."

"Shot and killed?" Red looked shocked.

"Yeah, I reckon." Beau sat down on a stump, taking another swig.

Julianne felt her heart lurch as she backed away from the crack she'd been peeping through. She sank down onto her bedroll and, pulling her knees to her chest, she wrapped her arms around them. *Levi's father had been shot?* Probably killed?

How had this happened? Why? What was going on in this world? Innocent girls were held hostage and honest judges were shot and killed. Tears for the man who'd been so kind to her at the Mayor's Picnic filled her eyes. Curling up into a ball, she rolled over on her bedroll and sobbed hard.

18

It wasn't until the next afternoon that Julianne heard the news about Levi. Watching through the crack, as the brothers gathered round their campfire, swapping stories, and drinking whiskey, she was shocked to hear Beau telling about how Levi Stanfield had been sworn in as the replacement judge for his father yesterday morning.

"Most folks were just laughing about it, calling him *Junior Judge*." Beau chuckled then took a swig. "But no one's gonna take it serious. Some folks are even placing bets on how long Junior Judge will be around. I would've liked to get in on that action." He laughed more loudly. "But I reckon that wouldn't be fair."

"Why wouldn't it be fair?" As Red sloshed some whiskey into his tin mug, there was a flash of light, a few seconds later it was followed by the loud boom of thunder.

"Sounds like a thunder-boomer coming our way." Beau looked upward.

"Some mighty dark clouds too. We're in for some rain."

"Grab up your bedroll," Beau told him. "We're gonna join the little lady."

Julianne watched in horror as the brothers scrambled to grab their things and the next thing she knew, they were invading her space. "Cozy in here." Beau held a lantern up to look around. "Hope you don't mind company."

Rain was pounding down on the roof so furiously it was hard to hear, but taking her bedroll to the farthest corner, she pulled it around herself and sank to the floor.

"You sit in front of the door," Beau ordered his brother. "Make sure she don't try to sneak out."

Red plunked down, leaning his head back into the door with a thud.

Beau held the half full bottle out toward Julianne. "Maybe you'd like a little snort of hooch to warm you up."

"No, thank you." She looked away.

"Then maybe you'd like *me* to warm you up," he offered. "I'm good at keeping gals warm."

"Aw, Beau," Red said. "Leave her be."

"But I got a fancy for yeller-haired girls." Beau was getting to his feet.

"Is that part of Danner's plan too?" Red stood too, grabbing away his bottle and locking eyes.

"Wha'd'ya mean—Danner's plan?" Beau sounded angry and Julianne wondered if they were about to fight again. And if so, it might be her chance to sneak out the door.

"Ya keep saying we're supposed to keep her till Danner comes," Red challenged. "Think ya get paid if you mess with her?"

Beau shrugged, but sat back down, looking at the floor. Red did the same, his back still blocking the door.

Fighting disappointment, Julianne turned her attention to Beau. She knew he liked to be the center of things, and she wanted to know what he'd been talking about earlier. "I heard you mention something about taking bets on the new judge in town. What's that about?"

He looked up with interest. "You mean Junior Judge?"

"Yes. Who's this Junior Judge?"

"Judge Stanfield's boy. And that's what he is. A *boy*."

"Reckon that makes you a boy, Beau?" Red challenged. "Levi Stanfield is a fair bit older than you."

"Well, for a judge he's a boy," Beau shot back. "That's what everyone is saying too."

"Then why is he a judge?" Julianne asked.

"Cuz his pa got shot." Beau's dark eyes glared at her.

Her reaction was diverted by another bright flash that sent slats of light into the shack, followed by a boom that rattled the floor.

"That was a good one." Beau laughed.

For a moment, it was only the rain, and Julianne tried to think of a way to get Beau talking about Levi again. "So did you bet?" she asked.

"Bet?" Beau looked confused.

"Yeah," Red jumped in. "You said they was a wagering on how long Junior Judge would last. You bragged you'd win. So did ya even bet on it?"

"Nah, didn't have time."

"Why did you think you could win?" Julianne asked with what she hoped sounded like bored disinterest.

"Because *I know*."

"You know *what*?" Red prodded.

"I know when he'll get his." Beau snickered as he snatched the bottle back from Red, taking a long swig.

"Get his what?" Julianne kept her tone calm despite her pounding heart.

"Same thing his pa got." Another flash and boom seemed to accentuate Beau's statement, and Julianne blinked to keep tears from coming.

"How'd'ya know that?" Red challenged.

"Too many questions are wearing me out." Beau leaned back. "You watch that door, Red. I'm takin' a little snooze."

For the next hour or so the three of them remained in the shack. But aside from the pounding rain and loud crashes of thunder, no one spoke. Finally the storm had passed, and Beau woke up enough to kick his brother.

"Get away from that door, lazybones. I need to get me some air."

Red stumbled to his feet, letting his brother out first. Then gathering up his belongings, he followed, solidly latching the door behind him. But some of their stuff, including the lantern, remained. Julianne was just getting up, ready to grab up their things, toss them in the corner and catch them on fire with the lantern. Her hope was the flames would make them return, and while they dealt with the fire, she'd sneak out the open door. But before she could toss the lantern onto the pile, Beau burst in.

"Give me that." He grabbed the lantern then yelled at Red who was on his heels. "Get our gear outta here before this fool girl burns the whole place down." He swore at her as they rescued their stuff. "Better watch it, Julianne. You could've gone up in smoke."

After only three days, Levi was starting to feel comfortable on the bench. Not only with the cases he was hearing, and passing judgment on them, but with his own personal safety. Nothing the least bit threatening had happened. Even the scoundrels like Royal Dayton seemed to be giving him space.

It seemed everyone in town had swallowed the story that the judge remained unconscious, hanging by a thread, and would soon be gone. Funeral plans were being discussed at the courthouse. Levi accepted condolences with a solemn expression. And felt more judgelike with each passing day.

"I have news," Marshal Rivers said as the two left the courthouse together that afternoon.

"Good news?" Levi knew the deputies were trying to track the criminal who'd shot his dad. Perhaps they'd found him, and this ordeal was over.

"Sorry to say, it's very concerning news."

"My dad?" Levi looked at the marshal.

"No, no. Orville is fine. So fine he wants out of the hospital. We might try to sneak him out tonight. He's resting quietly all day in preparation. That's one reason I'm taking you home with me now." He turned them down a quiet side street that led to his house.

Levi was curious about the other reason but wanted to know more about his dad first. "So you'd allow him to go home? To the farm?" Levi didn't like the sound of that. He'd hired a fellow to watch the house and animals, but it didn't seem a safe place for either Dad or himself right now.

"No. We'd bring him to my house to continue recovering. Gwendolyn actually suggested it. Naturally, your mother loves that idea."

"She would. So, tell me, what is the concerning news?"

"The folks from the Double W returned from their cattle drive this afternoon."

"Yes?" Levi thought of Julianne, thinking he'd like to ride out to see her.

"Miss Blackstone was not with them."

"Not with them?" Levi grabbed the marshal's arm and stopped walking. "What are you saying? What happened?"

"She left to join them on Saturday. Just like everyone at the ranch confirmed. But she never made it up there to join them. Since no one up there even knew she was coming, they had no idea anything was wrong. We were all equally surprised."

"So this whole time—since Saturday—Julianne was not with them on the cattle drive? And she was not at the ranch? And according to her parents, she wasn't there either? Where is she?"

"That's the big question."

"Maybe she really is at her parents. They did act strangely when

I was there on Sunday. Except that Caleb told me she went on the cattle drive." Levi felt confused.

"I haven't spoken to her parents yet. But I hoped you could go with me."

Levi nodded to the street that led to their neighborhood. "We're not far."

"I know."

As they walked toward the Blackstone house, Marshal Rivers told Levi his plan. "Let me do the questioning. At least to start with. You just watch and listen. I know you're good at that. If you think of anything else to add, after I finish, go ahead and jump in."

Levi just nodded, as the marshal rang the bell. The maid came quickly, looking surprised to see the lawman with Levi. "We're here to speak to Mr. and Mrs. Blackstone," Marshal Rivers said in an authoritative tone.

"Come in." She glanced nervously over her shoulder.

"Who is it?" Mrs. Blackstone asked from the hallway behind her.

"Mr. Stanfield and Marshal Rivers, ma'am. Come to see you and Mr. Blackstone."

Julianne's mother appeared with a startled expression. "Please, come in," she said quickly. "Ellie, go get my husband." As the maid left, Mrs. Blackstone led them to the front room, offering them seats.

"What we have to say shouldn't take long," the marshal told her.

Jefferson entered the room with a very curious expression. "What is going on here?" he asked in a slightly arrogant tone.

"Where is your daughter? Miss Julianne Blackstone?" the marshal directed to him.

"With her sister Delia," he answered with nonchalance. "They went on a cattle drive. I'm not sure if they're back yet or—"

"Your daughter did not go with them on the cattle drive. Her sister hasn't seen her in well over a week."

"What?" Mrs. Blackstone reached for a chair and, sinking into it, she clung to its arms. "Where is Julianne then?"

"Why don't you tell us what you know?" The marshal pulled a chair next to her. "When was the last time you saw your daughter? What were the circumstances?"

"I saw her on Saturday," she began in a trembling voice. "She came home from the Mayor's Picnic. She was upset."

"Why was she upset?" he pressed.

"Because of something between her and I." She glanced nervously at Levi.

"Because you feigned a buggy accident to control her?" he supplemented.

She nodded. "Yes. That's true. I did. But I apologized. She was upset, and she said she was going to live with Delia. She asked to take my buggy. The last thing she told me was she was going on the cattle drive. I assumed that's where she went."

The marshal turned to Jefferson. "What about you? When was the last time you saw your daughter?"

"At the Mayor's Picnic." He no longer sounded so pompous. "She left with, uh, a friend."

"What friend?"

"Royal Dayton."

"That's true," Mrs. Blackstone added. "Royal brought her here. That's when she and I had words. But Royal was gone by then."

"And she took herself out to the ranch?"

"I watched her with my own eyes. I saw her leave in my buggy." Mrs. Blackstone had tears in her eyes. "What has happened to her? Where is she?"

Marshal Rivers stood to look directly at Jefferson. "From what we know, your daughter made it to the ranch. She visited with folks there then got on her horse and headed up the trail to join her family."

"But you said she wasn't with them."

"Because she never made it up there. Something, rather, *someone* must have waylaid her on the way."

Mrs. Blackstone gasped. Holding her hands to her face, she let out a sob.

"Why?" Jefferson asked. "Who would do that?"

"That's what I want you to tell me, Mr. Blackstone. Who would have motive to keep your daughter from going up to meet her sister and family?"

"I don't know what you're getting at." Jefferson's eyes grew dark. "If you're accusing me, you're barking up the wrong tree. Julianne is my only daughter. We may have had our differences, but I'd do nothing to harm her."

"Then you do think someone *has* harmed her?" Levi couldn't help but take over and the marshal kept quiet.

"I didn't say that."

"But it's possible?" Levi felt more like a lawyer than a judge now. "Do you know anyone with reason to wish harm to your daughter? Perhaps to keep her quiet about something?"

"Answer the question," the marshal insisted.

"Am I on trial here?" Jefferson narrowed his eyes. "Should I be calling my attorney."

"Yes," the marshal told him. "That's a very good idea."

"Especially if you have something to hide," Levi added.

"Fine, I shall do that."

"So you do have something to hide," Levi goaded him. "Perhaps one of your business or political friends? But I wouldn't advise you to protect them. That doesn't shine a very good light on you as a father."

"Jefferson!" Mrs. Blackstone stood with fire in her eyes. "If you refuse to help these men to find our daughter, you are no longer welcome in my house."

"*Your* house?" He glared at her.

"I have paid for everything here with earnings from my dress shop. Yes, other than what the bank owns, this is my house. And I mean it. If you can't help your own daughter, you are not welcome here."

"Then I will take my leave." And without another word he turned and left.

Mrs. Blackstone collapsed into the chair, sobbing. And Levi and the marshal exchanged glances then Levi stepped in. Putting a hand on her shoulder, he spoke gently. "I want to find Julianne as much as you do, Mrs. Blackstone."

She looked up with watery eyes. "You do?"

"Of course, I do. And the marshal and I will do everything possible to find her. But if you know of anything that can help us, we need to know it. Now. Time is of the essence."

She sat up straight, putting a hand to her cheek. "Let me think. I could be wrong, but I believe something happened between Julianne and Royal. I watched them from this room on Saturday. They were speaking outside the front door. Julianne appeared to be saying things that Royal did not appreciate. Royal is normally a very congenial dignified person, but I could tell he was angry. For a moment I almost thought he was going to slap my daughter. If he had, wheeled chair or not, I'd have run out there and confronted him."

"What do you think Julianne was saying to him?" Levi asked quietly.

"I couldn't hear a thing, but it almost looked as if she were making an accusation. She shook her finger at him, like a scolding."

"Is it possible she knew about something he was doing?" the marshal asked. "Something she threatened to expose?"

Mrs. Blackstone took in a slow breath. "I'm not privy to all my husband's associates and dealings, but I do know they have been working on something very secretively. It has to do with the purchase of property outside of town. A farm, I believe." Now she told him the names of the men who'd been coming to the Blackstone house to plan this deal and the marshal wrote them down.

"Look." Levi pointed out the front window as Jefferson climbed into a buggy with an armload of paperwork. "He obviously didn't want us to see whatever it is he's taking."

"May I use your phone?" the marshal asked Mrs. Blackstone.

"Of course." She pointed him to it. And while he called his office, asking for a deputy to follow Mr. Blackstone, Levi spoke to Julianne's mother.

"I don't know what's happened to your daughter, but we will find her."

"Please, do everything possible. I'm so sorry for the way I treated her. And for the way I treated you as well," she tearfully told him. "All I want is for Julianne to be safe. If there's anything I can do, please, let me know."

"We'll keep you informed," he promised as he went over to the marshal, who was just hanging up the telephone. "You do the same with us."

"Yes. Call my office if you learn anything new," the marshal told her.

As soon as they were outside, Marshal Rivers turned to Levi. "You're not safe now. We can't trust Jefferson Blackstone. For all we know, he will turn his friends on you too."

"I don't care if I'm safe," Levi told him as they hurried down the street toward town. "I want to go find Julianne."

"My men are on it. Right now I want you to go to the hospital and stay with your father. I'm concerned for both of you. It seems whatever is going on here is bigger than we realized."

"But I—"

"No arguing. I'll get you safely to the hospital and you stay there until I come or send a message. Do you understand?"

Levi didn't like it, but he did understand.

"You might not fully appreciate that you are more valuable to us in the courtroom right now than you would be out searching for Julianne."

"I don't know."

"Hearing the cases you're hearing this week is no small thing,

Levi. I'm sure it all has something to do with whoever has taken Julianne."

"Then you believe someone has taken her?"

"Don't you?"

Levi nodded. "I think it's the same guy who shot my dad. And I think he's just a paid puppet. Someone on top, like Royal Dayton, is the one pulling the strings."

"I agree. It'll take more than one of us to gather up all the pieces of this mess." The hospital was in sight now. "And I thank you for your help with the Blackstones. I wouldn't have gotten that far with them if you hadn't jumped in. Jefferson Blackstone is a hard one to figure. For a moment, I really thought he cared about his daughter, and then he just turned on us."

They both walked in silence for a bit then Levi turned to the marshal. "Do you think Jefferson Blackstone might've turned because he wanted to protect his daughter?"

"What do you mean?"

"Suppose Jefferson really didn't know what his associates were up to in regard to Julianne. What if he just put two and two together now? Maybe he thinks by protecting his friends, he will protect his daughter?"

"I see where you're going, and I'll keep that in mind." They stopped in front of the hospital. "Stay safe, Levi. Keep your dad safe too. Maybe he'll have some advice for us. He knows partly what we're up against."

"I'll ask him." Levi started up the steps. "You stay safe too," he called. As he ran up the steps, he thought about the names Mrs. Blackstone had just given to the marshal. Some were not surprising in the least, but some felt straight out of the blue. He was eager to tell Dad what was going on. The marshal was right, his father would have something to say about it.

But his deepest thoughts were with Julianne right now. As he went up the stairs to his dad's floor, he wondered where she could be. Had anyone hurt her? Had they simply hidden her away…or something worse? Stopping in a quiet corridor, he leaned against the wall and closed his eyes. With tight fists, he begged God to *keep and protect her and help the lawmen find and rescue her and bring home the woman he loved. Amen.*

19

Although Delia wasn't blaming herself for Julianne's disappearance, she felt partially responsible and ready to do whatever it took to find her.

"I knew something was off when we went to visit Mother," she told Wyatt as they walked down to the corral. "I wish you'd let me go with you to—"

"No." He firmly shook his head. "Looking for a pair of armed and dangerous outlaws is not women's work."

"Women's work?" She grabbed his arm. "Did you really just say that to me, Wyatt Davis?"

His crooked smile looked sheepish. "Look, Delia, I know you can keep up with any of those men. You just proved it driving cattle." He nodded to where a dozen of their hands and horses were already ready to set out on a search. "But you're the mother of two children. Who missed you a lot while we were on the drive."

"I missed them too."

"And wouldn't you rather be here with them, just in case anything happened?" He frowned. "We don't know where those outlaws might be hiding."

"Do you think it's nearby?" She glanced around their property.

"I don't plan to leave the ranch until I'm sure you and the children are safe. But until we get to the bottom of whatever is going on, I want you and the children to stay here. And indoors. Caleb and Cash will remain behind to keep a watch on things while the rest of us are searching."

"I know you're right, Wyatt. It's just hard to sit at home when I know Julianne's out there somewhere."

"We *think* she's out there," Wyatt clarified. "We don't know that for sure."

"Julius seemed fairly certain after talking to Deputy Garson."

"Good thing Julius was riding up ahead today, otherwise he would've missed Garson."

"I've never seen Julius so fired up about something." She looked down to where Julius was gathering the men in a circle. He'd taken the lead on organizing the search. And considering everyone was still worn out from the trail ride, the men looked eager and ready to go. Wyatt and Delia joined them, standing just outside the circle.

"I need your attention, men," Julius called out. "Thank you for being willing to help us with this search. Deputy Garson has some instructions. I want everyone to listen carefully."

"Thanks." Garson stepped into the center of the circle. "First of all, we're looking for two men. One is riding a black and white paint. He's average height and dressed like a regular cowhand. We believe he's armed with a rifle, and that he's the man who shot Judge Stanfield."

"Judge Stanfield?" Delia gasped to hear this.

"That's right." Garson nodded. "The judge was shot on Saturday afternoon and the shooter was spotted leaving the scene. Our best tracker followed his trail. It cut through the Double W and joined up with another rider. Together they rode up to the cattle drive trail just a few miles from here. But because of all the cattle drive hoofprints, we were unable to track where they departed the trail. But our men are out there now, all proceeding in different directions." He waved a map.

"And you think these same men kidnapped Julianne?" a hand called out.

"That is our suspicion. We now know that the shooting occurred very close to the same time Miss Blackstone set out on the trail to meet up with you folks. And as we all know now, she never made it up there." He glanced at Delia. "Our assumption is that she was abducted by the same man who shot Judge Stanfield."

The men started rumbling amongst themselves. Clearly they were as outraged by this news as Delia and Wyatt.

"Are there any questions?" Garson asked.

"Is the judge dead?" someone called out.

Garson frowned. "It's likely."

"When do we leave?" another one shouted.

"I've divided this map into sections, and I want two men to partner up to cover one section." Garson told them. "Take what you need for the day. And I want every man armed. Be aware that these outlaws are considered dangerous. We will search the remainder of the day and meet back here at six o'clock to see what we've learned. Questions?"

But the men were already getting on their horses.

"One thing more," Wyatt called out, removing his hat. "Let's ask God to bless our search. We need His help to find Julianne." He led them in a heartfelt prayer, asking God to keep them safe, and to protect Julianne, and to lead them to her.

Delia watched as the men partnered up, got their assigned sections, and began setting off in various directions. Finally, Wyatt and Julius left, and Delia was standing alone in the corral with tears in her eyes. "Please, help them, God," she prayed. "And help Julianne. Bring her home safely. Bring them all home. Amen."

On the sixth day of her captivity, Julianne knew it was Thursday—

and the third day of July. She felt more desperate than ever to get out of here and since Beau was getting ready to go into town, she knew this might be her best chance to attempt an escape. All she needed was a plan to get Red's sympathy. With Beau gone, she might be able to sway Red her direction.

"We need more supplies," Beau told Red as he loaded his horse.

"We got enough food for two more days," Red argued.

"Maybe, but we're outta whiskey." He tightened his saddle cinch.

"You're up to something." Red sounded suspicious.

Beau just laughed, sliding his rifle into the case on the side of his saddle.

"Why are ya taking Pa's rifle to go into town?"

"I might need it."

"Ya got your revolver," Red pointed out. "No need for a long gun in town."

"Man never knows what he might need."

"Ya never took no rifle last time. You're up to something, and ya better tell me what it is."

"I'll tell you all about it when I get back."

"No." Red reached for the paint's reins. "You'll tell me now or I ain't gonna be here when you get back. And the girl'll be gone too."

"Come on, we've been over this. No girl, no money. Remember?"

"Look, Beau." Red's voice always got squeakier when he was scared, and it was squeakier than ever. "They gotta be looking for the girl by now. I'm like a sitting duck here. They figure things out I could be dead. You said we'd only keep her out here a couple days, but it's been a whole lot more'n that. I gotta bad feeling."

"And I gotta meet with Danner at two." Beau used his tough voice. "If I don't get there, this whole thing ain't gonna work out right."

"Is he paying you today?"

"Maybe." Beau got into the saddle.

"I don't believe you. You're up to somethin'." Red stood in front of the horse like he thought he could block it. "I bet you ain't even comin' back."

"Outta my way." Beau pushed his horse past.

Red pointed to the gear strapped to the back of the paint. "You're lightin' out on me. Leavin' me here stuck with the girl. The lawmen'll show up and I'll be in a heap a trouble."

"I got a job to do, Red. You just shut your trap and stay put and I promise I'll be back. And I'll be back with money this time. A fifty-fifty split too. I swear, Red, ya gotta trust me." He dug his heels into the paint and took off in a cloud of dust.

Julianne watched as Red kicked a stone then swore. Next he picked up a piece of firewood and hurled it straight at the shack. Jumping at the noise, Julianne knew how she was going to handle him. Waiting until she was sure Beau was a fair distance away, she called out to Red.

"Wha'd'ya want?" he yelled back in an angry tone.

"I want to talk to you."

"I don't wanna talk to you." He picked up another piece of firewood. "Don't wanna talk to no one. I just wanna kill somethin'." Using the heavy stick like a club, he slapped it across his palm, pacing back and forth by the fire.

She gulped. Hopefully he didn't mean her. Discouraged, she sat down and prayed. After a few minutes, she heard the door unlock and Red came in. He didn't have the stick in his hand, but he had out his gun. "Wha'd'ya wanna talk about?" he asked in his toughest squeaky voice. If she wasn't so frightened, it might've been funny.

"I think you're in a bad place, Red." She stood, backing up to the wall farthest from the door, which was still partially open, so he wouldn't think she was trying to escape.

"Why ya saying that?" He narrowed his eyes.

"I heard what Beau told you just now. I saw how he loaded up all his gear, even his rifle. I'm not surprised you're suspicious."

"Yeah, well, he has to go meet someone in town."

"But he's not coming back, is he?"

Red shrugged.

"You're smarter than this, Red. You have him figured out. You know he's going to get paid off by Danner. He's not even going to give you the two hundred dollars he promised."

"How'd ya know about that?"

"These walls have cracks to hear through." She poked her finger in a knothole. "Do you realize it's been six days since you brought me here?"

"Six days?" He looked shocked.

"That's right. And that means my sister and all her ranch hands got back from their cattle drive yesterday. Do you know what that means?"

He shook his head.

"They know I'm missing. They'll set out to find me. Right now there are probably two dozen armed men combing the land all around the ranch. I'm sure they're nearby right now. And that stand of aspens and this little shack are easy to spot. You're right, Red. You are like a sitting duck. They will shoot first and ask questions later." She knew she was exaggerating, but Red didn't have to know.

He pursed his lips as if thinking hard.

"Do you really think your brother's coming back?"

He let out a long, frustrated sigh. "I dunno."

"Last night he was talking about Independence Day, Red. Do you remember that?" The truth was they'd been talking quietly, the fire had been popping loudly, and she hadn't been able to hear every word.

"Yeah. He's got plans for the Fourth of July." Red brightened. "Fireworks and everything."

"That's tomorrow, Red. You really think Beau is coming back to take you to the Fourth of July celebrations tomorrow?"

Red scowled then kicked at the dirt. "I reckon I know why he took his rifle to town."

"Why?" she asked gently.

"He said it was gonna be Independence Day for the judge."

"But the judge is dead."

"Not that judge. Beau said for the new judge. He said there'd be firecrackers and guns going off around town, and it'd be Independence Day for the new judge." Red's pale eyebrows drew together, as if realization was setting in. "Beau said he was gonna set him free, just like he'd done for his pa."

Speechless, Julianne tried to conceal her shock at this implication. Beau murdered Judge Stanfield and planned to kill Levi too.

"I think Beau took the rifle to shoot him."

Julianne leaned against the wall, trying to keep calm, trying to think. "Did you know that Beau killed Judge Stanfield, Red?"

He sadly shook his head. "No. I reckoned my brother was kinda on the lawless side, but I never took him for no murderer."

"He'll be hanged if he's caught," she said quietly.

"What about me?" He locked eyes with her.

"Right now, you're guilty of kidnapping, Red. But if you let me go and turn yourself in, I can speak in your defense and I'm sure the law will go easy on you." She felt an urgency—they had to get away from here fast, but she didn't want to get Red too stirred up.

"Do ya really think so?"

"I really do." She took a cautious step forward. "You know Beau won't be coming back for you. If he shoots the new judge, he'll get his money from Danner and run as fast as he can. You'll never see him again, Red. Well, unless he gets caught. Then you'll see him swinging from a rope."

Red holstered his gun, stepping back. "I gotta get outta here." He opened the door wide. "You're free to go."

"Thank you." Still wary, she cautiously moved toward the door.

"I'm real sorry, Miss. Sorry about everything." He looked more like a boy now than ever.

As much as she just wanted to escape this horrid place, and get away from him, she felt a pang of pity. She paused by the campfire and looked him square in the face. "You have a choice now, Red."

"A choice?" He looked confused.

She nodded toward the aspens. "I know you're about to make a run for it."

"Yeah?"

"That'll make you look more guilty than you are."

"Then what'll I do?"

She sighed. "The only way you'll get out of this mess is if you stick with me."

"Do ya mean it?" He studied her. "You won't turn me in?"

She squinted into the afternoon sun, realizing that she didn't really know where she was or how to get back to the Double W. "You can trust me, Red. Get me safely back to my sister's ranch, and I'll tell them the true story. I'll speak in your behalf. You're not a murderer, Red. I don't think you're even a real kidnapper. You just got caught up in Beau's scheme."

He nodded as they continued toward the horses. "I didn't know what I was getting myself into when Beau asked me to help. He promised me money and I never stopped to question. If'n I'd known what he was up to, I'd surely said no."

As she bridled Dolly, Red continued to ramble about his brother, admitting that Beau always went his own way, and often got away with doing wrong, but never anything like this. Julianne lifted her saddle then almost fell backward. She knew she was weak, but she could do this.

"Let me help ya." Red took the saddle, hoisting it onto Dolly's back. While he saddled his own horse, Julianne tightened her cinch and breathed deeply. She was free again. Or almost. She had to make it back to the ranch.

They had barely started out when Red continued telling his story, going over every part about him and Beau, as if he needed to speak his piece. Her weariness made it hard to pay close attention, but when he mentioned the part about Beau going to meet his friends at the Mayor's Picnic, her ears perked up.

"He never asked me to come," Red said glumly, "but that weren't unusual. Beau likes runnin' 'round, but not me tagging along."

Julianne thought that was probably a good thing.

"Then Beau rushed home kinda early. I figured he'd be gone all day with his friends."

"Do you know his friends?" she probed.

"Just by name. Don't really know 'em socially. Ma says they're all a bunch a bad apples."

"She probably appreciates that you're not like that, Red."

"I dunno." He sadly shook his head.

"So what happened then?" She really didn't have energy to talk, felt too tired to do much more than just ride, but for all she knew this might be Red's best chance for a full confession. She felt certain Delia's ranch hands would be out searching by now. She just hoped no one would turn vigilante or get trigger happy.

Red continued about how Beau came home in a big hurry, all excited. "Ma and me were having our midday meal when Beau burst in and snatched up Pa's rifle. He loaded it right there in the kitchen. Course, Ma got real worried. But Beau just explained 'bout this big job."

Red turned, changing course so that they were going alongside a ridge. He explained how their family was barely scraping by. "We needed money bad so when Beau said he'd pay me good to help him, he didn't have to ask twice. He was in a big hurry. Told me go get Rowdy ready while he put on his work clothes."

"Is Rowdy the paint?"

"Yeah. I got both our horses saddled up, but when Beau came out, he said he was headin' out first. He told me to go pack us some camp supplies. Enough for a couple days. That's 'bout all we had in the house anyway. Ma got all worried and started to question. Beau just laughed and told her we'd be shooting jackrabbits for a rancher. It was a lie, but I didn't know it then. And it made Ma happy."

Julianne remembered how Beau manipulated Red by saying their mother was in danger if Red didn't follow orders. "You love your ma, don't you?"

He let out a long sigh. "Ma ain't gonna like this. Not one little bit."

"What about your pa?"

"He's dead. Me and Beau. We're all Ma's got."

"I'm sorry."

For a few minutes they rode in silence. Hearing a hawk screech overhead made them both jump and, seeing the slump in Red's shoulder, like he was carrying the weight of the world there, Julianne encouraged him to continue telling her his tale.

"After Ma went back inside, Beau was ready to go. He told me to bring my gun and head for the Double W Ranch. I reckoned that's where we'd be shooting jackrabbits. Beau told me to cut across the Circle Z Ranch cuz it's quicker."

"So you didn't take the main road?"

"Nope. And before Beau lit out, he told me just where to meet him on the Double W."

"Where was that?" she asked, trying to stay focused but feeling bone tired and hoping she'd make it all the way back without falling off her horse.

"Where the mountains come down and the creek runs by, there in the pines." He turned to look at her. "Do ya know the spot? It's right pretty there. Nice and cool."

"Yes. Good spot to water your horse." And shady and concealed, she thought, a good place for someone to hide. She held on to her saddle horn with one hand, keeping her eyes on Dolly's neck and mane. "So Beau was there?"

"I figured he'd be there, but no sign of him. I got off my horse and waited a spell. Then Beau got there, and he was kinda riled up. Rowdy was sweatin' and pantin,' but Beau wouldn't even let him drink."

Julianne slowly nodded. "In a hurry?"

"Yep. Beau led us deeper into Double W land like he knew where he was going. We got up there, you know, where the cattle drivers had just gone through. The dust was still in the air."

The hair on the back of her neck stood up as she remembered this part, unsure she even wanted to hear it again, except it seemed good for Red to tell her. Besides, they were coming into Double W land now. It wouldn't be long.

"We stop up there, and Beau says we gotta wait." Red's voice was getting squeakier, as if he was anxious. "Beau's kinda antsy, watchin' for somethin'. Then he gets quiet like and tells me we're gonna capture this girl. I ask him why and he says this girl's been trespassing and stealing cows, and she's wanted by the law."

"I get it." Julianne could imagine Beau making up a story like that.

"Beau said if we brung her in, we'd get big money from this bounty hunter named Danner. He said it was a big reward, and I'd get two hundred dollars all my own just for helping."

"And the girl you were going after, of course, was me."

"I gotta admit I weren't so sure 'bout Beau's story just then and there. Ne'er heard 'bout no girl cow rustlers afore. But then I saw you out riding. Not side-saddle like most women. You looked like a real cowgirl with your lasso and bedroll and everything, but all alone. I thought that was strange. And not too far ahead of you was some strays. Like maybe you were going after one."

Julianne remembered feeling there were strays nearby and hoping she'd find a hand rounding them up. Maybe even her brother, and they could've ridden on together. But that never happened.

"So when Beau told me to jump you, I did." Red shook his head. "I'm right sorry I did too. It's been nothin' but a heap a trouble ever since."

Despite her tiredness, she was curious. "So then you and Beau took me away. Did you know where you were taking me? Or why?"

"I thought we were gonna meet up with the bounty hunter. Maybe he was out there in the grazing land. Maybe he was out catching other rustlers, maybe friends of yours. I thought maybe we'd meet up the next day. But when that never happened, I started gettin' suspicious. Beau always gets mad at me for askin' too many questions. He's always telling me I'm stupid, just cuz I ask questions."

"Your questions were justified," she said. "And I don't think you're stupid."

"Really?" He looked surprised.

"Well, you were stupid to believe Beau. He really strung you along."

"I know. By the time I started figurin' stuff out, I was kinda stuck."

They were just rounding the edge of the rim rock when she saw two riders up ahead and coming toward them. Unsure of how to handle this, she glanced at Red. He looked understandably nervous, and his Adam's apple rose and fell.

"Them your folks?" His voice sounded squeakier than ever.

She adjusted her cowboy hat to shield her eyes from the sun then squinted to see better. "Yes," she said in relief. "That's my brother Julius and my sister's husband Wyatt." She waved toward them, hoping to show she was in no danger. "Don't worry, Red. These are good men. They'll hear out your story just like I've done."

"I hope you're right. I sorta feel like lightin' on outta here right now."

"Don't! That would be the stupidest thing you ever could do, Red. And a good way to get yourself shot." She locked eyes with him. "I'm your friend. I know that's probably hard to believe, but you can trust me."

He gulped. "All right, if ya say so."

Wyatt and Julius galloped their horses toward them, but Julianne warned Red it was probably safer for them to walk their horses. "Until we can assure them I'm all right."

"Should I hold up my hands?" he asked nervously.

"I don't think so." She noticed his holster. "But give me your gun."

"My gun?" he questioned.

"They won't shoot an unarmed man." She held out her hand.

He removed it and seemed grateful to be rid of it. "I never planned on using it. Honest. You coulda run, Miss Julianne. I never woulda stopped ya."

She nodded. "I know."

When the men got to them, she held out the gun as if to show that Red was not dangerous. "This is Red," she said quickly to Julius who was trying to hug her and remain seated on his horse. "He helped me escape."

Wyatt, who was next to Red, reached out for his hand. "Well, thank you for that, Red. You got a last name?"

Red looked conflicted as he shook his hand. "It's Bueller," he said in a very squeaky voice. Now he shook Julius's hand too.

"We've been scared witless over you. Your sister's in a real panic," Wyatt told Julianne. "Where you been? What happened?"

"I'm all right," she assured them, forcing a smile. "Just really worn out."

"You look like something the cat dragged in," Julius teased.

"Let's get you home," Wyatt said gently. "You look exhausted."

"And filthy." Julius slapped her back, sending the dust flying. "But I'm sure glad to see you, sis." He put a hand on her shoulder. "Glad you're safe."

"Thanks." She tried to sit straighter in the saddle but felt light-headed as she gripped the saddle horn with one hand.

"If I didn't know better, I'd think you just got back from a cattle drive," Julius teased as the ranch house came into sight.

"A very long cattle drive," she said quietly.

"We're almost there." Julius reined his horse closer to hers. "You look kinda pale, sis. Sure you can make it?"

"I, uh, I think so." She felt her hand slipping from the saddle horn…felt everything slipping…and then darkness.

20

DELIA HAD THE MEN CARRY JULIANNE UP TO THE GUEST ROOM WHERE she immediately began to peel off her sister's filthy clothes, tossing them into a sodden heap by the door. Julianne was partly conscious, trying to talk but not making sense.

"Let's get you cleaned up a little," Delia told her. "Then we'll talk." She dipped a washrag into the warm soapy water Ginger had just brought up and gently began to wash a week's worth of grime from her little sister's hands and face, taking special care with the cut on her hand.

"Help Red," Julianne murmured.

"Red?" Delia was confused. That was the name of her kidnapper. Why should they want to help him?

"Levi. Help Levi," Julianne muttered, eyes still closed. "Help him."

"How can we help Levi?" Delia asked quietly as she unbuttoned a shirtwaist that had once been white but was now tan colored from dirt.

"Tell him." Julianne opened her eyes as if startled but couldn't seem to focus. The poor girl was clearly exhausted.

"You need food and rest," Delia said gently. "Then we'll talk."

"Warn them," she said again as Delia pulled a clean nightgown over her dirt encrusted blonde curls.

"Warn who? About what?" Delia kept her voice calm as she helped Julianne to lie back on the bed.

Julianne said nothing, just stared at the ceiling. Ginger entered the room holding two mugs. "I've got bone broth and chamomile tea with honey. Let's see if we can get some of this down her, poor thing."

They took turns spooning broth and tea into Julianne, who was semi-conscious and still rambling incoherently about Levi and Red. The mugs were about half emptied when it became clear Julianne couldn't even keep her eyes open let alone swallow.

"Let her rest," Ginger suggested.

"You're right." Delia put the spoon back in the mug and stood. "But I don't want to leave her alone. She's been through so much. I'm worried."

"I'll stay with her," Ginger offered. "You need to be with the children. Billy is awfully worried about all this. Daisy is getting them ready for bed, but you should spend some time with them."

"I'm sure you're right." Delia sighed sadly to see her sister lying there so helpless looking. "Dr. Muller should be here soon. The men promised to bring him back here right after they delivered that awful Red Bueller into the marshal's hands."

"Did Julianne say anything about him?" Ginger whispered. "Was she hurt in any way?"

Delia shook her head with uncertainty. "Not that I could tell, but I couldn't ask her. Not now. She's barely holding on."

"Do you think Bueller is the one who shot the judge?" Ginger asked.

"Julius seemed pretty certain he's part of their gang."

"Gang?"

"According to Deputy Garson there are more involved."

"So we still need to be on guard?"

"I'm afraid so." She opened the door. "Thank you for sitting with her, Ginger. If she comes to or asks for me, please, come get me."

Delia took one last look at her sister. Her skin was so pale and her features so lifeless she could be mistaken for dead. Thankfully, she wasn't. Hopefully there was nothing seriously wrong with her.

Because of the holiday tomorrow, followed by the weekend, Levi allowed court to run overtime. It wasn't easy listening to the cases being brought before him because he was distracted by his concerns for Julianne. Yet, at the same time, he listened intently because these cases had been brought by miners who'd been cheated out of their claims. And the claim-jumpers, sneaky men like Danner and Martin and Rigby, seemed to have several things in common. They all used the same less than reputable surveyor to "prove" they owned the claims, they all used the same slick Denver lawyer to defend them, and they were all associated with Royal Dayton. Levi wasn't just hearing cases, he was collecting evidence.

Weary from a long day, it was going on seven by the time Levi removed his black robe. Accompanied by Deputy Wells, he went straight to the hospital to check on his father. His plan this evening was to make sure Dad was still doing well and then he and Deputy Wells would ride out to the Double W to see if there was any news about Julianne. He'd already been out there this morning before court began. Wyatt Davis had assured him they would keep him posted. More than anything, Levi wanted to help look for Julianne, and with three days of no court, he planned to join the search parties. He'd already packed up his saddlebags to take out to the ranch and hoped to bunk with the cowhands.

Levi and Deputy Wells were just heading up the hospital steps when Marshal Rivers, two deputies, and Dr. Muller came bursting out the door.

"What's going on?" Deputy Wells asked the marshal.

"Miss Blackstone's been found," the marshal said. "One of the kidnappers is in jail right now, and we're headed out to the Double W where I plan to hear the girl's accusations against him so I can charge him."

"Not until I've examined her," Dr. Muller added. "I'm sure she's been through a lot. She may not be ready for questions until tomorrow."

Marshal Rivers seemed to consider this. "I reckon I could wait until morning. That'd give me time to question the Bueller boy."

"Bueller boy?" Levi asked.

"One of the kidnappers," the marshal said. "They're brothers." He rubbed his chin. "Come to think of it, I probably should stay in town."

"Well, I'm heading out to the Double W," Levi told him. "I can talk to Julianne for you?"

The marshal nodded. "She'd probably tell you more anyway." He pointed to Deputy Wells. "I want you to stick around town. See what you can find out about the other Bueller boy. His name is Beau, and it sounds like he's working for a fellow named Danner."

"Rich Danner?" Levi asked him.

"The boy didn't mention a first name."

"Rich Danner's been accused of claim-jumping," Levi said. "He was in my court yesterday."

"This gets more and more interesting." Marshal Rivers nodded to Deputy Garson. "You go on out to the ranch with Levi. There's probably a chance Beau Bueller could still be hiding out near there. See if Miss Blackstone can tell you where they were holding her. Maybe organize another search party in the morning."

"And I'll keep an eye on the ranch house tonight," Garson said. "That Beau Bueller might have more tricks up his sleeve."

"I hope not, but you might want to let the ranch hands know to be on the lookout. And if anything changes here in town, I'll send word." The marshal looked up and down the street. "Things will be extra busy tomorrow with the Independence Day celebrations. I might want you back in town by then."

Levi glanced up at the hospital. "I'd like to let my father know why I'm not visiting him tonight."

"He won't be up there much longer," Marshal Rivers said. "My men are going to secretly sneak him out after midnight."

"To your house?" Levi asked hopefully. "With Mother?"

"Yes, I think it's safer. Too many people coming and going in the hospital."

"Can you explain to Dad why I'm not able to see him tonight?"

"You bet. I'll send a message from my office." He put his hand on Levi's shoulder. "And I don't want you to think we're out of the woods just because we got one of the kidnappers. For all we know, this could really heat things up. Sort of like poking the hornets' nest. So you be careful out there."

Levi assured him he'd watch his back. The marshal with Andrews headed back to his office, and Deputy Garson went to get his horse, promising to meet up with Dr. Muller's buggy before they left town. By now, knowing Julianne was there, Levi had scrapped his plan for riding his own horse to the Double W, opting to ride with the doctor instead. He just wanted to get there as quickly as possible. He was torn between relief and concern. Glad Julianne was safely with her sister, worried about her condition after her ordeal. Six days with those outlaws. What might she have suffered?

On the road out of town, with Deputy Garson trailing them, Levi tried to distract himself from fretting over Julianne by inquiring about his dad's health.

"Judge Stanfield is making a steady recovery," Dr. Muller assured him. "He should be back on the bench in about a month or so. Think you can hold up for that long?"

Levi nodded. "Longer if necessary. But I'd rather see my dad back on the bench. That way I can get back to practicing law."

"I hear you've been doing a good job, Judge Stanfield," Dr. Muller said. "I have no doubt that someday that bench will be yours for keeps."

Levi wasn't sure he'd want it for keeps. Right now, all he wanted was to see Julianne, to make sure she was all right.

"I know you're worried about the girl," the doctor said as he snapped the reins to speed up his horse. "Marshal Rivers told me that you and she are, well, good friends."

Levi just nodded.

"She's been through an ordeal. There's no saying how it may have affected her, Levi. I'm telling you this, not to worry you, but just to help you understand. Something like that can change a woman. Be prepared, son."

Again Levi nodded.

"Whatever you do, go easy on her. If you question her too hard about what went on, she could shut down on you."

Levi had already considered that. He'd studied legal cases against criminals who'd abducted women. He knew it could get very ugly. But he was determined, no matter what Julianne had suffered, he would stay by her side. He loved her. Nothing would ever change that.

21

Delia was so relieved when Dr. Muller arrived. "Please, come see her at once," she said as she met him at the door. She told him about the wounded hand as she led him upstairs. "I cleaned and bandaged it, but you should look at it too. And we only gave her broth and tea."

"That sounds wise," he assured her. "I wouldn't offer solid foods until she's had a good rest."

"Julianne is not herself at all," Delia continued. "She so tired she can hardly keep her eyes opened, but she's so agitated she can't settle down and rest. She keeps rambling about things but makes no sense. And she's trying to get out of bed as if she needs to go somewhere. It's very distressing."

"I'm not surprised," he said quietly as she opened the door.

"Oh, good." Ginger stood. "Julianne's having a hard time."

"You go on out," Delia told her. "I'll stay with the doctor."

Ginger's sigh was weary. "Poor girl."

"Need to go." Julianne was climbing out of bed. "Need to tell him."

"Not right now." Dr. Muller took her arm, helping her back into bed. "You can tell him later. Right now, we're going to examine you to make sure you're all right."

Delia sat in the chair by the window while Dr. Muller listened to Julianne's heart and checked her temperature and several other things. All the while, he spoke calmly and comfortingly, assuring her that everything was fine and that she would feel better soon. "You just need a good night's sleep," he told her. "I'm going to give you something to help with that."

"Levi," Julianne said again. "Need Levi."

"There she goes again," Delia said.

"Levi Stanfield?" The doctor poured out some medicine.

"Yes." Julianne sat up almost fully alert. "I need to tell him."

"Levi Stanfield came here with me," the doctor told her.

"Here?" Julianne looked hopeful. "Levi is here?"

"Yes." He held out the spoon. "Now if you take your medicine, I'll send him up to talk to you."

She opened her mouth, and she'd barely swallowed when she asked about Levi again. Dr. Muller closed his doctor's bag and turned to Delia. "I better keep my promise. I'll go down and send Levi up."

Delia followed him out of the room, standing on the landing and talking quietly. "I didn't realize Julianne knew Levi Stanfield, well, other than perhaps meeting him up here years ago."

"Seems she and Levi have been spending some time together in town. I think he came out here looking for her, but you folks were probably out rounding up cows." His eyes twinkled. "I do believe that Levi is courting your sister."

She smiled. "Well, he has always struck me as a fine young man."

"How about I send him up now?" The doctor grinned. "Might be just the medicine she needs?"

"Can I ask you a question first?" Delia felt uncomfortable but needed to know.

"Of course."

"Is Julianne going to be all right? I mean did anything happen to her while she was being held captive…anything a sister should be aware of?"

"She was obviously deprived of food and water, and I doubt she got much sleep. And of course, she's been through a traumatizing experience, but she's young and resilient. So other than needing a good bath and some healthy food, I suspect she will be as right as rain by tomorrow. To put it plainly, I'm not concerned that she's been violated in the manner that you are suggesting."

"Thank you." Relief washed over her as Delia went back into the room. Julianne was still sitting up in bed. Apparently the medicine hadn't started to work yet because she looked more alert than ever.

"So, Julianne. I hear that you and Levi are good friends?" Delia smiled. "That's nice to know."

"I wanted to tell you. Wanted to talk to you." She sighed. "He's really here?"

"The doctor is sending him up." Delia reached for a bed shawl, wrapping it around Julianne's shoulders and tucking the blanket up over it. "But you can't visit with him for too long. You need your rest. I'll invite Levi to stay overnight so that you can talk to him again in the morning when you're feeling better."

Julianne's eyes looked misty. "Thank you."

Delia heard a light tapping on the partially opened door. She went to greet Levi. "Julianne is eager to see you, Mr. Stanfield."

He thanked her and, looking nervous, he explained he'd spoken to the doctor just now. "He seems to think she'll be fine, that she just needs food and rest."

Delia nodded. "Yes. And I told Julianne you couldn't visit for too long. The doctor gave her medicine to make her sleepy. But I hope you'll stay the night. Then you can spend more time with her tomorrow."

"I'd like that."

"I'll leave you with her." Delia smiled. "But I'll leave the door open."

Levi quietly stepped into the room. Seeing Julianne in bed with a gray shawl over her shoulders, looking so pale and weak, frail and tired—nothing like the vivacious pretty girl he was used to bantering with.

"Hello?" He came closer, trying not to appear shocked by her changed appearance.

"Levi." Her eyes opened wider.

"Mind if I sit?" He nodded to the chair near her bed.

"I'm glad you're here." A shy smile brightened her face.

"I was so relieved to hear you were safe." He sat down. "I couldn't wait to see you. I hope you're feeling better. I'm sure it must feel good to be home."

She nodded slowly. "Very good."

"I hope you'll tell me more about your ordeal when you're stronger. I know you're worn out and need your rest, but I just wanted to come up and say hello."

"Levi." She reached out a hand. "I need to tell you…" Her voice drifted off and her eyes got a faraway look then fluttered closed.

He took her small cool hand, holding it between his hands to generate some warmth into it. "You don't need to talk now. You should probably just rest."

Her eyes opened again, as if trying to stay awake. "Need to tell you…" Her head drooped forward, as if falling asleep.

He knew he should go and let her sleep, but he didn't want to let go of her hand.

She looked up again, but her head was weaving back and forth, clearly struggling to stay awake. Her medication was probably starting to work. "Need to tell you," she stammered. "In town…fireworks…the judge…shooting…careful." Her head slumped forward again.

Levi tried to make sense of her strange ramblings as he released her hand, laying it back on the bed. Then he gently leaned her back into the pillows and, tucking the blanket up around her chin, kissed her forehead. "Good night, Julianne. Rest well." He stood up straight, just watching her for a long minute. He didn't want to leave but didn't want to worry her sister by staying too long. "God bless you, darling," he whispered as he quietly left the room.

Feeling greatly relieved, Delia had gone downstairs to reassure Julius and Wyatt that Julianne was going to be just fine.

"You don't know how glad we were to hear that," Wyatt said. "Dr. Muller told us the good news right before he left."

"She's really all right?" Julius asked with a furrowed brow. "Are you sure of that, Delia? Because she looked like death warmed over when we carried her upstairs. She was with those blasted villains for almost a week. Who knows what they might've done to her."

"The doctor assured me she will be fine," Delia said firmly.

"Well, those hooligans who took her aren't gonna be fine. I can't believe I didn't see right through that Red. When I first met him, I actually thought he was one of the search party guys and that he found her. I actually thanked him. Now, I want to kill him."

"Oh, Julius."

"I do. If Deputy Garson hadn't taken him away when he did, me and the other hands probably would've beat the stuffin' outta him."

"That's not a fair trial," Wyatt told him.

"I don't care. Julianne is my sister and I—"

"She's my sister too," Delia declared. "And it won't help her to hear you going off like this, Julius. Let the law and the court settle it."

"Speaking of court, why is Levi Stanfield up there?" Julius asked with understandable curiosity. "Isn't he Judge Stanfield's boy?"

"It seems that our sister is being courted by young Mr. Stanfield."

"When did that happen?" Julius asked.

"Apparently while she was living in town with our parents, she and—" Delia stopped at the sound of Billy calling from the top of the stairs.

"I'll see to him." Wyatt headed up.

"Let's go into the other room." Delia pointed to the main living room. "Now I'm thinking about our parents."

"What about them?" he growled.

Delia didn't really want to think about this, but it was the reasonable responsible thing to consider. "Shouldn't we let them know Julianne is safe?"

Julius scowled. "Why?"

"Because she's their daughter and I'm sure they're worried."

"The only thing Father would worry about was that he might not be able to marry her off to one of his rich friends now."

"Oh, Julius."

"You know it's true."

She wondered how he'd heard of that, but didn't want to ask.

"Look, tell 'em if you want, Delia, but I want nothing to do with them. I'm not even on speaking terms with my father. I'm surprised you are."

"I was thinking more about Mother. I'm sure she's been worried."

"The only thing that she's been worried about is not having Julianne around to wait on her hand and foot, and to work at her blasted dress shop." He threw up his hands. "I'm tired, Delia. It's been a long hard week and I don't want to think about my parents. I'm going to bed."

She patted his back. "You must be exhausted, Julius. You gave it your all on the cattle drive. And barely home and taking the lead with the search parties. You deserve a really good night's rest, little brother."

His expression softened. "I guess I'm kinda beat."

"Tomorrow's Independence Day," she reminded him. "So it'll be minimal work around here."

"Too bad we canceled our barbecue. Might've been fun."

"Wyatt suggested we have the barbecue on Sunday. In the meantime, there'll be no shortage of food around here. Daisy's been baking for days."

"Some of the fellas are going into town tomorrow afternoon. There's supposed to be fireworks and stuff. I might go with 'em."

"Well, you boys stay out of trouble." She shook her finger then smiled.

"Sure thing." He made a sly wink. "G'night, sis."

She wanted to suggest he might check on their mother while in town, let her know that Julianne was safe, but she suspected that'd only put the growl back into him. Instead she told him good night then went into the kitchen to make a pot of tea. Daisy and Ginger were just finishing up cleaning the kitchen.

"Looks like it's been a late night for everyone." Delia got down the teapot.

"What'd the doctor say?" Ginger asked eagerly. "Is our girl all right?"

As she measured tea, Delia reassured them that Julianne was going to be fine. "She's just exhausted from her ordeal. The doctor gave her medicine to help her sleep tonight. And she'll need good food and rest tomorrow." She poured hot water into the pot then set up the tea tray with three cups and saucers. She hoped that Levi would want to sit and visit with her and Wyatt for a bit.

"How about some cookies to go with that." Daisy held out a small plate of sugar cookies, but instead of the usual white dusting of sugar, some were dusted in red and blue.

"These are so pretty," Delia told her. "How did you do this?"

"Just a little food dye to color sugar crystals," Daisy said proudly. "For Independence Day."

"Well, you are the clever one." Delia smiled and thanked her, carrying the tray out to the living room where Wyatt and Levi were standing and talking. "You gentlemen interested in some tea?" She set the tray on the table in front of the couch.

They both thanked her then sat down, waiting as she served them.

"Levi was just telling me that he's been taking his father's place in the courtroom."

"As a judge?" she asked in surprise.

"A temporary judge," he clarified.

"You mean until they find a replacement for your father?" She frowned. "Oh, that's right. I was so sorry to hear about that. Your family must be devastated."

"It's been a difficult week." Levi reached for a cookie. "I've been hearing a lot of cases. I didn't even finish in the courtroom until after six tonight. And then I came straight here."

"Straight here?" she questioned. "Does that mean you've had no supper?"

He held up a cookie and smiled.

"Oh, Mr. Stanfield—"

"Please, call me Levi."

"Only if you let me go make you a plate of food."

"I don't want to trouble you."

"Trouble? We have a kitchen full of food. Why there's fried chicken, potato salad, and all sorts of things." She was already standing.

His eyes grew wide. "That sounds wonderful. To be honest, I haven't had much appetite all week. Not since my father was shot and Julianne went missing."

"It must've been a terrible week for you."

"Not one I'd like to repeat."

As she went back to the kitchen, her heart went out to Levi. The poor man had been through a lot. But at least he hadn't lost Julianne. She filled a generous plate, musing over whether their relationship was as serious as she assumed. But hadn't he made a special trip out here just to check on Julianne? And if Delia was any judge of character, that serious young judge had a very good chance with her sweet little sister. Wouldn't that be something—Julianne and a judge! Already Delia was imagining a lovely summer wedding with a huge reception out here on the ranch. Half the town would probably come. But then she remembered the sad news about Levi's father. Perhaps a winter wedding would be more suitable.

22

After Delia left to get Levi something to eat, he took the opportunity to speak candidly with Wyatt. "Julianne was trying to tell me something when I was up there just now. I could tell the medication was taking effect because she was having difficulty talking. But some things she said were concerning, and I'm not fully sure what she meant."

"What did she say?"

"She didn't speak in a complete sentence, but only in single words. She said town and fireworks and shooting and judge and careful." He frowned. "I believe I can trust you, Wyatt, but what I'm going to tell you needs to be kept quiet for now." He explained how they were letting everyone think his father had died. "It's to keep him safe. But hearing Julianne trying to warn me, I think she must know my father's still in danger. I'm worried the outlaws might still try to kill him. And the marshal plans to move him from the hospital tonight. I'm concerned he won't be safe now."

"First of all, I'm glad to hear your father is alive, but I understand your concern." Wyatt rubbed his chin. "How about I go speak to

Deputy Garson while you eat something? See what he thinks about this."

"Thinks about what?" Delia asked as she brought in a large plate of food, setting it on the table in front of Levi.

"I just want to tell Garson about something Julianne told Levi," Wyatt said lightly. "Probably nothing, but it might help with the case."

"This looks delicious. Thank you." Levi dug right in, hoping his full mouth would give him an excuse not to answer her questions. To his relief, she just chatted with him while he ate. When he was done, he thanked her again, quickly excusing himself. "I need to speak to Deputy Garson."

"And Wyatt can get you set up in the guest cottage." She looked tired. "I'm going to turn in. It's been a very long day."

He told her good night then went out to where Wyatt and Garson were talking on the porch. "We need to send word to town," Garson told Levi. "You're right. The marshal needs to know that there's risk in moving the judge tonight."

"I'll go," Levi said. "But I'll need to borrow a horse." He looked at Wyatt.

"Of course." Wyatt nodded.

"You can't go alone. I was ordered to stay with you." Garson frowned. "And to stay here and guard the ranch."

"We've got plenty of men here, plenty of guns, we can easily keep an eye on things. I'll assign the men to shifts tonight," Wyatt told them. "You both go to town."

With that settled, Levi and Garson prepared to leave. Since Levi was still in his courtroom attire, Wyatt loaned him riding clothes. And Wyatt even found another volunteer to ride to town with them. "Silas is our best marksman." Wyatt handed Levi a pistol. "You should be armed too, just in case."

The sky was just getting dusky as the three armed men headed toward town. Levi knew this ride could be dangerous, but hadn't he been in danger all week just sitting on the bench? In fact, he'd almost welcome an attack if that meant they could catch the outlaw.

Delia insisted on taking Julianne's breakfast tray up to her. Billy had been sneakily checking on his aunt because his important job was to quietly come down and tell his mother as soon as she woke up.

"Can I carry the tray?" Billy asked.

"I appreciate your willingness," she told him, but I have a more important job for you to do."

"What's that, Mama?"

"Aunt Julianne loves those pink roses—the ones growing by the front porch." She glanced at Ginger. "Ask Ginger to help you with the sheers and to cut your aunt a great big bouquet. Then have Ginger help you arrange it in my pretty crystal vase and take it up to Aunt Julianne's room. I just know that will help her to get well faster than anything." She pointed to his bowl of oatmeal. "But finish that first."

He grabbed his spoon. "I'm almost done."

By the time Delia made it up to Julianne's room, she was getting out of bed. "Julianne Margaret," Delia scolded. "Back into bed with you."

"I want to get dressed."

"Breakfast first." Delia smiled. "And you might as well enjoy eating it in your bed. It's not the sort of treat one gets every day." She waited, tray in hand.

Julianne sniffed. "Well, I'll admit I'm hungry and that does smell good."

"Oatmeal with applesauce, a soft boiled, and lightly buttered toast. I would've brought you bacon and eggs and hotcakes, but Dr. Muller recommended you take it easy on your first solid food."

"That looks good enough to eat." Julianne grinned as she climbed back into bed. As she started to eat, Delia poured them both a cup of tea and sat down.

"You seem more like yourself today."

"I feel more like myself." She bit into a piece of toast. "I'll feel even more like myself after a nice hot bath."

"Ginger is already heating water."

"I know Levi was up here last night. Well, unless I dreamt it. I didn't, did I?"

Delia laughed. "No, he was up here. But Dr. Muller had given you that sedative and I think you were feeling the effect."

"I remember trying to tell him something, I hope he understood. Anyway, I can explain it to him better today. After I've had my bath." She dipped her spoon into the oatmeal. "I must've looked a sight. I hope I didn't scare him."

"I'm sure he could see past your appearance. And considering all you've been through, well, you really don't look that bad." Delia sipped her tea.

"I'm embarrassed to say that I wish I had one of my pretty dresses from Mother's house to wear today. By the way, has anyone told her I'm back?" Julianne frowned. "Or did she even know I was missing?"

"She knew. Although they thought you'd gone on the cattle drive with us."

"Yes, that's what I said before I left. I was so angry at her. Did you know she and Father made up the whole thing about the buggy accident? Just to keep me there?"

"I heard about that." Delia shook her head. "Hard to believe."

"I thought about Mother while I was being held captive in that horrible shack. I know she loves me. And you and Julius too. I want her to know I'm all right."

"We'll send word to her today."

"And Father too, I suppose." Julianne scowled. "Although I'm not sure I care whether he knows or not. He's involved in some pretty dirty dealings."

Delia pointed to the food. "Why don't you eat now and tell me about that later."

Julianne obeyed, taking a bite of toast. "But I need to tell Levi about some of these things—it's very important," she said with her mouth full.

"All right, Miss Chatterbox." Delia smiled and stood. "I think you'll do more eating and less talking if I'm not in the room. How about I get your bath started?"

Julianne nodded eagerly as she spooned in a big bite of oatmeal.

Satisfied her sister was going to get some nourishment, Delia went to the bathroom to discover Daisy was already getting it ready.

"I'm just so glad Julianne is back." Daisy laid out a towel. "I was so worried about her that I did some real honest to goodness prayin'."

"I think we all did." Delia thanked her then went downstairs to find Ginger and Billy just finishing up their arrangement of roses.

"That's beautiful," she told them.

"Can we take 'em up to her now?" Billy asked.

"Of course." Delia glanced around. "Where's Lilly?"

"Wyatt carted her outside." Ginger nodded toward the porch.

Delia went out to find Wyatt giving Lilly a horsy ride on his knee. "Someday you're going to have your own pony, little Lil. You'll ride over hill and dale just like Mama."

"I see you're starting to train her already," Delia teased as she stood next to him. Then, looking across the ranch land, she felt a wave of worry. "Is it safe to be out here like this? What about that other kidnapper?"

"I've got men posted around. I'm keeping an eye out too."

"Just the same, I think I'd feel better if we stayed in."

Wyatt stood. "Let's go in."

"Where's Levi?" she asked as she closed the front door. "Julianne's eager to talk to him this morning."

"Levi left last night."

"Last night?" She took Lilly from his arms. "Why?"

"Julianne told him something about the judge being shot today, and he was worried."

"But the judge..." She lowered her voice. "Isn't he dead?"

Wyatt looked conflicted. "Not everything is as it seems."

She frowned, knowing he was keeping something from her. "What do you mean? Is Judge Stanfield dead or not?"

He shook his head.

"He's alive?"

"I'm not supposed to say anything."

She smiled. "You didn't. I guessed. But I'm glad to hear it."

"Just don't let anyone else hear it. Marshal Rivers is keeping it under wraps for the time being."

"And Levi really did go to town?"

"That's true."

"Julianne will be greatly disappointed."

"How is she doing?"

"Much improved. But she's determined to talk to Levi. I made her promise to finish her breakfast and have a bath first. Now what will I say?"

"You'll have to figure that one out." Wyatt's brow creased as he stared out the front window. "I need to check on the men. A lot of them plan to go into town to celebrate the Fourth, but I need some to stick around here, to help keep an eye on things, just in case."

"Do you think that other outlaw is still nearby? Do you think we're really in danger?"

"Hard to tell." Wyatt frowned. "But because Julianne is here with us, Deputy Garson seems to believe we need to be on our guard." He sighed. "But I still don't understand why they kidnapped Julianne. Garson suspects it's because Julianne witnessed something in town, that she knew of something no one wanted made known. Have you had a chance to talk to her about any of the circumstances surrounding her abduction?"

"Not yet. But I plan to." Delia handed Lilly back to Wyatt. "Why don't you ride herd on this one until Ginger comes back down."

"And you'll find out what Julianne's story is?" He looked hopeful.

She nodded. Hopefully, if nothing else, this could prove a good distraction for not mentioning Levi's whereabouts. Because Delia had a strong feeling that Julianne would not receive this news lightly.

23

JULIANNE HAD NEVER FELT SO GOOD TO BE CLEAN AND DRESSED. Even though she had on an old calico farm dress—something Mother would never approve of—she felt like a new woman. She was perched on the edge of her bed, tugging on her shoes when Delia knocked on her door and came in.

"Well, look at you. Fresh as a daisy." Delia sat in the chair by the window. "No one would guess you just endured such a horrid week."

"Thanks. I feel so much better."

"Yes, but you still need to take it easy," Delia warned. "Dr. Muller said—"

"I need to talk to Levi," Julianne interrupted.

"You talked to him last night."

"I can barely remember last night. But I need to talk to him today, Delia. There's more I need to tell him. It's important."

"Well, not just yet." Delia pursed her lips as if she had something more to say.

"Why? Is something wrong?"

"No, but I need to talk to you first. That is if you're feeling strong enough. Are you?"

"Of course. I already told you. I feel perfectly fine. What do you want to talk about?" She sat up straight, studying Delia.

"We still don't know why you were kidnapped. What was their motive? Wyatt and the hands are on high alert here. They're worried that other kidnapper might show up and do something, well, dangerous. But Wyatt feels it might be helpful for him to know what happened and why. So that he can be more prepared to know what we might be up against. To take precautions. Do you understand?"

"Yes. That makes sense." So Julianne told a short version of how it happened, including where and when she'd been kidnapped, where she'd been taken. "At first I thought they wanted ransom money. I even offered to help get it. But Beau, the older brother, refused. And later on, Red, the younger brother—and the one who helped get me home—told me about how Beau convinced him that I was rustling cattle and—"

"What? You rustling cattle? You cannot be serious."

"Yes, it sounds ridiculous. But Red believed him. He thought they were capturing me for a reward. And to be fair, I was in my riding clothes and had my lasso. And I was alone and there were stray cows nearby. So I suppose it seemed believable. At first anyway. Red began to doubt it later."

"But they kept you out there for nearly a week. Why was that?"

"Because Beau had made a deal with a man named Danner. Apparently the plan kept changing and he was waiting for Danner to pay him—"

"So there are more men involved?"

"That's why I need to talk to Levi." Julianne suddenly stood. "I need to warn him that he's in danger and should stay—"

"Why is Levi in danger?"

"I'm not sure of all the facts, but I believe it's because he's replaced his father as the new judge. There were a lot of claim-jumping cases—and the claim-jumpers are greedy thieves that want their way. And that means anyone opposing them should be gotten rid of, as in dead." Julianne remembered what Beau said about fireworks. "And it's supposed to happen today. I heard Beau bragging how the judge will get his independence on Independence Day. He'll be set free just like his father was. That's what Beau said. That's why I need to speak to Levi. I need to warn him not to go to town."

Delia brightened. "Perhaps he was speaking of Levi's father."

"But Judge Stanfield is already dead." Julianne felt a wave of sadness.

"But what if he's not dead?"

"What do you mean?" Julianne leaned forward.

Delia lowered her voice. "He might not be dead, Julianne. But I'm not supposed to say that. The marshal wants it kept quiet for the time being. Safer for the judge."

Julianne felt a rush of relief. "Oh, that's wonderful news. I won't say a word to anyone. But I still need to speak to Levi. There are other things he needs to know. Things I overheard right before I was kidnapped. Important things." She held up a finger. "And I'm certain it's the very reason I was kidnapped. I had plenty of time to think these things over when I was imprisoned in that grubby shack. I'm pretty sure I've got it mostly figured out. So please let me go see Levi."

"First you need to tell me about all those things, Julianne. Wyatt and his men need to understand who and what we might be up against in protecting you here on the ranch. We need to know who we can trust and who we can't trust. For the sake of everyone, including your nephew and niece."

Julianne nodded somberly. "Yes, of course. How selfish of me." Now she began to pour out more details. She described Beau's appearance, and how he was associated with a man named Danner. "But there's more, Delia. I overheard something—another part of the scheme that I need to tell Levi about. Something they were trying to keep secret. And maybe it's not illegal, but it's wrong. Very wrong." She took in a shaky breath. "And my father is involved."

"Jefferson?"

"He's partners with Royal Dayton and a few others." Julianne quickly explained about the farmland purchase and plans to build a casino and other things. "The city won't allow it, but the location makes it appear to be part of town. But no one in town will approve of it."

"You're right. There are ordinances opposing that sort of thing."

"I already knew about it when I was at the Mayor's Picnic. And it was very disturbing, and I was eager to tell Levi. But he was gone. So I was talking to Judge Stanfield." She explained about how the buggy accident was completely fabricated. "I was so angry, I wanted to go home." She looked at Delia. "I mean home here with you. I wanted to go on the cattle drive. But Royal Dayton insisted on walking me back to Mother's house. And he was so aggravatingly smooth, so full of himself, acting like he could control me. But I could see beneath his slick surface. So I shot off my mouth, Delia. I told him I knew everything about the crooked land deal. And that I wouldn't keep quiet."

"That was quite bold."

"I could tell he didn't like it. He knew I could ruin their land deal, not to mention his bid for the senate seat."

Delia's eyes grew wide. "Oh, my goodness. That must've made him very angry."

"Enraged was more like it."

"So you think Royal Dayton was behind your kidnapping?"

Julianne nodded. "I suspect he's in cahoots with this man Danner. I'm sure they set it up right after I tipped off Royal. It was probably in the works even before I left town. I'm guessing that while Royal Dayton was giving his fancy campaign speech—did you know my father is his campaign manager?"

Delia shook her head.

"So while Royal enchanted his listeners, Danner was probably setting up his hit men. Red told me how his brother Beau came rushing home that day, and how they took off straight away. I know a lot of details. And I need to tell Levi." She stood. "I have to tell him now."

"You can't tell him now." Delia stood too.

"Why not?"

"He went to town."

Julianne sank back down on the bed. "No…no…no."

Delia sat by her, wrapping an arm around Julianne's shoulders. "He was worried about his father. You said something about the judge being shot and fireworks. Levi assumes his father was in danger."

"No." Julianne stood, facing her sister. "It's Levi who's in danger. It's the junior judge. That's what Beau called Levi. Junior Judge. And I'm sure Beau was the one who shot Levi's father. He nearly said as much. Beau believes Judge Stanfield is dead. And he said Junior Judge was going to join him. Today." Julianne was halfway to the door. "I have to warn Levi."

As she rushed downstairs, Julianne felt sickened, but continued anyway. At the foot of the stairs, she grasped the railing, trying to catch her breath…and to think.

"Julianne?" Delia held on to her. "Are you all right?"

"Just winded."

"You need rest."

"I can't rest," Julianne protested. "Not until I warn Levi."

"I'll send Wyatt or Julius to town," Delia told her. "They can warn him."

"I'm going too," Julianne insisted. "You can't stop me." She looked down at her dress. "My riding clothes. I need—"

"Your riding clothes are filthy. And you're not getting on a horse." Delia locked eyes with her. "Not unless it's over my dead body."

Julianne started to cry. "But what about Levi's dead body?" She grabbed her sister's hands. "Please, help me, Delia. I must go to town. Now. If you don't help me get there, I swear I will sneak out and go alone."

"Where are you going alone?" Wyatt asked as he came into the house.

Delia quickly explained the situation, and Wyatt immediately created a plan. "We will all go into town together. Delia, you get yourselves and the children ready. I'll tell them men who were about to leave to wait for us. We'll all leave straight away—together There is safety in numbers."

Suddenly everyone was scrambling, and it wasn't long before carriages and a wagon were loaded and, surrounded by a number of ranch hands on horses, they all caravanned to town. Julianne rode with Julius in the one horse buggy, keeping the top up in order to help conceal her identity. Delia and Wyatt and the children, along with Ginger and Daisy rode in the carriage up in front of them. As grateful as Julianne felt for everyone's help and protection, she could only think of Levi and, closing her eyes, she prayed over and over *God, keep him safe*.

To her relief, her normally chatty brother wasn't in a talking mood as they rode to town. She wasn't sure how much he knew about her reasoning for coming today, but he'd been surprisingly kind and protective, even suggesting she try to nap on the way to town. Delia must've said something to him, but Julianne figured she could enlighten him regarding her concerns for Levi later. In the meantime, all she could do was lean against his shoulder and pray.

When they finally reached the outskirts of town, where more carriages and wagons lined the road, she sat up straight and, adjusting the brim of her hat to screen her face, looked around. This was where they'd all agreed to go their separate ways. Julianne felt relieved to see the carriage with Wyatt and Delia and the others departing their company. She knew they'd be safer if she wasn't near them.

"Looks like everyone's on their way to celebrate Independence Day," Julius observed as he pulled the horse to a stop to make way for a family crossing the street.

Julianne nodded. "Quite a crowd."

"Billy's sure looking forward to seeing some fireworks." Julius sounded as if he was trying to keep the conversation light. Probably for her sake.

"I hope the noise won't scare Baby Lil."

"Or the horses."

Julianne spotted Mayor Redding walking with an entourage of city officials. Probably on his way to some celebratory gathering. Would Levi possibly be there?

"So wha'd'ya plan to do in town?" Julius asked.

"I'm not really sure." She paused for a moment, trying to decide how much to tell him. "But I need to find Levi," she blurted.

"I know that. But where do you plan to look?" he asked.

"I honestly don't know, Julius." She surveyed the throngs of people clogging the sidewalks and streets. "He could be anywhere."

"So what do you think is going to happen?" Julius asked as he pulled the buggy to a stop. "I know you think Levi is in danger, but I never heard how exactly."

Turning away from the street and tipping her wide hat brim even lower, she spoke quietly toward his ear. "I'm afraid the man who kidnapped me, the one who's still running free, is in town today. And that he plans to shoot Levi."

Julius nodded grimly. "Oh?"

"And Levi could be anywhere."

"So where do we start?"

She stared into the busy street, hoping to spot Levi, trying to create some sort of plan for how to do this.

"How about we go to the marshal's office," he suggested. "You tell 'em your concerns and the marshal can let his men know to be on the lookout."

"Yes," she agreed. "Good idea. More eyes out there watching."

"We'll take a side street." He reined the horse to turn right, moving away from the crowds.

On this quieter street, she continued to peer up and down, hoping to spy Levi, praying that he would be safe. They were just turning onto another street when a string of loud bangs made the horse toss his head and Julianne jump. Julius calmed the horse then turned to Julianne. "Just firecrackers. Not a gun."

"How can you be sure?"

"Well, I reckon I could be wrong. But firecrackers have a different pitch. Sharper somehow."

Still, she remembered what Beau Bueller had said about firecrackers and shooting a gun…and the way he'd laughed about it. What if she were too late? What if Levi was right now, wounded and bleeding, or worse?

Julius pointed to the marshal's office. "How about I let you out in front? I'll find a place to park the buggy and meet you inside."

She looked both ways down the street then climbed from the buggy and hurried into the marshal's office. The gray-haired man at the desk introduced himself as Deputy Andrews. "How can I help you, ma'am?"

"I'm Julianne Blackstone and I need to speak to Marshal Rivers," she told him. "It's vitally important."

The deputy's brow creased. "You're the girl that got kidnapped."

"That's right."

"You shouldn't be in town. Not all by yourself."

"I'm not alone, but it's imperative I warn someone. Levi Stanfield is in grave danger."

The deputy was on his feet now. "Come back here." He guided her into a private office then picked up the telephone. "I'll call Marshal Rivers's home. That's where Levi and his, uh, mother are staying."

"Thank you."

She waited while he called but could tell by the conversation that neither Marshal Rivers nor Levi were there. "If either of 'em get in, tell 'em to call the marshal's office at once," he finally said. Hanging up, he turned to her. "Sorry, Miss. They're not at the Rivers's house."

"Where do you think they might be?"

"Hard to say. I know the marshal's got most of the deputies out on the street, they're on the lookout for Beau Bueller and—"

"Beau Bueller's the one who plans to shoot Levi," she said urgently. "Today."

"You know this for a fact?"

"I heard him say it."

"Well, I'm the only one here in the office. But we need to get the word out on—" The sounds of loud voices in the front office stopped him. Reaching for his gun, he cautiously cracked opened the door. Standing behind the deputy, she noticed Julius and a couple of the ranch hands out there. She pushed past the deputy to go out.

"There you are." Julius looked relieved to see Julianne. "I brought some help with me. We're thinking we can all go scouting around town for Levi."

"This is my brother Julius and some of our friends," Julianne explained to the deputy.

Deputy Andrews holstered his gun and shook Julius's hand. "We sure could use some help." He quickly organized the men, assigning different sections of town to be searched. "And if you see a deputy, make sure you let him know what's going on."

"Or if you see Levi," she injected. "Make sure he gets out of harm's way."

Everyone was starting to leave again, and Julianne trailed behind Julius. "Where do you think you're going?" he demanded.

"I'm going out there to look too."

"No, you're not." Deputy Andrews put a firm hand on her shoulder. "You're staying right here, young lady."

"But I can help—"

"No." Julius firmly shook his head. "If that kidnapper sees you on the street, you'll be in as much danger as Levi."

"Not only that, you'll be putting the folks around you in danger too," the deputy warned. "You're staying put."

Feeling helpless, but knowing she had no choice, Julianne watched as her brother and the hands all left. She began pacing back and forth in the front office, hoping something might distract the deputy long enough for her to get away.

"I admire your courage," Deputy Andrews told her. "But if you really care about Levi Stanfield's safety, you'll sit down and be quiet." He led her back into the private office and pointed to a chair. "After all you've been through with those Bueller boys, you oughta know this is serious. Why go out on the street and complicate matters? Let the men flush out the town without having to worry about your welfare too."

She sighed. "I suppose you're right. But it's hard to sit by and do nothing."

"You did something. You let us know that Levi is in danger. That's enough." He reached for the telephone again. "I have an idea."

She listened as he asked someone to do him a favor. "Come by the office and I'll explain." After he hung up, he told Julianne that his daughter was on her way. "Adelaide will take you on up to the marshal's house. You can wait there with Levi's mother and Mrs. Rivers. Chances are Levi will be showing up there before too long anyway. And I promise you, if I hear anything, I'll call up there directly and let you know."

She reluctantly agreed to this plan, asking him to let Julius know of her whereabouts. And it wasn't long until Adelaide Andrews showed up in a shiny red buggy and, just like her father had promised, transported Julianne up to the Rivers's home. Their house wasn't located too far from Julianne's parents' property, but she had no desire to see her parents just yet. Not her father anyway. Perhaps she might want to speak to her mother again…someday.

24

Deputy Andrews must've called ahead to the Rivers's house because Mrs. Rivers was waiting at the door for her. "Come in, come in." She waved to Adelaide then quickly ushered Julianne into the front room where Mrs. Stanfield was seated.

"You sit yourself down, Miss Blackstone, and I'll bring us in some tea," Mrs. Rivers told her. "I believe you're acquainted with Mrs. Stanfield."

"Yes, we've met," Julianne gave the marshal's wife a weak smile. "But please call me Julianne."

"Yes, of course, Julianne. Now you just make yourself at home. I know you've been through quite a terrifying experience. In fact, I'm surprised you're out and about so soon. I should think you'd be home resting."

"Well, I was, uh, concerned about something." Julianne didn't want to worry poor Mrs. Stanfield.

"You come and sit with me, Julianne." Mrs. Stanfield patted the sofa. "We have some catching up to do."

Feeling like the baby chick suddenly being sheltered by a pair of mother hens, Julianne sank into the sofa with a weary sigh.

Mrs. Stanfield placed a hand on Julianne's forearm. "You must be worn to a frazzle, dear girl. We all heard about what happened, and we've been praying for your safe return. Thank the good Lord you're all right."

Julianne nodded. "And I'm so glad to hear Judge Stanfield, your husband is all right."

Mrs. Stanfield's pale brows shot up. "What?"

Julianne covered her mouth in embarrassment. "I realize I'm not supposed to know about it or say anything, but I assumed you already—"

"Yes, dear. I know. But we must keep quiet. Until the culprit is found."

"I know who did it," Julianne confided. "At least I think I do."

"Really?" She blinked. "Who?"

"One of my kidnappers. Beau Bueller." She almost added that Beau was hoping to do the same thing to her son but managed to keep this to herself.

"My husband suspected that very thing." Mrs. Rivers set down a tea tray. "But he's still trying to put all the pieces together."

"He should talk to Red Bueller," Julianne suggested. "Red told me the whole story in detail. And he had nothing to do with shooting the judge, and he didn't even realize he was involved in a kidnapping until it was too late." She told them about the cow rustling story and, despite the seriousness of the situation, the women chuckled.

"Imagine a pretty little thing like her rustling steers," Mrs. Stanfield said to Mrs. Rivers. "It is amusing."

"So what brings you to town today?" Mrs. Stanfield asked. "And so soon after escaping your difficult ordeal?"

Julianne thought hard. "I was worried about a friend. Beau Bueller spoke of another diabolical plan while I was held captive, and I wanted to warn the marshal about it. Something that was supposed to happen today."

"And my husband is apprised of this?" Mrs. Rivers asked.

"Deputy Andrews promised to get word to him, and the others." She took a sip of tea. "I wanted to go out looking too, but they wouldn't let me."

"Well, I'm glad of that," Mrs. Stanfield told her.

"Is Levi out there looking too? With Marshal Rivers?" Julianne didn't want to appear overly nosy, but she really needed to know.

"My husband asked Levi to visit his chambers today. He's concerned over these upcoming court cases and wanted Levi to look into them." Mrs. Stanfield glanced at the mantle clock. "Levi left less than an hour ago."

"Did he go alone?" Julianne asked.

"Yes. And since it's a holiday, he wasn't worried about anyone disturbing him."

"And the courthouse is quite safe and secure?" Julianne remembered the tour Levi had given her of the building. It had seemed fairly solid. But what if someone saw him on the street, watched him go inside? Someone who wanted to permanently silence the young judge? Already her heart was pounding hard.

"Why are you asking about this?" Mrs. Stanfield looked worried.

"Yes, *why*?" Mrs. Rivers demanded.

"Levi is the one I was worried for, and why I came to town today," Julianne quickly spilled her story. "While I was held captive, I heard Beau Bueller make threats against Levi. I tried to warn Levi last night, but the medicine Dr. Muller gave me muddled my mind and I'm afraid Levi didn't hear me right, and then he was gone so I couldn't tell him, so I came to town."

Mrs. Rivers was already going for the telephone. "I'm going to call my husband's office. I'll let Deputy Andrews know to send someone to the courthouse."

"Yes," Julianne said eagerly. "Beau Bueller is a dangerous man. He must be stopped."

Mrs. Rivers explained the situation to Deputy Andrews. "And Levi is alone in the courthouse right now. He may need help. Please, hurry." She hung up with a furrowed brow. "He's going to check on it himself."

Mrs. Stanfield stood. "I'll call the courthouse. It won't ring through to the judge's chambers because no one's at the front desk. But perhaps Levi will hear it and answer." With the receiver against her ear, she waited for a while then sadly shook her head. "No answer."

Poor Mrs. Stanfield looked more worried than ever now. And feeling partly to blame, Julianne attempted to comfort her. "Levi will know what to do. He's the smartest man I know," she told his mother. "I'm sure he's being very careful. He knows there are dangerous men about. I know he'll be on his guard." She suddenly remembered the bitter contempt she'd heard in Beau's voice. "I hope and pray he will."

"That's exactly what we need to do," Mrs. Rivers declared. And right there in her front room, the three women all bowed their heads and prayed for Levi's safety and for the criminal to be apprehended.

Now to further distract Levi's mother, Julianne inquired about their small farm. She told her about how much she enjoyed being on Delia's ranch. "It's more than just a cattle ranch," she said. "It's also a working farm."

"Yes, we've visited out there before." Mrs. Stanfield's eyes lit up. "Winston Williams was friends with my husband. I always admired the way he ran his ranch. And your sister is doing a wonderful job of carrying on the tradition. I've tried to emulate the Double W in a small way on our farm." She sighed. "But Orville and I are getting too old to be farmers. And lately we've been discussing moving back into town." She explained about a small house they had owned since his days as a lawyer. "It may be time. Things around here seem to be changing so—" She stopped at the sound of several loud bangs.

"That's just the neighbor boys lighting firecrackers again," Mrs. Rivers assured them. "No need to fret over it. Just having some fun."

But Julianne noticed Levi's mother's expression had become worried again, and despite her efforts to appear unconcerned, Julianne felt anxious too. She remembered Beau's talk of firecrackers and shooting the Junior Judge. Was Levi really safe?

Levi hadn't been in the judge's chambers for long when he heard the telephone ringing in the reception area. Thinking someone forgot today was a holiday, he returned to perusing the papers on Monday's claim-jumping case, as well as something regarding an old case involving Dayton Springs. He'd been so glad to hear Dad take an interest in these cases, he'd eagerly come over to the courthouse. His plan was to take some of these papers home so his father could go over them more thoroughly. Despite his physical weakness, Dad's mind was still sharp as a tack and any insight he had would be helpful to Levi next week.

Levi was just sliding a file folder into his briefcase when he heard a noise. Not the phone this time, but a loud clank and clunking sound—almost as if someone had just forced open a door. Perhaps he was just edgy or being overly cautious, but shutting off the light, he grabbed his briefcase in one hand, and the gun from the holster in the other. And backing into the dimmest corner of the office, he waited in the shadows and strained his ears to listen.

Through his partially opened door, he heard the hollow sounds of footsteps echo down the hallway. Someone had definitely entered the building. Unless it was his imagination, the footsteps had a haughty sound, like someone strutting. The hair on the back of his neck stiffened as he decided they'd likely broken in. From the sounds of it, right through the front door, which despite its size and bulk was not as secure as most folks imagined. He quietly moved toward the chambers' door, staying along the shadowy wall of bookcases.

When he reached the door, he paused to listen again. The cocky footsteps were getting closer but hadn't yet turned the corner. He glanced at the gleaming revolver in his hand. He knew how to use it and wasn't a bad shot, but he'd never shot a man. Never wanted to. He knew he'd shoot to defend his mother or father or anyone else he cared about. But was he willing to take another man's life to defend his own? He wasn't sure. And he really didn't want to find out.

He pushed the chambers' door open a little wider, peering out to see no one coming down this hallway yet, but the footsteps were definitely getting louder and closer. And it sounded like just a single man. Perhaps someone who didn't quite know their way around the courthouse. He wanted to believe it wasn't a criminal, but something inside warned him otherwise, and he preferred to err on the side of caution. But could he reach the back exit, slide his key into the lock, and let himself out before whoever it was got there? It was a chance he had to take.

Turning the light on in his office, he left the door cracked open then stealthily crept down the short hallway. At the back door, he tucked his briefcase under one arm and removed the key from his vest pocket and, still holding the revolver, started to slip the key into the door.

"Hold it right there, Junior Judge. Hold it, or I'll shoot!"

Levi's back was to whoever was behind him, but he tried to remain calm. No fast moves. "You don't want to shoot a man in the back, do you?" he said in an even tone. "Even an outlaw should have more self-respect than that."

"Then turn around," the man growled. "I know ya got your gun drawed. We'll make it a fair match, Junior Judge." He made an evil sounding chuckle.

Levi considered the options. He was good with a gun but had never considered himself fast. He knew the outcome of a shootout wouldn't be good. But would he prefer to be shot in the back? He suddenly thought about Julianne and how brave she'd been while held captive by the Bueller brothers. Most likely this was Beau Bueller behind him right now. Wouldn't he rather die trying to outshoot this arrogant lawless punk than be shot in the back?

"I said turn around!" the man yelled. "What're ya? Yeller? Come on, Junior Judge, don't make me plug you in the back."

Levi steadied the gun in his hand and, his finger ready on the trigger, he started to spin around when he heard a loud bang. His ears ringing from the sound, he continued to turn. Expecting to feel a surge of pain somewhere in his back, he was determined to shoot this criminal, even if it was the last thing he ever did. But the man was already crumpling to the floor. Coming up quickly from behind him was Deputy Andrews, his gun drawn.

"Are you all right?" Andrews asked Levi as he kicked the revolver away from the man on the floor.

"Yes," Levi called back, stunned to realize he hadn't actually been shot.

Andrews bent down to check the condition of the wounded man. "He's alive," he said as he removed the second gun from the outlaw's holster. "Looks to be Beau Bueller too. No surprises there."

Carefully holstering his own pistol, Levi slowly approached, stunned to see the outlaw wasn't much more than a boy and writhing in pain.

Two more deputies ran down the hallway toward them, guns drawn, ready for action. "I got him," Deputy Andrews called out to them. "He's still alive. You fellows get him to the doc."

They each took one arm, pulling the man to his feet.

"You can take him out the back door." Levi hurried to unlock it, holding it open as they dragged the wounded man out. "It's closer to Dr. Muller's office." After they departed, he turned to thank Deputy Andrews. "How did you even know I was in here…or in danger?"

"Got a call from the marshal's wife. She said Miss Blackstone was concerned for your safety. Seems she had good reason too."

"Julianne Blackstone?" Levi asked in wonder.

"Yep. She's up at the Rivers's house right now."

Still clutching his briefcase, Levi headed for the back door. "That's where I'm headed too."

"I'll take care of things in here," Andrews was assuring him, but Levi was already on his way out, with one thing on his mind. He needed to thank Julianne for helping to save his life.

25

Julianne was so glad to see Levi alive and well, and to hear the news that Beau was captured, that she almost forgot all the things she wanted to tell Levi. But after he reassured his mother he was fine, and handed off some legal papers to his father, the two of them slipped outside, sitting down to visit in Mrs. Rivers's pretty flower garden.

Piece by piece, she told him about the things she'd overheard in her parents' house. "And I foolishly threw that right in Royal Dayton's face," she admitted. "Not my finest hour, I'm afraid."

Levi was actually writing these things down on a little pad he'd removed from his vest pocket. "What time do you think that was?"

"I left the picnic early," she said. "So I doubt it was even one o'clock yet."

"And what time did you leave town to go to the Double W?"

"It was really quick. I'm sure I was on my way there before two. And I drove the buggy fast."

"And my father was shot around three." He wrote that down. "What time did you leave for the cattle drive?"

"I'm not sure. It was late in the day, but I remember thinking I could make it up there before dark."

"Well, it all seems to line up. Even if we don't get a full confession from Beau Bueller, we know he took orders from Rich Danner. And we know Danner is a friend of Royal Dayton's. It seems entirely feasible that Royal is behind the whole thing. With his hat in the ring for the upcoming election, he certainly has more motive than anyone. And Dad has some suspicions about his involvement in one of the first claim-jumping cases. Might even explain how he was able to finance all his businesses in Dayton Springs. That was the primary reason I went to the chambers, to gather up some paperwork."

He looked at her. "Is there anything else I should know? I'd like to get this all into Marshal Rivers's hands as soon as possible. He'll want you to make a full affidavit later, but for now this is enough for him to pull in Dayton for questioning."

"Yes, definitely get that to the marshal."

"Royal Dayton is scheduled to make a speech this afternoon. Hopefully the word about Beau Bueller being shot and in custody hasn't leaked out yet, but you never know. News like that could scare Dayton off." Levi stood, pocketing his notepad.

"Be safe out there," she told him.

"I will. But don't worry. I think the real danger is past now."

"I have one more question," she began then stopped, "but maybe it could wait until later."

"If it's relevant to this case, go ahead." He waited.

"About my father." She grimaced at the word *father*. "It's no secret he's friends with Royal, not to mention his campaign manager, but I don't really know how involved he might've been in all the criminal activity, Levi. And it worries me."

He slowly nodded. "It's obvious that Jefferson's interest in the casino land was for his own personal profit. A quick way to make easy money. At the expense of this town. Unethical perhaps, but it wasn't illegal." He seemed to study her closely. "Do you have reason to believe he's involved in the criminal aspects of this case?"

"I thought about it a lot while I was being held by the Buellers. I might not have much respect for my father. I know he's an arrogant self-centered supercilious man. But I can't believe he's a criminal. I just don't think he could've approved of having his own daughter kidnapped like that."

"How about I look into your father's involvement?" His expression, as usual, was hard to read. It was possible he suspected her father was guilty but didn't want to say as much to her. And if that were true, how would it affect his relationship with her? It wouldn't look good for a respectable judge to be involved with a criminal's daughter.

"Thank you. I appreciate that." She forced a meek smile.

He reached out to touch her cheek and for a short hopeful moment, she thought perhaps he was actually going to kiss her, but instead his hand moved down, and a sad sort of smile crossed his lips. "I'll see you later, Julianne."

"I'm not sure how long I'll be in town today," she told him. "The deputy promised to tell Julius I was here at the Rivers's place, and I suspect Delia will want to get the children home before their bedtime. Especially now that we know most of the danger is past."

"Most of it," he agreed. "But I do think you'll all be safer out there on the ranch." He reached for his hat, then tipping it to her, took his leave. And for some reason, seeing his back, walking away from her, she felt very close to tears.

After delivering his notes to Marshal Rivers, followed by a long conversation, Levi headed for the Blackstone house. Unsure of what sort of reception he would get, he braced himself when the door opened. It was the maid again, but after he introduced himself and asked to see Mr. Blackstone, she hedged.

"Is he at home?" Levi pressed. "Or perhaps I can speak to Mrs. Blackstone."

"I, uh, I'm not sure they're home to visitors right now."

Suddenly he wondered if they'd even heard about Julianne's return. He knew they weren't on good speaking terms with their family members. "I have news regarding their daughter."

"Miss Blackstone?" The maid looked interested now.

"Yes, can you please let them know I need to talk to them?"

"Yes, sir." She nodded. Then leaving the door ajar, she hurried off. And, not expecting an invitation, Levi let himself in. But waiting in the foyer, he suddenly remembered the last time he'd been here. Royal Dayton had been lurking in the shadows. Perhaps he was here now. Levi remembered that he was still wearing the holster and revolver loaned to him by Wyatt. Hopefully he wouldn't need it.

Levi checked his pocket watch, relieved to see it was around the time when Mr. Dayton would be delivering his campaign speech in the town square. Unless he was being questioned by Marshal Rivers right now.

"Hello?" a male voice said.

Levi turned to see Julianne's parents approaching. Dressed as if they were going out, their expressions were full of questions and, unless he was mistaken, anxiety.

"You have news of Julianne?" her mother asked with troubled eyes.

"I do." He glanced at Jefferson, trying to read him.

"Then, please," Jefferson commanded, "tell us."

"Where are your manners?" his wife asked in a sharp tone. She turned to Levi. "Come into the parlor." Not waiting for his answer, she took him by the arm, leading him into the dimly lit room where the drapes were closed. "Please, sit down."

"Please, tell us," Jefferson said again. "What do you know?"

Levi took his time to sit down. "Shall I assume you haven't heard then?"

"We've heard nothing." Mrs. Blackstone's expression grew more anxious. "What do you know? Is she safe?"

Levi waited, studying Jefferson closely, trying to determine what the man did or did not know. "I'm surprised you haven't heard anything," he directed to Jefferson. "I thought you were well tuned into the gossip, rumors, and hearsay that float around this town. Perhaps your sources are letting you down?" He waited again.

Jefferson looked flustered now. "I haven't been out of the house in days," he declared.

"Really?" Levi almost believed him.

"That's true," Mrs. Blackstone said. "Jefferson has been staying very close to home. We both have. We were hoping to get word of Julianne. Please, if you know something, don't keep us in suspense." Her eyes filled with tears. "Even if it's bad news, I would rather hear it than this not knowing."

But Levi wasn't ready to divulge yet. "You say you've been staying home and yet you're both dressed up, as if you're about to go out."

"That was Jefferson's idea." Jane dabbed her eyes with a lace-trimmed hanky. "He wanted to make an appearance at the Fourth of July speeches. I'd agreed to go with him then changed my mind. I really don't like being out in public just now." She narrowed her eyes at her husband. "I'm surprised you do."

"I have a commitment to keep," he growled. "You know I'm expected to show my support for Royal." He checked his watch. "As it is, I'll probably be late."

"Are you sure Royal will be there?" Levi asked.

"Of course, he'll be there. He's to deliver his speech following the mayor." Jefferson, clearly agitated, stood up.

"Unless he's being detained."

"Detained?" Jefferson's dark brows drew together. "Why would he be detained?"

"For questioning?" Levi kept his tone even.

"Questioning for what?" he demanded.

"Please, stop with this cat and mouse game," Mrs. Blackstone insisted. "What has become of my daughter? I demand to—"

"Why would Royal be questioned?" Jefferson interrupted.

"Quite possibly a number of things." Levi locked eyes with him. "It's quite likely you'll be called in as well."

"If this is about our land development deal, save your breath." Jefferson folded his arms in front of him. "It's fallen through."

"You must be very disappointed," Levi continued. "Although I'm sure that it wouldn't have helped Royal Dayton's bid for the senate seat if word got out about his involvement in such an unscrupulous scheme."

"It doesn't matter now anyway," Jefferson shot back. "The deal is off, and our primary investors have left town."

"The Bronsons?" Levi remembered their name from the information Julianne had shared. "Maybe they didn't appreciate the criminal elements attached to the scheme."

"What criminal elements?" Jefferson glared at him. "What we planned to do was perfectly legal. Sure, some folks wouldn't have liked it, and it wouldn't have been approved in town, but it was all going to happen outside of the city limits. You're a judge, you should know that the law couldn't touch us with a ten-foot pole."

"That wasn't what I was referring to." Levi stood up to face Jefferson. "I am referring to the criminal elements that Royal Dayton is allegedly involved in."

"What criminal elements?" he demanded. "If you mean his property in Dayton Springs, that was all done legally."

"According to Dayton. But there are some miners who beg to differ. But I'm not referring only to that. Do you know about Dayton's connections to a man named Danner?"

"Rich Danner?" He shrugged. "That's not secret."

Levi just nodded, keeping his eyes fixed on Jefferson as if he was hearing his case in the courtroom. "And do you know about Danner's relationship to Red and Beau Bueller?"

"I don't recognize those names. Bueller?"

Levi believed him.

"Why are we talking about people we don't know?" Jane stood up shaking her fist. "I want to know about Julianne! You said you had news."

"The Bueller brothers kidnapped your daughter," Levi told them. "We already have a confession from one of them. It's believed the other one shot my father. And today, in the courthouse, he attempted to shoot me." He watched Jefferson closely. "I don't suppose you've heard about that."

Jefferson mutely shook his head.

"And Julianne?" Mrs. Blackstone asked with a tremor in her voice.

"She is safe."

Julianne's mother sank back into the chair with a loud sigh.

"I don't understand," Jefferson's tone was softer. "What does this have to do with Royal?"

"Royal Dayton will be questioned by Marshal Rivers. Based on the evidence gathered, he is suspected of setting up your daughter's kidnappers."

"No, not Royal!" Mrs. Blackstone shook her head. "I can't believe he'd do such a thing."

Levi was still focused on Jefferson. "What about you? Do you think he could do such a thing? Would he go to such extremes to protect his name? To protect his run for the senate seat? To protect his investments? Would he risk the life of your daughter to get what he wants?"

Jefferson sat down slowly, as if deflated, his head hung down and his hands dangled loosely by his sides.

Levi continued. "Julianne overheard all your plans for the shady development, Jefferson. She confronted Royal with that information on the day of the Mayor's Picnic, when he walked her home. Royal was enraged that she wanted to go public with it. He returned to the picnic to give his speech, but first he spoke to someone, didn't he, Jefferson?"

Jefferson looked up.

"Did you see Royal talking to Rich Danner at the picnic? Before he gave his speech?"

Jefferson just nodded.

"And then Danner left?"

He nodded again.

"Did you know about this?" Mrs. Blackstone stood, jabbing her husband in the shoulder. "Did you know they were planning to abduct Julianne?" She jabbed him again. "Answer me, Jefferson, did you know?"

"I didn't know," he muttered, "but it all makes sense now."

"It was your fault!" she yelled at him. "If Julianne had been killed, it would've been your fault. You brought those men into our lives. Just because you wanted to be important and respected and wealthy. You invited the devil into our home, Jefferson Blackstone! I don't know if I can ever forgive you."

"I'm going."

"Where are you going?" Levi asked.

"Away. Far away."

"Not before you talk to Marshal Rivers," Levi told him.

"Why should I?" he asked. "You already know the whole story. My ignorance left the door open for Royal to take advantage. I can see that now."

"Your ignorance and your arrogance!" his wife shouted at him. "I don't care if you do go away—far away—I've had enough of you!" She started to storm from the room then stopped to look at Levi. "Julianne?" she asked. "Where is she? Can I see her?"

"I'll let her know you want to see her," he said gently. "Just know that she's safe." After Mrs. Blackstone left the room, Levi asked Jefferson if he was ready to go make a statement in the marshal's office and, to his relief, Jefferson did not resist. The last thing they needed was for Jefferson to go telling his friends about what he'd just heard.

And Levi had been prepared to make a citizen's arrest and use his firearm to motivate Jefferson to go with him. But as they made the walk through the busy town, he was relieved that hadn't been necessary. Jefferson had seemed truly surprised by some of this and, unless Levi was wrong, he almost seemed sorry. For Julianne's sake, he hoped so. Time would tell.

26

As it turned out, Marshal Rivers had been unable to round up Royal Dayton. Somehow the senate candidate must've gotten wind of the Bueller brothers' incarceration and confessions.

"Royal never showed up for his campaign speech," the marshal informed Levi that evening. "Not only that, but Rich Danner made himself scarce as well. My men are still looking, but rumor has it both men have left town."

"That figures."

"I did get a full confession out of Jefferson Blackstone," the marshal said. "And the story about Dayton and Danner will be on the front page of Monday's paper. Not only about their botched property deal, but their possible connection to your father's shooting and the kidnapping."

"Their names will be mud in this town. Not that they'll be around to know it."

"Tongues will be a flapping, that's for sure, and you can bet that Dayton's bid for the senate has fizzled by now."

"Good for Colorado." Still, Levi didn't feel like celebrating. "So what did you do with Jefferson Blackstone?"

"There wasn't really anything I could hold him on. He may bear some moral responsibility, but according to his affidavit, he hasn't broken any laws. Unless something new comes up, he's free to walk." The marshal shook his head. "Sounds like he might too. Probably for the best."

Levi wasn't so sure. "Speaking of walking, I think I'll take one. Might even pay Jefferson Blackstone another little visit."

"He may be gone by now, Levi. He seemed in an awful hurry."

Levi shrugged as he put on his hat. "We'll see."

The sun was low in the sky by the time he knocked on the Blackstone's door. The maid answered it again, but instead of questioning him, let him in.

"I'd like to see Mr. Blackstone," he told her, but before she left, Jefferson came down the stairs with a valise in his hand.

"Looks like you're clearing out," Levi said.

"Might as well. I'm pretty much washed up in this town." He set his valise by the door to pull on his coat and hat.

"That must be a pretty big blow to your pride." Levi tipped his head to one side. "I suppose it's easier to just run away than stick around and eat humble pie."

Jefferson looked irritated, but his voice remained calm. "There's nothing left for me in this town. Going back East."

"And what is there back East for you?"

He shrugged. "At least I can hold my head up."

"Holding your head up for what? For whom? What about your family? Your children? Julius and Julianne? Your wife? You can just leave them behind?"

"They're better off without me."

"They might be better off without the part of you that's arrogant and superior and proud. But what if you humbled yourself, Jefferson? What if you used this opportunity to become the man your family could respect and maybe even learn to love?"

"I don't know how to do that." Jefferson actually sounded sincere. "I wouldn't even know where to begin."

"Seems like you could be on the way to learning right now," Levi said gently. "When a proud man gets knocked down, it's a chance for a humble man to rise up."

"I don't know." He picked up his valise.

"Right." Levi stepped out of his way. "You know what I do when I don't know what to do?"

"What?"

"I ask God to help me figure things out."

"And does that work?"

"So far so good." Levi smiled.

"Well, I'll give it some thought." Jefferson looked back into the house. "But not here. Not now."

Levi watched him go outside to where his carriage was waiting. And with the sun sinking low into the western sky, he watched Jefferson Blackstone drive out of town. But as he watched him, Levi prayed, asking God to pick up the pieces of a selfish but broken man and rebuild him into something better. As Levi walked back up the hill, he heard the sounds of fireworks and looked back to see explosions of color bursting in the sky. The town was kicking up its heels and celebrating, but Levi just wanted to go someplace quiet. Someplace he could think.

Julianne returned to the ranch with most of the others. Only a few hands had decided to remain in town for the nighttime festivities, which everyone knew would involve fireworks and firewater and could lead to anything. But to Julianne's relief, Julius wasn't one of them.

"It was an exciting day," Julius said as he drove the buggy.

"But you said you missed out on most of the celebration parts."

"Yeah, that's what made it exciting. I got to work with the deputies and Marshal Rivers. That was exciting."

"Let me guess, so now you want to be a lawman?"

He grinned. "Maybe so."

"Well, there's no reason you couldn't be." She turned to look at him, still marveling at how her twin brother had grown from a boy to a man while she'd been gone. "In fact, I think you'd make a good deputy."

"That's what Marshal Rivers said too. He told me to come in and talk to him about it sometime."

"Do you think you'd like that better than being a ranch hand?"

He shrugged. "It's been fun working with Wyatt and the guys, but we mostly do the same thing every day. Well, except at brandin' time, or when we drive cattle. That can get exciting." He jabbed her with an elbow. "Or when my sister gets kidnapped. That's pretty exciting too."

"A little too exciting for me."

"Marshal Rivers said he heard I did a good job searching for you."

"Well, you and Wyatt found me."

"That wasn't hard since you were coming back to the ranch. But Deputy Garson told him how I put together a plan for the men to go looking. He said I showed initiative. I'm not even sure what that means, but it sounded good."

"It's like gumption."

"Yeah, I like the word gumption better." He laughed. "Anyway, I want to go in to talk to Marshal Rivers. You know, after things in town calm down. Did I tell you that Beau Bueller's gunshot wound wasn't serious? Reckon he started to turn just as Deputy Andrews came up from behind and shot him, so it kinda glanced off and never hit anything vital. They said they'd bandage him up and toss him in jail by Sunday. In the meantime, he's got two deputies watching him in a locked room in the hospital."

"I know he's a lowdown dog, but I'm glad he didn't get killed. Even more glad that no one else got killed."

"He's a dirty rotten scoundrel and I wouldn't of cared if he had gotten himself killed. He can't be charged for murder since no one died, but he'll still be charged for attempted murder. Two accounts. That's lawman talk."

She just nodded.

"And those other men we were looking for must've got away. We thought we had that Danner man cornered, but it turned out to be the wrong guy. And that Royal Dayton, the one running for the senate, he never even showed up to give his speech. Lucky for him cuz we were gonna grab him for questioning. Deputy Garson reckons he skipped town. Maybe the others did too."

"Did you know our father was Royal Dayton's campaign manager?"

"What?" Julius looked shocked. "I knew he was into politics, but I didn't know that."

"He and Royal and a few others were involved in some pretty shady business dealings."

"Is our old man gonna get locked up?" Julius looked worried. "Might not look good for a lawman to have his pa in jail. I hope the marshal doesn't hold that against me."

"Levi told me he doesn't think Father did anything illegal. Just unethical."

"Meaning they can't lock him up?"

"Apparently."

"Well, that's a relief. Not that I'd care if he was locked up. Just not in these parts. Maybe he can go back to Pittsburgh and get himself locked up there." He laughed.

"Do you really think that's funny, Julius? I mean really?"

He scowled. "Better to laugh than cry in your beer. Don't ya think?"

"You're probably right. But you know what, Julius? Right now I'm feeling sorry for our mother."

"You kidding? After what she did to you? Tricking you into believing she was crippled and all that?"

"I know. But she was sorry afterward."

"That's like punching a guy in the jaw then being sorry cuz it's broken."

"She is our mother."

"I don't know, Julianne. Sometimes I wonder if we were orphaned at birth and then adopted by Mother and Father. Cuz I don't see how we're much like 'em. And Delia sure ain't nothing like Mother."

Despite herself, Julianne had to laugh. But she was serious because she really felt compassion for Mother. Yes, she'd made some ridiculous mistakes, but Jefferson had been greatly to blame for that. And Mother had seemed genuinely sorry when Julianne had confronted her.

Back at the ranch, after the children were put to bed, Julianne asked Delia about Mother. "I feel like I should try to see her," Julianne admitted. "It's as if she's been caught in the middle of my father's scheme. I actually feel sorry for her."

"I can understand that." Delia filled their teacups. "But even if you did go see her, what can you really do? I mean with Jefferson there, shadowing her and controlling things, what good would it do?"

"I wondered about bringing Mother out here for a spell."

"Just Mother?" Delia's brows arched.

"Yes. Just Mother. It would give her a break."

"I'm sure she needs one." Delia sighed. "No offense, Julianne, but Jefferson would wear anyone out."

"No offense taken. I know my father well. Good grief, Julius was just saying he hoped Father goes to jail. Not here, mind you, that would embarrass Julius. But he thought back in Pittsburgh would be just fine, not that they'd take him."

Delia frowned. "Julius isn't far from the truth, Julianne."

"What do you mean?"

"I never wanted to say anything when you and Julius were young. But Mother confided in me that the reason they never returned to

Pittsburgh was because Jefferson's gambling had gotten them into trouble. Not just losing the house and everything, but all of you had been threatened if he didn't repay his debts."

"I always had a feeling there was something going on." Julianne sighed. "And knowing his interest in this casino development, and being so friendly with Royal, who owns casinos, well, I figured Father hadn't given up that habit."

"I've wondered about that too. And I've warned Mother more than once to keep her dress shop profits out of his hands, but I don't know if she heeded my advice."

"I know the shop's been profitable. And Helena can manage the business just fine, as well as keep Father's hand out of the till. If Mother would just let her."

"Our fashionable mother is convinced Helena is not sophisticated enough to keep up the La Mode image."

Julianne couldn't help but giggle. "Once Father's scandal goes public, Helena's image might seem much improved."

"Poor Mother. I hope this doesn't ruin her dress shop. But I do think you're right." Delia nodded. "Mother should definitely come out here until things cool off. She might even enjoy the barbecue on Sunday. But not Jefferson. I'm not ready for that."

"No, I'm not either." And after all that Julianne had been through this past week, she knew she'd have no trouble standing up to her father. He'd made his bed. It was about time he took a nice long nap in it.

Levi was surprised to see Julianne being driven through town the next morning. He recognized the old ranch hand Caleb at the reins of the wagon, but curious as to their destination, he followed them in his dad's carriage. It soon became clear they were headed for the Blackstone house. Interesting.

Levi was somewhat comforted that Julianne's father was gone, but knowing the other players hadn't been rounded up, he was still on alert—they all were. So he decided to park the carriage down the street and wait. Caleb just dropped Julianne off, tipped his hat then headed back to town. Levi would've preferred the old cowhand remained. Although he'd seen Jefferson depart yesterday, he couldn't be certain. And what if Royal or Danner were still about?

Levi drove the carriage up to the house and, taking his time, got out. He wasn't sure what he'd do or say, but he felt his presence might be helpful. The maid answered the door and he asked to see Miss Blackstone. Soon both Julianne and her mother appeared.

"Levi," Julianne exclaimed, "what are you doing here? Is anything wrong?"

He removed his hat. "I was sort of wondering the same thing. Everything all right here?"

"Yes." Julianne smiled. "Mother just told me that my father has left. We aren't sure where, or if he's coming back."

He nodded. "Yes, I knew about that. But I'm surprised to see you back in town."

"I've come to convince Mother to go out to the ranch with me," she told him. "I feel she needs a break." She turned to her mother, who looked worn out and wan. "Please, Mother, Delia wants you to come too. And it's the barbecue tomorrow. And your grandchildren would love to see you. Please, say you'll come."

"I don't know." Her mother twisted a handkerchief in her hands. "I should probably stay here and—"

"And what? Feel miserable. You know that Helena can manage La Mode."

"But I haven't been in there for weeks now. Who knows what might be—"

"How about if I go in for you?" Julianne offered.

"Would you?" Mrs. Blackstone looked hopeful.

"If it would convince you to go out to the ranch for a spell."

"Yes," she said eagerly. "But do you think you could go in today?"

Julianne glanced at Levi then back to her mother. "I was hoping we'd drive your little buggy out to the ranch together, Mother. I already let Caleb go back and—"

"How about if I drive your mother to the Double W?" Levi offered. "That way you could spend the afternoon at the dress shop."

"Yes," Mrs. Blackstone agreed. "That would be fine. Thank you." She reached for Julianne's hand. "If you're at the dress shop, it will help my customers to see that I'm still part of things. Do you know what I mean?" She suddenly seemed to take notice of Julianne's durable looking calico dress. "But would you mind changing first?"

Julianne frowned. "I'll go change." She held up a finger. "If you'll start packing your things." Her mother promised, then Julianne called out to the maid. "Please, Ellie, can you help Mrs. Blackstone pack some bags? Enough for a couple of weeks?"

"Yes, Miss," Ellie agreed as Julianne hurried up the stairs.

Mrs. Blackstone turned to Levi. "Do you think I'm doing the right thing?"

He wasn't sure how to answer. "I'm surprised you'd care about my opinion."

"I respect your opinion," she said somberly. "I know you're an intelligent and sensible man. After all, you're a judge—and a trustworthy one too. I trust your judgment."

He nodded. "I do think you're doing the right thing, Mrs. Blackstone. Visiting your family will be good for you. And I'm sure Julianne's presence at your dress shop will be most reassuring to both your employees and your customers. I think it's a very sensible idea."

She sighed. "Thank you."

"May I use your phone to call my parents while you're getting ready? I was on my way to check on our farm, but I'll explain the trip will take a bit longer."

"Yes, of course."

By the time he finished explaining his plan to his mother, Julianne was coming down the stairs. Although she'd looked fetchingly pretty in her farm dress and straw hat, she was sophisticatedly beautiful in her topaz blue dress and stylish hat. In fact, he wasn't sure which version he preferred.

"How about if I give you a ride into town," he offered. "Then I'll come back for your mother."

"Oh, I'm used to walking," she told him.

"You look far too elegant to walk by yourself." He smiled.

On the trip to town, Levi told her a bit about his encounter with her father last night. "How do you think your mother will do without your father around?"

"I'm not sure. Sometimes she seems strong…sometimes it's hard to tell. She didn't seem to know where he'd gone or when he'd be back." She tugged at a glove. "What about the marshal? Won't he want to question my father?"

"He did question him yesterday."

"But he didn't see any reason to put him in jail?"

"No. Like I said before, it was unethical, but not illegal. And I'll warn you it will all be in the newspaper on Monday."

"We figured it would. That's why we think Mother will be better off at the ranch. I know this has been hard on her."

"It must be hard on you too, Julianne. You've been through so much. I was surprised to see you in town today. Surprised at your willingness to help at your mother's shop." He slowed down in front of La Mode. "Quite frankly, I'm impressed. You seem to be made of sturdy stuff."

She laughed. "I suppose I should take that as a compliment."

He felt embarrassed now. "Maybe it's because your image, especially when I first met you, was that of a refined lady—now I'm not saying you're not—but you're also a very resilient young woman."

"Who can ride a horse." She grinned as he pulled to a stop. "And rope a cow."

He nodded. "I guess I'm saying I'm impressed."

"Then thank you." Her brow creased. "But I have a question for you."

"What's that?"

"I know our family is going to experience even more humiliation. Goodness, poor Julius is almost beside himself with worry it will ruin his chances to become a deputy—"

"He wants to be a deputy?"

"Yes, well, what I want to know, Levi, is won't you be embarrassed to be associated with us? I mean because you are a judge with a solid reputation to uphold. For you to be observed with any of the Blackstone family—like even right now—well, it seems it could be detrimental to your image."

"I'm not the least bit worried." He smiled as he hopped down from the carriage, going around to help her down. As he reached for her hand, Julianne released what seemed a relieved sigh.

"Thank you," she told him. "And thank you for transporting my mother out to the Double W. Delia will be expecting her."

"How about if I pick you up later this afternoon?" He smiled. "Around three?"

"Would five be too late? I don't know how long it'll take for me to evaluate how the business is actually going."

"Five is perfect." He tipped his hat. "Perhaps I can convince you to stay in town, to join me for dinner?"

She seemed to consider this. "That would make for a late ride back to the Double W. And then you'd still have to drive back to town. I have an idea. When you get my mother, tell her I will remain in town until tomorrow. I'll stay at her house and get things in order for while she's gone. Then, if you don't mind, you can deliver me to the Double W tomorrow." She held up a finger. "And it's their big barbecue day—would you join us? And your parents too?"

"I'm not sure Dad is ready for travel, but Mother might enjoy the outing. As well as meeting your mother."

She looked surprised, but just nodded. "That sounds nice. And, again, I thank you for taking Mother out there. I greatly appreciate it. Can you please let her know my plans to remain in town?"

He promised to do so then got back into the carriage. There he watched as she gracefully entered the dress shop. Not for the first time, he marveled at the many diverse facets of her personality. Farm girl, cowgirl, refined lady, typist, intelligent, capable, kind, resilient…he didn't care if her name *was* Blackstone. He wouldn't even care if her father had been the notorious Jesse James, or if her brother joined up with the Rogers Brothers Gang. Julianne was Julianne and, if he had his way, she might one day be *Julianne Stanfield.* Not that he had ever expected to marry this early in his career, but the idea was growing more and more appealing.

27

JULIANNE HAD EXPECTED A SURPRISED RECEPTION AT THE DRESS shop, but after a couple of hours and a lot of explaining, her mother's employees seemed to adapt themselves to Julianne's presence. Still the customers were another challenge altogether. Most of them seemed to know of her kidnapping. Some stared at her as if she were a sideshow freak. Some were just politely curious. Others felt they had the right to hear the full story, refusing to accept her condensed version. After a few hours, weary of the attention, she managed to keep herself busy straightening and organizing, while maintaining a very low profile.

It was nearly closing time when she overheard a pair of customers gossiping about a woman passing by the shop. Screened by the cheval mirror next to the hat counter, they were unaware Julianne was even there.

"I just don't see how that woman can hold her head up in public," the older one said in a hushed tone that was still quite audible.

Julianne glanced out the front window to see a worn-out looking, gray-haired woman carrying a basket of what looked like hand-knit socks. Perhaps she was a peddler, but who purchased wool socks in July?

"Shameful!" the younger one said.

"That Mrs. Bueller never could control those boys. Not after her husband passed. I always said they'd come to no good."

Julianne felt a rush of conflicting emotions. Anger at the judgmental women for being so mean-spirited, compassion for poor Mrs. Bueller, and confusion for what she was about to do.

"Excuse me," she told Helena. "I have an errand to run." And without getting hat or gloves, she hurried out to the street and called out to the woman. "Mrs. Bueller?"

The woman turned with a fearful expression.

"Excuse me." Julianne forced a nervous smile. "May I speak with you?"

"What for?" she asked with a suspicious tilt of her head.

"Are you selling those socks?" Julianne pointed to the basket.

"Yeah, but nobody wants 'em." She fanned her flushed face. "Too hot out for selling socks."

"I'd like to buy some."

Mrs. Bueller blinked then scowled. "Nah, you're a fancy lady. You don't want 'em."

"Yes, I really do. You see, I live on a ranch with a lot of cowboys, including my brother. And they're always needing good socks." Julianne pointed to the dress shop. "If you'll come with me, I'll pay you in there."

"Me in that fancy place?" The woman looked appalled.

"Yes, it's fine. My mother owns the shop."

"Oh, I dunno." She shook her head, backing away.

"Come on." Julianne took her by the elbow, leading her into the shop where the two stunned customers openly stared. "Right this way." Smiling at the flabbergasted women, Julianne led Mrs. Bueller into the backroom. "Please, sit down." She pointed to a chair by the worktable. "I'll be right back." To ensure the woman didn't run off, Julianne took the basket with her.

She returned with some cash and a glass of water. "I know you're Mrs. Bueller." She sat across the table from her. "Do you know who I am?"

She just shook her head then eagerly drank the water.

"I am acquainted with your sons."

Mrs. Bueller set the glass down with a loud clunk. "*You* know Beau and Red?"

"I spent the last week with them." Julianne took in a deep breath. "I'm the one they kidnapped."

Mrs. Bueller's pale eyes grew large. "Oh, my Lord. Oh, dear, oh my." She stood.

"Please, sit back down. I have something to say to you."

Mrs. Bueller sank into the chair. "I'm so ashamed. So terrible ashamed."

"What your boys did is not your fault." Julianne pursed her lips. "Any more than it's my fault that my father is a scoundrel."

Mrs. Bueller leaned forward. "What?"

"My father has done some bad things. Sometimes I feel ashamed because of him. Just like you might be feeling ashamed now. But it's not right to blame yourself for someone else's bad choices."

Mrs. Bueller's eyes were welling up. "But they're my sons. I'm their ma. Seems I shoulda raised 'em better."

"Did you teach them to do bad things? Did you encourage them to shoot or kidnap people?"

"No, of course not. I took 'em to church every Sunday when they was boys. Henry went sometimes…before he died. Then Beau got big and didn't wanna go no more. Red would still go sometimes."

"See, you tried," Julianne said. "You did your best."

"I knew Beau had some friends that were trouble. I worried when he'd come home late. But I never ever dreamed my boys could do somethin' like they done." She took another sip of water. "And I had a bad feeling this last time. I asked Beau what he was up to, and he got a job with some rancher."

"Shooting jackrabbits?"

Her eyes got wider. "That's right."

Now Julianne told her the whole story, taking care to show Mrs. Bueller that she believed Red got pulled into Beau's scheme. "Red thought they were catching a cattle rustler. And he questioned Beau all the time. Red even helped me escape. And he felt sorry about the whole thing."

"That sounds like Red." She pulled out a gray handkerchief. "Breaks my heart he's locked up."

"I don't like painting Beau in a bad light, but he knew what he was doing. He shot Judge Stanfield and attempted to shoot the judge's son. But it was because a man named Rich Danner was paying him. Perhaps you know Mr. Danner?"

She sadly shook her head. "Never heard of him till a deputy asked me, just the other day."

"I'm sorry Beau got shot, Mrs. Bueller, but I'm glad it's not serious. Still, he will likely be convicted. He'll probably spend a lot of time in prison."

"I know, I know." Head bent down, she sobbed quietly.

"But I'd like to help Red."

She looked up. "You would?"

"Yes. I want him to get a fair shake. And I have friends who I think can help."

"After all my boys done to you, why are you being so kind, Miss Blackstone?"

Julianne thought hard. "Aren't we supposed to love our enemies? Not that I see Red as an enemy. In a strange way, I think of him as a friend." She couldn't say the same for Beau, but that was where loving one's enemies got real.

"I'd be most grateful if you could help Red. He's always been a real good boy. Always could count on him." She wiped her eyes.

"Beau, he's always been a handful. Headstrong and full of himself. Too good-looking for his own good. He never did listen to me. I used to warn him, pride comes before the fall. Reckon he had to learn the hard way."

Julianne thought of her father, maybe he had to learn the hard way too. She heard the door behind her open and looked to see Helena peering in, eyeing Julianne and her guest curiously.

"We're getting ready to lock up and go home," Helena said.

"Go ahead and go. I'll lock up."

"Are you sure?"

Julianne gave Helena a firm nod. "Yes, of course. You and the girls can go now. I know how to lock up."

"All right." She gathered her things then called in Lizzie and Rowena to do likewise. Naturally, they were curious too, but neither of them questioned her. After they left, Julianne reached for the sock basket.

"Aw, you don't really want to buy those," Mrs. Bueller said.

"Oh, yes, I do." She examined a pair. "They seem very well made. I can't wait to show them to the ranch hands." She wanted to say as a thank you for the way they all went searching for her but knew that would make Mrs. Bueller feel worse. "We're having a little celebration tomorrow, and I'll make a gift of these." Julianne counted them out then laid out what she felt the socks were worth.

"That's too much."

"For this quality of work?" Julianne shook her head. "That's a fair price."

"I don't know what to say."

Julianne stuck out her hand. "How about we say we are friends, Mrs. Bueller."

As they shook hands, Julianne inquired about her needlework skills.

"I made this." Mrs. Bueller pointed to her plain blue dress. "I know it ain't nothin' fancy, but all these tucks here are done by hand."

Julianne examined the small stitches. "Very nice. We can use a dependable seamstress for the shop." She explained how a lot of young girls worked awhile then got married. "If you're interested, we can talk again on Monday." She looked at the clock and stood. "Someone is giving me a ride and I better lock up." She walked Mrs. Bueller through the shop and, seeing Levi waiting in the carriage, waved. "I'll be right out," she called to him.

Mrs. Bueller grabbed her hand again, squeezing it tightly. "You're just like an angel sent from God," she said. "You truly are."

"Will I see you on Monday?"

Mrs. Bueller nodded with teary eyes. "Yes! Thank you!"

Julianne put a hand on her shoulder, looking into her eyes. "And remember, you're not to blame for other people's bad choices. You're not to be ashamed."

She nodded. "You remember those words too, sweet girl."

As Julianne got her hat and things, she did remember those words. She was not to blame for her father's bad choices, and she had no reason to be ashamed.

It wasn't until driving Julianne and his mother to the barbecue on Sunday that Levi finally got Julianne to tell him about the mysterious woman in front of her mother's dress shop yesterday. "You know I'll keep asking," he said.

"Goodness," Mrs. Stanfield said. "Now, my curiosity is bubbling over too."

"I know she wasn't a customer," Levi continued to press. "But she seemed so very grateful. I'm dying to know what was going on."

"If you must know that was Mrs. Bueller."

"What?" Levi turned to look at her. "The mother of Beau and Red?"

Julianne simply nodded.

"Did she go there to see you?" his mother asked in a worried tone.

"No. I actually ran out to the street to see her. And I forced her into the shop." Julianne held up a cloth bag. "She had socks to sell. I bought all of them for our ranch hands. They are really well made and—"

"You can't be serious." Levi knew there was more to the story. "Tell us what really happened."

And so she shared an almost unbelievable story about how she'd befriended the mother of her abductors. "And that brings me to another thing," she finally said. "We need to help Red."

"Help Red?" his mother sounded slightly aghast.

Julianne explained to her how Red had been in the dark about the whole thing, and how he helped her escape, and how it was unfair to incarcerate him. "And Mrs. Bueller needs him with her. Red shouldn't be in jail. He was a victim of circumstance."

Levi laughed. "Maybe you should become a lawyer."

Julianne laughed too. "Maybe I'd like that."

"A woman lawyer," his mother mused. "I think I'd like that too."

"So unless I can find someone to represent Red's case…" She looked imploringly at Levi. "I suppose I'll just have to take it on myself. That is unless I find a judge that I can influence."

"Oh, I think we can find someone to represent Red," he told her.

"Of course, you can," his mother said. "Now you've got me feeling sorry for him and his mother."

Julianne, obviously fueled by his mother's sympathy, now told them about how she'd offered Mrs. Bueller a job. "She's a fine seamstress. She's coming in to meet with me on Monday to discuss it further."

"But will you be there on Monday?" Levi asked as he turned up the long driveway of the Double W. "I thought you planned to live out here on the ranch from now on."

"I've been thinking about that. Of course, I need to speak to Mother first, but I feel I can be of more help living in town and working at the shop. Women's clothing is not my favorite thing, but

I think it might be good for me to stay there awhile longer. And good for my mother too."

"And will you also be doing some typing there?" his mother asked.

"Of course," Julianne told her. "And perhaps I'll take up a correspondence course on law. Do you think they have such things?"

Levi and his mother both laughed.

"I'm serious," she told them.

"I've no doubts about that." Levi winked at his mother. "What did I tell you about this woman?" He pulled up to the house, getting down to help his mother and Julianne. "I'll go park the carriage," he told them. "And meet up with you later." He watched Julianne link her arm into his mother's and, as the two of them went up to the house together, he thought to himself—it was as if she was already family.

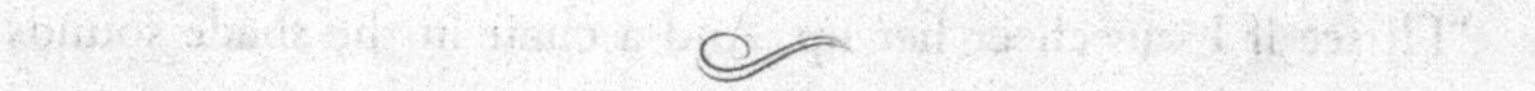

While Levi tended to the carriage and horses, Julianne eagerly led his mother to where the crowd was gathered between the barn and the house. She was so thrilled to see all her family and friends at the barbecue that she could hardly keep her feet from dancing as she went around greeting everyone. She proudly introduced Levi's mother to Miranda and Jackson and their two little boys, then continued on to a few others that she didn't think Mrs. Stanfield had met.

"I'd love to see if anything has changed in the gardens and orchards and whatnot," Mrs. Stanfield told Julianne.

"And I'd love to show you." Julianne led the way, proudly showing her some of the new workings of the farm, pointing out some new irrigation that Wyatt had implemented and a few other innovations.

"I've dreamt of doing some things like this on our own little farm," Mrs. Stanfield said longingly. "But I'm afraid Orville and I are getting too old to maintain it. And although Levi won't continue being a judge after his father returns to the bench, he'll still be busy with his law career." She bent down to examine one of the chicken feeder devices. "Although he does love the farm."

"I can understand that." Julianne sighed. "Despite my offer to manage Mother's dress shop in town, I'll miss being out here."

Mrs. Stanfield linked her arm in Julianne's. "Thank you for the tour. I expect we should get back to the party."

As they returned to the yard, Julianne spotted her mother sitting by herself. In a chair almost hidden on the shady side of the house, she looked unhappy.

"There's someone I'd like you to meet," Julianne said. "It's my mother. And she's been through some difficulties of late." She glanced at Levi's mother. "Of course, you have too. And I do admire how bravely you've faced everything."

"I'd love to meet your mother."

"Perhaps you can encourage her," Julianne said quietly. "She looks to be feeling a bit glum."

"I'll see if I can cheer her up. And a chair in the shade sounds perfect to me," Mrs. Stanfield told her.

Julianne performed the introduction then secured another chair for Levi's mother. By the time she returned, the two women were visiting rather amicably. Mrs. Stanfield was complimenting Mother on the shop, praising the cashmere shawl Levi had purchased there. "It's the perfect weight for a cool summer evening. I just love it."

Satisfied the mothers would be all right, Julianne spotted Levi now joining the crowd near the punch table and excused herself. Still feeling a bit nervous about having Levi's sweet, refined mother alone with her somewhat unpredictable mother, Julianne hurried over to join him.

"What do you think?" she asked him, nodding to where the two women were still visiting.

"Perfect." He hooked his arm into hers.

"You mean putting our mothers together?" she asked.

"No, I mean you." He laughed then pointed to where some musicians were just warming up. "And I do recall you promising me a dance or two at this barbecue. You know, to commemorate the first time we danced together so many years ago. I hope you plan to make good on your word."

"Of course, I do." She grinned. "But first I want to introduce you to a few people." She took him around, but instead of calling him Levi Stanfield, she introduced him as "Judge Stanfield." Naturally, this created some good-natured ribbing about young judges and so on, but Levi took it in stride.

"You seem pretty young to be a judge," Miranda said teasingly.

"I like the idea of a young judge," Jackson told his wife.

"It's only temporary," Levi clarified. "My dad will be occupying the bench again. Probably by the end of summer."

"Then he'll go back to practicing law," Julianne informed them.

"Well, I think you two make a very handsome couple." Miranda declared. "Julianne and the judge."

"Miranda." Julianne gave Miranda a look to suggest she'd overstepped.

But Miranda just winked back. "I'm not the least bit surprised you'd be the one to snag yourself a judge. You were always the smart one." She patted Julianne on the back. "I was surprised you didn't go to a real university like Delia did."

"I wanted to, but my parents wouldn't agree." Julianne still felt her cheeks warming at Miranda's assumption that Julianne and Levi were a couple but tried to hide her embarrassment by changing the conversation's focus. "Miranda, didn't I hear that you're keeping the books for your husband's new mining company? That must be quite a task."

"It used to be a lot easier," Miranda told her. "But when the mine showed color things got a little crazy. Jackson says we can afford a real bookkeeper now, but I don't trust any outsider to manage our money."

"Have you had any trouble with claim-jumpers?" Levi asked.

"Oh, sure," Jackson told him. "But I grew up in the mining business. I know how to handle them."

"Yeah, you just send them packing." Miranda pointed to where two young couples were looking for others to join them in a square dance. "Come on, Jackson, you promised me you'd dance." She pointed to Levi and Julianne. "Maybe Julianne and the judge can join us."

"You don't have to ask me twice." Levi grabbed Julianne's hand. "How about you?"

She grinned. "Of course!"

After a day of dancing and visiting and eating and then dancing and visiting and eating some more, Julianne couldn't remember when she'd had a better day. Everything about it felt very nearly perfect. But the sun was going down and some of the partiers were already calling it a day. As sad as she was to see it end, Julianne suspected Mrs. Stanfield was tired and ready to get home to her husband, but when Julianne hinted of as much, she just waved her hand.

"Is it too dark for you to show Levi the gardens and orchards?" Mrs. Stanfield asked. "I was telling him how much I'd like him to see the innovations."

"There's still some light in the sky," Julianne said. "Would you really like a tour?" she asked Levi.

"I'd love one."

"Go, go," his mother urged. "I'll be fine."

Again, Levi looped his arm in hers. "Lead the way, my lady."

She gave him the same tour she'd given his mother, only quicker this time since the light was fading fast. Finally they were in between the gardens and orchards and Levi paused, tilting his head up to the sky. "Look at those stars," he exclaimed.

Doing likewise, she looked up. Then he bent toward her, landing a very tender but passionate kiss onto her lips. "I hope that was all right," he said afterward.

"Well, yes, it was fine." She felt happy but slightly flustered to imagine what others would think. After all, Levi was a respectable judge.

"I probably should've asked you first."

She smiled at him. "I would've said yes."

So he kissed her again. And then he stepped back and, holding on to her hand with both of his, he got down on one knee and looked up. Was it the reflection of the night sky or were there real stars in his eyes?

"Julianne, I love you. I have known for a while that I love you, but like a good judge, I was weighing everything, pondering and thinking, then planning for just the right time. I thought that would be when I returned to practicing law, but then you went missing and I felt I couldn't wait another minute. Julianne Blackstone, will you do me the honor of becoming my wife?"

For a moment she was too stunned to answer, and poor Levi looked seriously perplexed. "Yes, Levi, I will marry you. I love you too. I think I've loved you since that day you danced with me at Delia's wedding so long ago."

He stood to kiss her again and this time she felt herself melting into his arms. Finally, realizing it was probably getting late, she asked if they should rejoin what was left of the party. "Perhaps we should make an announcement?" she said with uncertainty. "Or at least tell our mothers?"

"My mother already figured it out. That's why she wanted me to take you on the moonlight garden tour." He laughed. "But you're right, we should make an announcement. I can just hear Miranda's reaction. Julianne and the judge are going to be married!"

Westward to Home

Book 1

Delia and the Drifter

Available Now!

Book 2

Miranda and the Miner
Available Now!

Also by Melody Carlson

The Legacy of Sunset Cove

Harbor Secrets
Riptide Rumors
Surf Smugglers
Turning Tides

The Mulligan Sisters

I'll Be Seeing You
As Time Goes By
String of Pearls
We'll Meet Again

Dear Daphne Series

Home, Hearth, and the Holidays
A Will, a Way, and a Wedding

Whispering Pines

A Place to Come Home To
Everything I Long For
Looking for You All My Life
Someone to Belong To

Second Chances

Heartland Skies
Looking for Cassandra Jane
Shades of Light
Armando's Treasure
Thursday's Child
Built with Love

CPSIA information can be obtained
at www.ICGtesting.com
Printed in the USA
LVHW042059150622
721365LV00013B/467